THE NIGHT BEFORE

Also by Wendy Walker

Emma in the Night
All Is Not Forgotten

THE NIGHT BEFORE

WENDY WALKER

ORION

An Orion paperback

First published in Great Britain in 2019
by Orion Fiction,
This paperback edition published in 2019
by Orion Fiction,
an imprint of The Orion Publishing Group Ltd,
Carmelite House, 50 Victoria Embankment
London EC4Y 0DZ

An Hachette UK company

1 3 5 7 9 10 8 6 4 2

A CIP catalogue record for this book
is available from the British Library.

ISBN (Paperback) 9781409190035

Printed and bound in Great Britain by Clays Ltd, Elcograf S.p.A.

www.orionbooks.co.uk

In loving memory of
Estel Herbowy Kempf (1915 – 2017)

ONE

Laura Lochner. Session Number One.
Four Months Ago. New York City.

Laura: I don't know if this is a good idea.

Dr. Brody: It's up to you, Laura.

Laura: What if you try to fix me and I end up more broken?

Dr. Brody: What if you don't?

Laura: I'm scared to go back there. To the past. To that night in the woods. A piece is still missing.

Dr. Brody: It's up to you. Only you can decide.

Laura: It was in my hand. The weapon that killed him. But that night didn't change me. That night made me see what I've always been.

Dr. Brody: Then let's start there. Tell me about the girl you've always been.

TWO

Laura. Present Day. Thursday, 7 P.M.
Branston, CT.

Lipstick, cherry red.

I choose the color because it's bright and cheerful. It's optimism in a tube. And that's exactly what I need tonight.

The guest bathroom at my sister's house is impossibly small, with slanted ceilings and a tiny oval mirror. The lipstick hovers on the edge of a pedestal sink.

I put it on first so I won't change my mind, rolling that optimism right across my lips. Next comes the concealer. Two stripes under my brown eyes, and the dark circles from weeks of insomnia disappear. Rose blush colors cheeks that have not seen the sun for far too long.

Insomniacs sleep during the day.

My sister, Rosie, gave me a pretty dress to wear. Black with tiny flowers.

Wear a dress for a change. It will make you feel pretty.

Rosie just turned thirty. She has a husband and a toddler— Joe and Mason. They have a house in the hills of Branston, six miles from downtown. And one mile from the place where all of this started. The street where we grew up. Deer Hill Lane.

Rosie says she doesn't have any occasion to wear the dress. The skirt gets in her way when she's chasing after Mason and she's too tired to do much of anything at night except grab a beer in the strip mall at the edge of town. She says this like she misses having nothing better to do than put on makeup and dresses. But really, she doesn't need the dress or the occasions to wear it, because her days are filled with bear hugs and belly laughs and sticky kisses on her face.

Her husband, Joe, doesn't care. He adores her. Even now, after thirteen years together. After growing up together on the same street. Even with Mason sleeping in their bed, and an old house in need of constant repair, and Rosie never wearing a dress.

He adores her because when they were young, she wore lots of pretty dresses for him and that's the person he still sees.

That's the kind of person I need to be tonight.

I search for my phone in a pile of towels and clothing that lie on the bathroom floor. When I do, I pull up the profile and un-chain the hope. *Jonathan Fields*. His name sounds like a song.

Jonathan Fields. I found him on a dating website called findlove .com—an actual website. The name says everything about it. Jonathan Fields is forty. His wife left him a year ago because she couldn't get pregnant. She kept their house. He drives a black BMW.

That's what he told me.

Jonathan Fields spoke to me on the phone. He said he didn't like emails or texting because it was too impersonal. He said he hated online dating but that his friend met his fiancé on findlove .com. It was not one of those hookup apps. No swiping allowed. The profile takes an hour to build. They have to approve your

photos. Jonathan Fields said it was like having your grandmother
fix you up on a blind date, and this made me laugh.

Jonathan Fields said he liked the sound of it.

I liked the sound of his voice, and remembering it now actually sends a surge of warmth through my body. I feel my mouth
turn up at the corners. A smile.

A fucking smile.

I told him a lot about my job, and this made it easier to tell
him very little about me.

I have an impressive résumé after jumping through hoops all
my life. *Princeton . . . an MBA from Columbia . . . a job on Wall
Street!*

"Wall Street" is one of those terms that won't leave this world
no matter how antiquated it's become. I work in Midtown, nowhere
near Wall Street, which sits at the very bottom of Manhattan.
And the firm I work at isn't quite as sexy as Goldman Sachs. I
sit at a desk and read stuff and write stuff and hope to God it's
not wrong, because other people at our firm will make trades and
deals upon the advice I give. Me, a twenty-eight-year-old who
needs a shrink to tell her how to behave.

Jonathan Fields works at a hedge fund downtown, so he understands about my work.

That's what he told me.

I didn't tell him about my childhood here, running wild in the
woods behind our house with the neighborhood kids. Me and
Rosie—and Joe, whose family lived up the street until he went to
high school and they moved closer to town.

And I didn't tell him why I've stayed gone all these years.

I don't use social media, not ever, so it's not like he can check.
I didn't tell him my father's last name. Lochner. Google still finds
Laura Lochner and the things she did, or didn't do—they can

never decide—years ago. I've used my middle name, my mother's last name, since I left this place. Heart. Laura Heart. Isn't that ironic? Named after the one thing inside me that feels broken.

Omissions are not lies.

Rosie took Joe's last name, *Ferro*, so there are no Lochners from our clan left in all of Connecticut.

I did tell him that I drive my sister's minivan. It's blue. And humiliating. I'm shopping for a new car, but *I've just been so busy*.

There's a knock at the door. I open it and find Joe looking at me sheepishly. He's still in his suit from his law office, but he's loosened his tie and undone the top button of his shirt. Joe stands six foot two and can barely see through the frame of the door without ducking. His stomach bulges at the waist of pants that have grown too small. But he still manages to be handsome.

"I'm supposed to tell you to wear the dress," Joe says, as though talking about women's clothing has just cut off his balls.

My sister's voice echoes from downstairs. "Wear the damn dress! The one I gave you!"

Joe smiles and hands me the glass of bourbon he cradles in his hands. "The mouth on her, I'm telling you. Our kid is gonna be so fucked up."

I feel the smile growing and I want to cry. Joe loves my sister. She loves him. They both love Mason. *Love, love, love.* It's all around me, making me regret staying away so long. But then also reminding me why I have. The love is here, but it always feels just beyond my reach.

I take a sip of the bourbon.

"Yeah, well, that was a given, right? You married a Lochner," I say.

Joe rolls his eyes. Shakes his head. "I know. Is it too late to get out?"

"Kind of."

Joe sighs. He glances at the dress hanging on the shower rod. "All right. Just wear the dress. And this guy—he'd better not be a douchebag or I will kick his ass so hard. . . ."

I nod. "Got it. Dress. Ass kicking."

Then he adds, and my smile fades, "Are you sure you're ready for this?"

I've returned home because of a man, a breakup, and that's all they know about it. I haven't had the courage to tell them more. They're happy to have me back. More than happy. And I don't have the stomach to see that change by revealing another bad chapter in my life. The fact that they haven't pressed me for answers tells me they're expecting the worst—and that they don't really want to know. Maybe they need to believe I've changed as much as I do. Maybe we will now be a normal family because I'll stop being me.

Still, I know it must seem a bit extreme, taking a leave of absence from a competitive job, a grown woman moving in with her sister, just because of that. One breakup, and with a man they'd never met or even heard of. How serious could it have been? I feel this question seeping from Rosie's skin every second of every day.

I consider Joe's question. *Am I ready for this?* I look at him and shrug. "Probably not," I say.

Joe replies with sarcasm. "Awesome."

We had this same conversation before I came upstairs. Joe walked in circles, wiping counters, listening to the hum of the dishwasher, feeling satisfied that he'd put everything back in order after being at work all day. (He's neat. Rosie is not.) He's a happy hamster running on his wheel.

Just have fun. Don't make too much of it. I would walk across glass to be free for a night!

Rosie punched the side of his arm, and he sighed dramatically like he was nostalgic for his single life. They both like to do this. Rosie in the kitchen making me coffee, complaining about the long day ahead. Joe in the kitchen at night, just the two of us, each having a bourbon, pulling back his floppy black hair so I can see the receding of his hairline. *Look!* he says. *Can't you see it! I'm balding from boredom!*

But all I see is the truth. I see it when they fold Mason in their arms, or steal a kiss when they think they're alone. It's all just talk.

It's the way happy people talk when they want to make the rest of us feel better.

Our friend Gabe was over as well, lending advice. Gabe was the fourth lifelong compatriot in our childhood band of thieves. He lived right next door with his parents and older brother, until the brother went to military school and then enlisted in the army. Now Gabe lives in that same house where he grew up. He bought it from his mother after his father died and she moved to Florida.

It's odd how the three of them are all still here. Right where I left them a decade ago.

Gabe got married just last year to a woman he met through work. *Melissa.* She was a client of his, but he never talks about that because it's *awkward and unseemly*—his words. Gabe does IT forensics, sometimes for suspicious spouses like Melissa had been when they first met. He found the evidence that led to her divorce and now she's married to Gabe.

He's happy, but not the kind of happy that makes you talk shit about it. I imagine it will take more than a baby to get him there. Melissa was broken, and Gabe likes to fix things—people, especially. But Melissa is an outsider to Rosie and Joe, and to me now that I've come home. She moved here from Vermont to be with her first husband and now she's here for Gabe. It's difficult to see her in three dimensions.

It doesn't help that she is tolerated here rather than welcome, though we all try to hide it. She's tall and stick thin and that makes Rosie feel short and fat, even at five four and 130 pounds. Melissa doesn't like how much Joe swears, her back arching every time he drops the f-bomb. Which, of course, makes Joe say it more. He managed to use it four times in one sentence last week at a barbecue. And me—well, I'm a single woman with a lifetime of stories lived with her husband. She's too simpleminded to understand our friendship.

So, as Joe says every time she leaves and wants Gabe to follow, *Fuck her.* The band of thieves from Deer Hill Lane is a tough crowd.

Gabe stayed today, after Melissa left. He gave me a cheeseball wink and said something encouraging like, *Laura will eat this guy for lunch. She's always been fierce and fearless.*

I tried to smile. But the truth is, I left a great job because a man broke my heart. Not so fierce and fearless after all, am I? Not exactly Lara Croft or Jessica Jones, kicking ass and taking names. Men falling at my feet—*but I have no time for them because I have to save the world.*

This talk, like the ones before it, stopped before we got to the good part. To the bad things this fierce and fearless girl has done. Right here, in this town.

Mason calls out for Joe. His voice melts my heart. Rosie probably put him up to it. I can hear her—*Mason*—go call for Daddy! She's enjoying a glass of wine.

Joe rolls his eyes.

"Want me to leave the bourbon?" Joe asks.

"Which one of us needs it more?" I reply.

"Good point."

Joe takes the bourbon and leaves me with the dress and the makeup.

And the mirror.

I did not find Jonathan Fields right away. I was a novice on findlove.com and did everything wrong. The first mistake was being honest in describing myself. I said I was *independent but compromising*. I preferred *tequila to chardonnay, scuba diving to sunbathing, sneakers to high heels*. I said I didn't know if I wanted children. Cringe.

And the worst, most colossal mistake—the pictures. They were current and unfiltered. Me on a hike with an old friend. Me playing with Mason on the front lawn. Me standing in the kitchen in a T-shirt, my mousy brown hair in a ponytail. No boobs showing, not even my poor excuse for them.

I thought they were attractive—the pictures, that is (I'm not a good judge of boobs). All of it, the entire profile, was me. The old me.

When we were just kids who ran through the woods like hooligans, thoughts of romantic love a million years away, our mother used to hold court in our kitchen. One day Rosie and I came inside undetected. I can't recall what we needed from the house, but we stopped at the foot of the kitchen door when we overheard her say my name to Gabe's mother, Mrs. Wallace. I was six, Rosie eight. They were drinking coffee.

I don't know. . . . She was just born that way. Born with fists for hands. It's hard to love a girl like that.

I've never forgotten it, that expression. *Fists for hands.* Or the conclusion she'd come to about my fate. Rosie pulled me away, back outside, where we were free and easy. She made a joke about it, about how our mother was always wrong about everything, anyway. Rosie was trying to protect me from words that should have been hurtful, but all I remember feeling was a sense of pride that our mother had bothered to see me at all. I had always felt invisible to her.

We never spoke of it again—about how hard it was to love me. Rosie got her hands on Joe and held on to him like the golden ring at the carousel. And I rejected everything remotely feminine, beating it all away with my fists for hands. The color pink. Smiles. Dresses.

In the race for love, she learned to walk and I'm still crawling. Though she's never stopped trying to teach me.

I find my reflection in the tiny oval mirror and give it a look of admonishment. My brown eyes and mousy hair.

No, no, no.

Nope. No looking back. *Lipstick, cherry red . . .*

Old Laura woke up every morning to an empty mailbox on findlove.com. Not a wink or like or message. So, in spite of the worry Rosie hides behind smiles, she helped me change my profile and the new me got a date with Jonathan Fields.

I put on the dress, wrapping it around my body and tying it at the waist. We've always been the same size, though Rosie has boobs and curves and high cheekbones and gold highlights that light up her face. Sometime I think I willed those things away too, when I was a little girl. Still, I let myself look in the mirror and see what I knew I would see. It is pretty. I am pretty.

I put on the one pair of high heels that's not in a box in the basement. Black pumps. I can't stop now.

Dark circles erased. Lips bright red. Rosy cheeks. Pretty dress. I'm feminine and fun-loving. Smart but obedient. Ready to move into some man's life like a new piece of furniture. *I look just as good in jeans as I do in a black cocktail dress.* That's what men say they want. That's what women say they are.

It feels dishonest, but what I feel doesn't matter. Not tonight.

Rosie has been teaching me—how to be sexy but not sleazy. How to be smart but not intimidating.

It's a game, Laura. Do what you have to do to get the first date. Then you can be yourself. People don't know what they want until it's right in front of them.

Yes. That's true.

Joe was more pragmatic.

Men don't read the profiles. They look at the pictures and measure their hard-ons.

Sometimes I think I will lose my mind trying to understand. The shrink told me that I would find it here, at home. The answer to this question about me and men. Me and love. Why I lack the skills to find it, and why I beat it away when it finds me. Me with my fists for hands. The girl no one can love. So here I am.

Our mother was beautiful and she did everything that was asked of her. She would have killed it on findlove.com. Even so, our father left her when I was twelve. He left her, left us, for a woman who was older than our mother. A woman who didn't wear dresses. He left us and moved to Boston with her. Now our mother lives alone in California, still trying to get past that first date.

Our father's name was Richard. He hated when people called him Dick, for the obvious reason.

I haven't seen Dick in sixteen years.

I'm tired of not knowing the answer about me and love.

But tonight I will not ask questions. I will not wonder why Jonathan Fields clicked on my profile—if it was because my new pictures gave him a hard-on or because he read my fake profile and it made him feel good about himself. I'm so tired of all of this. I just want to be done. I want it to be over. I want to stop fighting. I want to be happy like Rosie and Joe. So happy, I talk shit about it.

I take a deep breath and gather the cherry-red lipstick from the counter. I turn off the light. Walk out the door and down the stairs. I find Joe and Rosie in the kitchen, cooking something with too much garlic. Gabe has gone home to his wife, reluctantly no doubt. Still, I envy that he has someone waiting for him. He's torn, but he's also happy. Nothing is perfect. I would settle for that.

"Oh!" Rosie gasps. "You wore the dress!" She stops cooking and presses her right hand over her heart like she's about to recite the Pledge of Allegiance. She's not sure if she's happy that I'm going on a date. We've been walking this thin line of hope and worry since the day she came to fetch me in New York. But the fact that I've worn her dress somehow makes her feel better. Maybe it will just be a normal first date if I look this pretty.

"You look very nice." Joe nods with the approval of a teacher handing back a test. A teacher who's not a pervert. A test with a good grade.

"Thanks," I say with the smile that got lost upstairs.

I feel naked arms around my naked legs and look down to see a little creature looking up. "Lala," Mason says. He closes his eyes like he's savoring his knowledge of me, my smell, and my name (sort of) and how I will now bend down and pick him up and give him a giant kiss. He tires of it quickly and squirms away, bare down to a diaper, and filled with joy that is unstoppable.

I wonder if I ever felt that way. I can't imagine it.

Rosie gives me her car keys. "You'll be back, right? Otherwise I can call you an Uber. . . ."

I take the keys. I will not stay out long with this man. Just enough to entice him. Rosie has told me how this works, and I am finally going to get it right.

I take the keys to make sure of it. Driving your sister's minivan is better than not shaving your legs to ensure abstinence. I'll be home tonight.

"Don't forget the purse!" Rosie says. She points to a black purse that goes with the dress and that sits on the counter. "I emptied it for you."

I take the purse. I put the lipstick inside.

I walk to the side door that leads to the driveway.

"You'll be home?" Rosie asks again.

"Don't worry," I say.

I give them one last smile. They look at me across a room that has grown silent. I see a flash of hope wash over Rosie and it kills the hope inside me. Because right on its heels is the bone-deep fear that never leaves her when she looks at me.

I say nothing, swallowing the words.

You don't need to worry, because I'm not going to be me tonight.

I have not convinced her with the lipstick and the dress. But she'll see. I've left old me upstairs in the attic. I've done everything right this time. And I've chosen Jonathan Fields. A man with a proven track record in the sport of love and commitment.

Don't worry, Rosie. You'll see in the morning.

I am going to get it right tonight.

Even if it kills me.

THREE

Rosie Ferro. Present Day. Friday, 5 a.m. Branston, CT.

Something is wrong.

Rosie felt it the moment her eyes opened to the dimly lit room. The body of a two-year-old was curled up beside her. Mason was a heat-seeking missile when he found his way into their bed. Joe was gone, his covers pulled down, likely in a fit of frustration as he made a hasty exit to the couch in the family room downstairs. Their bed wasn't big enough for the three of them anymore, and neither of them had the energy to break Mason of the habit.

A night-light lit up the room enough to see his sweet, innocent face. White as snow with a mop of dark hair, like his father. A little man-child.

She pressed her cheek against his soft skin.

"Okay," she said to herself in a whisper. "Everything's okay."

But she didn't believe it.

She reached for her phone on the nightstand. It was five a.m, which explained the throbbing in her head. They'd gone to bed later than usual. Mason had been restless and hard to put down.

When it was done, after five stories and sitting by his bed while he dozed off, Rosie had washed down two Benadryl with a glass of wine. She knew her mind wouldn't rest unless she hit it hard.

Joe hadn't asked why. He already knew. She'd been on edge like this from the moment Laura had moved in. Rosie had driven the minivan into the city, helped her pack up her things like a mother bear rescuing her cub from the side of a cliff. And just like a mother bear, she hadn't stopped hovering and worrying, and yet trying to remain inconspicuous so she didn't make things worse. It was a task that had every nerve in her body ignited, ready to respond to whatever crisis unfolded next.

Joe had kissed her on the forehead as she lay in their bed, curled up in a ball, eyes staring at nothing. Her mind racing down rabbit holes of bad scenarios as she waited for the drugs and wine to kick in.

She's fine, Joe had said. *It's just a date.*

He'd gone back downstairs to watch whatever sports he could find and drink a beer. He seemed almost giddy as he left the room, having the television, and the entire downstairs for that matter, to himself for a change. Their house was small, and having Laura there had made it even smaller these past weeks.

Joe and Laura were always together somewhere—the kitchen or family room—their shared sense of sarcastic humor fueled by each other's company. And Gabe—he'd been coming over more often, it seemed—and without Melissa (thankfully, because Rosie had not gotten used to her). Joe was a different person around Laura and Gabe. He was that strong, good-looking kid who ruled the world. Or Deer Hill Lane, at least. It was in his voice and in his smile. Unbridled confidence. She missed seeing him that way. But time only moved in one direction. They weren't kids anymore.

Joe said he wasn't worried about Laura, and Rosie was done

fighting with him about the subject. He always had an answer, a comeback she couldn't refute.

You don't know her the way I do.

Really? I grew up with both of you.

But . . .

No buts . . . Is there one thing you know about Laura that I don't?

There wasn't—and yet hearing a story is not the same as living that story. Seeing it and feeling it and absorbing the intangible, indescribable things that settle into your gut somehow. Joe said he wasn't worried that she was already out on a date, a date with a stranger from the Internet, just weeks after fleeing her entire life because of some guy who blew her off after she'd *given him her heart*, whatever that meant.

Fact: Laura had never mentioned this boyfriend until she showed up back home. How serious could it have been? And yet he caused her to *take a break* from her job—a coveted job that wouldn't be waiting for her much longer.

It was undeniable that Laura had bad luck with men. For someone so smart, and Laura was that if nothing else, she kept making the same mistake over and over. What Joe couldn't seem to grasp, the intangible thing he couldn't feel, was the reason why. This latest breakup was just a symptom.

Or, perhaps, a warning.

Rosie pressed her lips against Mason's warm cheek then slowly snuck out of the bed. She tiptoed across the floor, down the hall and then the stairs to the family room. She found her husband on the sofa, his big, burly body trying to hide beneath a small throw blanket to keep warm.

From there, she went to the bay window and looked out onto the street, and to the short driveway to the right where she normally parked her car.

She stood there for a moment, looking. Searching. Down the street to the right, then to the left. Her mind kicking into the next gear.

She walked back to the sofa and placed her hand on Joe's arm until he stirred.

"What's wrong?" he mumbled. "What time is it?"

"Five," she answered.

"What's happened? Mason . . ."

"No, he's fine. Sleeping."

Rosie lay down on the small space left on the sofa, curling her body into his. He opened his arms and pulled her close. The warmth of him, the feel of his physical strength, made her sigh.

"Then what?" he whispered.

"The car's not back."

"What car?"

"My car. The one Laura took on her date."

Joe kissed her ear and laughed. "Good for her," he said.

Rosie pushed him away and sat up, looking back and forth between Joe and the empty driveway she could still see through the bay window.

"It's not funny!" she said.

"So she got carried away. So what?" Joe slid his hand across her thigh. "Maybe we should get carried away."

"Stop." Rosie pushed his hand off and stood up. Arms folded, shoulders tense with worry, she walked across the room to the window.

"Don't you think it's strange how she came back after all these years? Dating on the Internet. Staying out all night . . ."

Joe sat up now as well, pulling the throw blanket around his bare shoulders. "She's trying to figure things out, that's all. Maybe it's about time. Maybe she's tired of running."

Rosie considered this. Laura had left this town the second she graduated from high school. She'd never looked back. There had been "drive-bys" at the holidays. She'd sent gifts for Mason. She'd called and texted and emailed. But she'd never come to stay. When Rosie wanted to see her, she took Mason into the city and forced Laura to be part of their lives.

And now, suddenly, here she was. Wanting to change. Looking for the *right* kind of man. Wearing makeup and dresses. Taking advice from Rosie when she used to chastise her, calling her a *girl*, as if there were no insult that could sting more.

Come on! Stop being such a girl!

Christ, how she used to taunt them all into danger. Climbing trees taller than their roofline. Walking across the barely frozen pond.

Come on!

There was a nature preserve behind the houses on their street. Acres of woods, trails, and streams that had been their playground. Laura was the youngest and they had all taken to protecting her from herself, Rosie and Joe among them.

She'd eaten up the attention like a starving animal, from the neighborhood kids when she was younger, and, later, from the nuns at their Catholic school.

St. Mark's of the Holy Trinity. It was a joke in their Protestant family. The city had decent schools through eighth grade, but they got too big and unruly after that. Private schools were expensive. So were the houses in the smaller towns nearby, the more suburban communities, because their public schools got kids into the top colleges. Parochial school was the best option for families like Rosie and Laura's, especially after their father left.

The faculty had adored Laura. So when they caught her smoking in eighth grade, and doing other things every other year until she graduated, they would speak to her like a little lamb who was born without the instinct to herd. *There's a good reason to stay with the herd,* they would tell her. *Nothing less than survival itself.*

If you keep leaving the herd, the wolves will come.

Laura always had the same response.

Good thing I like wolves.

Rosie looked back at Joe.

"I'm going to check her room," she said.

"Don't do that." Joe was close to pleading.

"Why not?"

"Because if she did Uber home and was finally able to sleep, you'll wake her up. She hasn't slept well since she got here. She's turning into a zombie."

"But what if something happened?"

"It was just a date."

"With some guy from the Internet."

"That's what people do these days. And besides that, he's old as fuck and drives a BMW."

Rosie sighed. "I have a bad feeling," she said.

"You always have a bad feeling this time of year."

He wasn't wrong about that. It was barely September, but the distinctive smell was in the air, the changing seasons, fires burning, tugging at memories that would never find a place to settle. And once they crept from the back corners of her mind, they always played out to the end.

Cool night air. Smoke and heat blowing sideways from a fire. The branches popping, not quite dead. Not ready to burn . . .

"What if it's about Laura? What if it's a sign?"

Rosie walked back to the sofa and stood in front of him.

"Please don't wake her up. I can't take a sister fight at five in the morning."

"I have to check. I'll be quiet."

Joe grabbed her wrist, but then let go when he felt her pull away.

There were so many things they still didn't know about Laura's return. She never said his name—this guy who broke her heart. They called him "Asshole." Or, if Mason was in the room, "A-hole." That had been Joe's idea. Neither of them had wanted to press her for answers she wasn't ready to give.

But there were so many pieces of her story that weren't adding up.

For the first time in my life, I thought I had it right.

She said she'd been seeing a therapist, trying to break bad habits, change. But if she'd gotten it right, this man would not have disappeared.

The nuns at St. Mark's had been right about her, always leaving the safety of the herd. And Laura was right about herself. She liked wolves.

But Laura was no lamb.

Rosie stopped at the top of the stairs and let the memory play on.

Cheep beer in plastic cups. Cigarettes. Flavored lip gloss. Bug spray . . .

It was a tradition on the last day of summer, the last Saturday night before the start of school.

Branston was a small city, flanked by the Long Island Sound on one end and the rural woodlands of New York State on the other. Just at the northern border, before the woodlands and rolling farmland, was the public preserve and river gorge that backed up to Deer Hill Lane.

They didn't live far from it now, though Rosie had never gone back. Not in eleven years.

Every year it was the same. Dozens of local kids bursting at the seams with the excitement of change. It was in the air. A new season. A new grade. Getting older. Wanting new things. Dreading new things. Needing new things. Hope pushing up against fear like summer against fall. She could still conjure that feeling in her gut.

They'd parked their cars on a gravel road along its edge and walked to a small clearing. Music from someone's speaker had been drowned out by the clamor of drunk teenagers. She'd been a sophomore in college. Laura had been starting her senior year of high school. Joe hadn't been at the party that night. His family had wanted one last weekend at their house on the Cape. Gabe had already gone back to college. Of the four of them, it was only Rosie and Laura who had been at the party that night. And it was only Rosie who knew what it felt like to hear that scream in the woods.

Maybe that was enough remembering. Maybe it would leave her now.

Rosie walked quietly across the hardwood floor. The house was a Cape, built in the 1930s. The floors upstairs were bird's-eye maple, gorgeous but old, and every step created a noisy creak. She made it past her bedroom without waking her son, then continued down the hall.

Laura stayed in a small converted attic. It was at the end of the hallway, just past the guest bathroom. The lights were off, her door closed.

Rosie took another step, placing her foot down in front of her, gently at first, before shifting her weight.

Then she stopped, suddenly aware of herself, creeping around her house in a state of panic the way she had done when Mason was born. How many times had she woken him from a peaceful sleep just to make sure he was still breathing? Her fears were not normal.

Or maybe they were. Maybe there was good reason.

Rosie had been her sister's protector from the day she was born. It was in her blood, in her bones. But it had never been enough. In the end, she had failed.

The smell of the fire. The scream in the woods . . .

She would never forget it. She would never stop hearing it. The woods had been silenced in an instant. No one had moved. They'd all just frozen, wondering what they'd heard. Waiting to see if it would come again. And it did. A second scream. Rosie had looked around the fire, searching for Laura. Even as her legs had started to move toward the road where the cars were parked, where the scream had come from, she'd kept looking, hoping, that she was wrong. That the scream did not belong to her sister.

Two more steps and she was outside the attic door. She pressed her ear against the wood and listened for sound. The TV, maybe. Music. Laura sometimes fell asleep with things still playing. But the room was quiet.

She placed her hand on the doorknob and turned it gently. But it, too, creaked from age. So would the door jam as it twisted on rusty metal. There was no getting in the room without waking the person inside. But Rosie was too far gone to care, and the memory kept playing.

They'd run to the road, scattering through the woods to find the quickest path. There was no trail. It had been so dark. Someone had a flashlight and they'd turned it on. Someone else had gotten into a car and turned on the headlights. The screams had become sobs. Down the road were two figures. One standing and one on the gravel road, lying still . . .

Rosie pushed the attic door open, slowly, already talking herself down. They were not in the woods. Whatever she found in this room wouldn't mean anything. Laura was a grown woman. Maybe she got too drunk to drive and stayed at his place. Maybe she stayed to sleep with him. She'd promised to be home with the car, but people break promises like that all the time. Especially Laura. Especially when it came to men. Her good intentions were always overcome by the desire and longing that were never satisfied. And so what if she did sleep with him? Joe was right: the guy was older. Forty and divorced. Safe to the point of boring.

But all of this reasoning came and went without effect. The past, the scream in the woods. And that boy lying at her sister's feet. The memory played.

Running to her sister, breathless from screaming her name. *Laura!* Coming to her, that look on her face. Terror. Disbelief. And that boy on the ground. The blood pooling around his head. Laura's first love. The one who'd broken her heart. Dead.

This memory always played until the end. Always. Rosie blinked away the last image and looked for her sister.

Laura had been gone for ten years, but it didn't matter. Rosie was always waiting for the next tragedy to unfold.

The door open now, she flipped on the light.

And all she found was an empty bed.

FOUR

Laura. Session Number Six.
Three Months Ago. New York City.

Laura: Rosie thinks I bring this on myself. She says I'm the one breaking hearts.

Dr. Brody: What about that? What about the ones who did love you?

Laura: They didn't love me. They just thought they did.

Dr. Brody: Because they didn't know you?

Laura: Maybe. Rosie says I choose men who won't love me. I choose them *because* they won't love me. But why would I do that?

Dr. Brody: To prove a point.

Laura: What point?

Dr. Brody: It will be more helpful if you find the answer yourself.

Laura: Don't take this the wrong way, but I hate you a little right now.

FIVE

Laura. The Night Before. Thursday, 7:30 p.m. Branston, CT.

Jonathan. John. Johnny. Jack. As I drive downtown, I wonder what people call him.

There's traffic and I'm running late. Construction. One-lane road. Shit. *It's good to be late. Keep him waiting!* I tell this to myself. I can be one of those women who pull this off. Hide the eagerness. Hide the desire.

I think about texting him, but he said he doesn't like to text. I don't want to call, because that's a little extreme. And, of course, my phone is on low battery because I forgot the charger from my room. God forbid Rosie should leave one in the car.

He'll wait ten minutes. Won't he?

The minivan smells like Goldfish and apple juice. Rosie cleans it every week, but it makes no difference. I don't think she smells it anymore, she's so used to it, like the stale coffee that pervades the kitchen until Joe comes home from work and empties the pot.

The kitchen is Rosie's domain until then, and I usually find her there staring at nothing while Mason watches cartoons. She pours me the stale coffee (to chase away the bourbon hangovers from late nights with Joe and Gabe) and recites mantras from her days as a feminist, with the same breath that she gives me advice on how to be attractive.

You don't need a man, Laura. Not for anything.

At the risk of stating the obvious, it's easy to say you don't need something when you're holding it in your hands. She might as well tell me she doesn't need her coffee as she inhales her second cup.

Still, I consider her advice now as I feel the panic that he might leave because I'm ten minutes late.

I don't need a man.

The only trouble is that after years of wondering why it was so hard for me to find one, I finally had done just that—found a man who loved me.

He didn't stay long, but while he was here, he unlocked the door to a well of needs. And there were so many of them. The need to be held and touched. The need to laugh and cry and search another's soul. The need to be seen. To be known. Not the fierce and fearless warrior who conquered the world, but the little girl tugging on a sleeve or the hem of a coat, looking up. Always, always looking up with the foolish hope that someone would look back and be happy to see me there.

I am pathetic with my silly daydreams.

Jonathan Fields . . . do they call you Nathan? Or Nate?

I wonder if he's handsome in real life. I wonder if his hair is as dark and full as his pictures, his eyes as blue. His body as fit as it looks hidden beneath a shirt. I wonder if I will see that thing in his eyes that I love. Mischief. Just a little. Not the kind old me likes. Just enough to keep her quiet.

But whatever I see when my eyes first fall upon Jonathan Fields, I will not ignore it. I will not pretend he is the right man if there is clear evidence that he is the wrong man. And I will not invent evidence to prove he's the wrong man if he's the right man.

I am handicapped by a lack of instinct. Tonight will not be easy.

Jonathan Fields. I'm almost there.

Past the construction on Main Street. I make a left on Hyde, another on Richmond. I find a spot at a meter and pull in. We're meeting at an Irish pub that is just on the block behind me. On the left. It's nestled in between an upscale diner and an Italian place. They have seating outside in the summer. When we were kids, we used to get in with our fake IDs. I think it's harder these days. But maybe they've learned how to make better IDs. Ours were more pathetic than my daydreams.

I have so many memories from growing up in this town. They've been crawling out from every corner since the day I returned.

Jonathan Fields suggested this place. He said it was near his apartment so he went there a lot and the bartenders would give him free whiskey. Not that he couldn't afford whiskey. He made sure to throw that in, and I have not done anything with any of this information. I've left my scaffolding at home. There will be no inventions tonight. No reconstructions. No blind eyes. I had an excellent therapist, even if I was a terrible patient.

I open the vanity mirror and check my face. Mascara hasn't smudged. Cheeks are rosy. I apply some more cherry-red lipstick because I've been biting my lip. I rub some of it off my teeth with my finger. That's really *not* a good look. Lipstick on your teeth. Seriously. That could have been a fatal unforced error.

Damn it! Have I become my mother? I close the mirror and stare out the windshield, onto the street. After Dick left us, our mother couldn't sleep or eat unless she had a boyfriend, and she would go to the bottom of the barrel to find one. After Dick left us, she went out almost every night and I remember hating her for it.

How do I look, girls?

We don't give a shit, Mom. We have homework and tests and our periods and zits and the other tortures of puberty to deal with—alone—thank you very much.

I don't want to be someone I hate. But maybe that's what's required.

I feel that thing in my stomach. It's not quite anxiety. Not quite nervousness. It is distinct, a feeling specific to this set of circumstances—a first date after a bad breakup. It's hope, but it's so fragile. Hope on its deathbed. People gathered around it, saying prayers. A priest standing over it, reading last rites. Part of me has already grieved it. Part of me can't until it's totally dead, maybe even until it's been buried six feet under.

I need a drink ASAP.

Hand on the handle, door open. Grab purse, phone, keys. Close the door. Lock the car. It's 7:38.

I walk like I could give a shit about anything, across the street, down the block. My heart is beating faster and it's pissing me off. I breathe slower but it makes it worse. I can feel my cheeks getting redder than they already were.

A small group of people stands outside, smoking and laughing. They've clearly enjoyed happy hour drink prices. I walk around them and find the door, pull the handle. Step inside.

The bar is dark. Dimly lit. Wood paneling. There are tables in the back and loud music playing in the front, which is packed with people of all ages—except middle. Middle-aged people are home with their kids. It's Thursday night, after all.

I scan the crowd. Two naughty girls to my right, drunk and

slutty. Talking to three young executives. Douchebags. I wonder how that math is going to work out. To my left are five colleagues from a medical office. They're still wearing their cotton-candy shirts and badges. Dead center is the bar, lined with an assortment of men and women. No one is alone. Shit. Did he leave? Did he blow me off? No, no, no! The thought rips through me and I realize in an instant how vulnerable I am tonight.

It doesn't sit well, being vulnerable. It makes me feel like a wild animal trapped in a corner. Nothing left to do but fight its way out. It brings back memories of things I don't want to remember. So many mistakes. So many regrets. They come in flashes, sweeping in like Sarin gas, devastating every nerve in my body. Paralyzing me with self-hatred.

I realize now that I have started to believe in Jonathan Fields when he is nothing more than a name and a voice and a story on a page. I have let it all swirl around in my head and become a real person, like a kid with an imaginary friend. Insanity. Desperation. I've done it again. I haven't followed the instructions. This does not bode well.

I feel a hand on my shoulder and I turn.

"Laura?" he says. There he is . . . Jonathan Fields, saving me from myself. Saving himself from me, though he doesn't know it.

He's beautiful. I almost gasp, that's how beautiful he is. And I haven't even had a drink.

Blue eyes. Dark hair. Just like his pictures. Only his face has structure that the pictures didn't capture—the way his cheekbones frame his perfect nose. The way his smile pulls up higher on one side, more endearing than smug. And his body—that slender, fit body—it moves with masculine grace.

All of this rushes in and sweeps me away.

"Yeah. Jonathan?" I'm so perfectly collected right now. I don't know how, because the emotional 180 has nearly killed me. I want to crawl under the covers in Rosie's attic and disappear from the world.

His eyes scan me up and down. It's a little odd, to be honest, but if he's feeling any bit of what I'm feeling, nothing would be odd. I am blinded by a surge of adrenaline. I have no sense of myself.

Then he speaks.

"Sorry, it's just . . . well, you're really beautiful."

I let his words enter my brain for processing. I get my shit together. Clear the Sarin from my bloodstream. The adrenaline clears as well, and the words get through. They sound sincere. *Check*. And they explain his roving eyes. *Check*. All good.

I smile. I have to force myself. Voices echo in the distance. My sister's. The ghosts of my past. They tell me I shouldn't be here.

Go home. Get under the covers.

He looks around. His eyes pause on the back room with the tables. He loses his smile, but only for a second.

"Listen," he says. "This place is kind of crowded. I'd really like to go somewhere quiet where we can talk and get to know each other."

He's not wrong. It's loud and smells like stale beer. People are laughing too hard because they're drunk at seven forty-five on a Thursday. And he wants to talk. That's a good sign. I walk back from the ledge of an emotional inferno.

"Sure," I say. I smile again.

He touches my arm and leads me in front of him toward the door. As we're walking out, past the sluts and douchebags and cotton candy uniforms, I think I hear someone call his name. I try to look back where the tables are, where the voice came from, but he moves past me and waves me on to follow. When he gets to the door, he opens it and ushers me outside. Then to the corner of Richmond and Maple. He doesn't stop walking until we're in the parking lot of a CVS.

I follow, not asking where we're going.

I don't know why.

Well, that's not really true.

He turns to face me, a little winded. He looks over my shoulder, then back at me with a smile.

"Sorry about that. I just couldn't hear myself think in there. It's been one of those days."

I know exactly what to say.

"It's fine. I've had some of those myself. What do you want to do?" I'm so understanding. *It's all about you, Jonathan Fields.*

He points to a building just down the block.

"That's where I live. I'm parked in the garage. Want to take my car and go down to the water? There's a ton of places down there."

"Sure!" I say with enthusiasm. *Anything you want, Jonathan Fields.*

We start to walk.

"I hope you don't take this the wrong way, but I was so relieved when I saw you."

I get it now. He hid in the back somewhere until he could scope me out.

"So, what would you have done if I was old, fat, and ugly?" My tone is slick and I hate myself again. I hear Rosie. *It's not that hard—just be nice for God's sake!* Nice. Be nice. Not slick. Not irreverent.

But then he laughs. He finds my irreverence amusing. I fight to keep from making assumptions. Drawing conclusions. Maybe he's just nervous. People laugh when they're nervous. It doesn't mean he sees old me. Real me. And likes *her*. It doesn't mean anything. We just met. *Do not invent him.*

And—I'm the one who should be nervous. I'm walking now into an underground parking garage. Alone with this man. This stranger. No one else in sight.

He pulls out his keys and clicks the button. A Toyota sedan lights up. It's not the car I was expecting from a forty-year-old banker with no kids to feed. It's not the black BMW he told me about.

It's not that I care about money. I've fallen for all kinds of men. Teachers. Students. A handy man. It's just that it's not adding up. But what do I know about divorce and alimony and the cost of keeping a house and an apartment? Nothing. Well, maybe a little. It's not rocket science. Maybe his BMW is in the shop. I'm so very good at inventing stories.

But, anyway, it's too late. He opens my door and I get inside. The door closes and my stomach tightens.

This was supposed to be simple. I was supposed to be new me tonight. Just a girl who wore a dress and went on a date. My head is throbbing. I'm so tired from the emotional roller coaster of the past fifteen minutes. Facts are spinning around and around. The car. His story . . .

And that woman's voice from the back of the bar, calling after him as we made a hasty departure.

Please let me be wrong, Jonathan Fields.

Please be the man you said you were. *Please, please, please.*

Because I don't know what I'll do if you're not.

SIX

Rosie. Present Day. Friday, 5:30 a.m.
Branston, CT.

Rosie stood before the empty bed. She drew both hands to her mouth, open palms pressed to her lips to silence the fear.

She started to turn, run back downstairs to tell Joe that Laura really hadn't come home last night. But then she stopped. He would just repeat his theory about how she got *carried away*. About Laura being Laura.

So she began the search for her sister, alone.

It felt strange to be among Laura's things, and she paused to consider her actions. It was a violation. There was no way around it. She knew her sister at her core, but the outer layers that had been built around it these past ten years—she knew nothing of those. Only benign facts. What she studied in college. The basic tasks of her job as an analyst. A vague description of her office and colleagues. *Bitchy Betty. Hot Henry.* She had a best friend there, a woman named Jill. The two of them had made up nicknames for everyone else. It was funny, but impersonal. Rosie didn't even know if she'd been happy there.

When Rosie called her, and even when she'd gone in with Mason to see her at her apartment, they spoke of sandwich shops and political scandals and Mason not sleeping in his bed and the Stepford Wives at the mommy and me classes. Never about the layers—not Laura's. And not her own. Rosie hadn't even met her roommate, who never seemed to be there on the weekends. She had a boyfriend in New Jersey who had his own place.

Having Laura here, in her house, felt more like hosting a family friend who'd come for a visit than a family member. So it also felt strange to be in her room, looking through her private things.

And yet, at the same time, she *was* family, and Rosie was worried the way only family can worry because of the history they shared and the things she knew. And how those things now made her feel. The mother bear protecting her cub.

Something is wrong.

It was a familiar feeling. One she'd had since she wore braids and plaid kilts and would find Laura in her room, crying under her bed where no one would see her. Or up in that tree, fear overcoming the determination that made her start climbing.

No one remembers that Rosie had gone up after her more than once, swallowing her own fear to help her sister get back down. But that was the truth.

What is the truth now, Laura? Where are you?

She shook off the apprehension and let her eyes scan the room the way they never had before. Even when she'd come to find her sister here—bringing her food, bringing Mason to jump on her bed. Seeing if she wanted to go for a walk or a drive or sneak out for a drink after Joe got home. She'd been in this room dozens of times and yet never seen it beyond Laura. It was always just a setting, a backdrop. Now, it was transformed in her absence.

She looked around carefully. There were four coffee mugs, some empty, some with remnants days old. Also three dirty dessert plates. Four water glasses. Rosie gathered them slowly, methodically piling them on the floor just outside in the hallway.

Her eyes turned next to the unmade bed. The black eyeshades that lay across a pillow. The sheets and blankets tangled from restless sleep. Dreams. Nightmares, maybe.

Does the past visit you at night, Laura? Is that why you can't sleep?

She shook out the covers and then made the bed. Replaced the throw pillows that had fallen to the floor. Laura was everywhere in this room. Her smell. Her clothes, strewn about the pieces of furniture. A chair. A bedside table. Even the floor. They hung in the closet and draped from the shelves where they had been placed without any concern for folding. For order. And Rosie found herself straightening them as she checked the pockets, undoing the chaos in this room as though it might turn back the clock and bring Laura home safe and sound.

It was just after five-thirty when she sat at Laura's desk. A laptop was open, its screen black. Papers and books were stacked in piles. A notepad. Pens. Writings on paper.

Rosie looked through them, slowly at first, cautiously, as though Laura might walk through the door and see her. It was ridiculous. Of course she was looking for something, anything, that might tell her where her sister had gone. If for no other reason than she had Rosie's car and she had promised to have it back by morning.

Page after page, there was nothing but work. Notes and data about companies. She'd said she was staying on top of things. Rosie hadn't fully believed her.

She started then with desk drawers, finding most of them empty.

A stapler, but that was Joe's, when this had been his desk. Some more pens. Paper clips. Nothing personal. Not even a checkbook.

She closed the last one and sat back in the chair, her eyes now on the computer. She placed her finger on the track pad and swirled it slowly until the screen came to life. It wasn't locked.

She sat back then and stared at the screen, now filled with the color from a photograph.

Rosie was startled as she saw herself staring back, just ten perhaps, with Laura, who must have been eight. Beyond them, at the edge of the creek that ran behind their house, were two little boys. She knew them instantly.

One of them was Joe—strong and tan, his dark hair long, past his ears. How strange it was to see him as a boy, to be reminded that they'd been friends since birth, that they'd ever been friends like that, wild and free and young.

The other boy was Gabe, of course. He was the opposite of Joe—tall and slender, with a buzz cut. Each of them was so different, like they had been cast in a television show. Still, the four of them had been inseparable, and even though other kids came and went, they were the ones who'd stayed together until the end of junior high when Joe's family moved closer to town. Rosie hadn't seen this picture for years, since their mother had left for California. Laura must have had it copied and scanned. But when? And why? Laura hated everything about her past here.

They'd been collecting frog eggs that day, large masses of gray jelly with tiny black dots. They used to put them in buckets of water and wait for the tadpoles to hatch, which only happened once over the years. They'd been too young to know that the eggs needed to be fertilized after they were laid. It hadn't mattered. The excitement had been in the hunt and the waiting and, of course, the friendship that surrounded the adventure.

Rosie wore candy-striped shorts and a pink shirt with frills around the collar. Laura was in her tomboy attire by then—dirty jeans, torn T-shirt. Their skin was tan, their hair streaked blond from the sun. Rosie was smiling, a big wide smile right at the camera. Laura's face was not empty, exactly, but searching, her eyes not focused on the camera, but instead on the person behind it, holding it. Her eyes were on their father, her image out of focus because she was not the subject of the lens or the man behind it. Rosie was. Not Laura, though her eyes pleaded to have the camera turned her way, to focus on her. *Good Lord*, how this knowledge struck hard, as though it were the first time she'd found it.

She leaned forward and studied her sister.

How far back did it go?

The angry child, fits of rage, uncontrollable. Rosie tried to remember. It was forever. Their whole lives. Laura had bloodied her fists even back when she still wore pink, pounding them into a wall, breaking through the plaster. Rosie closed her eyes to see it clearly. Blood dripping on a snow-white arm. Tears streaking a freckled face. She couldn't have been more than six.

Had anyone else bothered to see her? The grown-ups in the neighborhood had their own lives. Couples sipping cocktails on someone's patio. Wives sipping coffee in the kitchens. Men drinking beer, their lawn mowers idling side by side on a Sunday afternoon.

A wave of guilt made her close her eyes.

Their mother told Mrs. Wallace that day in the kitchen that Laura had been hard to love, the little girl with fists for hands. With rage inside her. But maybe they had created the rage— all of them. She knew this now, having her own child. How easy it was to damage them with nothing more than words. Or indifference.

None of that mattered now. *Time only moved in one direction.*

Rosie started to click on the icons.

Two hours later, she heard the floorboards creaking. First came the slow, heavy steps of her husband. Then the quick shuffles of her son.

She heard her name being called.

First by Joe. "Rosie?"

Then by Mason. "Mama?"

Morning was here, though she tried to deny it. Even as the dark sky began to turn gray and then orange. Even as the clock ticked relentlessly on the table beside the bed. Minutes, then hours had passed with no headlights coming down the driveway.

"Rosie?" Joe was outside the door, knocking softly.

"I'm here," she answered.

The door creaked open. Joe stood in the hallway, holding Mason. As usual, he was bare down to his diaper. Mason hated clothing.

"Whatcha doin'?" Joe asked.

Rosie looked at him with wide, manic eyes. She could feel her expression and she could see its reflection on Joe's.

"She didn't come home."

Joe nodded. He let their squirming child down and he ran to Laura's bed and climbed on top of the covers. She had a fluffy down comforter and Mason liked the way it felt against his skin.

"Okay," Joe said calmly. "You been in here since before? When you woke me up?"

Rosie didn't answer. She looked at her son, then back at her husband. Suddenly she felt as crazy as the person he was seeing.

"Hospital?" Joe asked.

"Four times."

"Her phone . . ."

"Every fifteen minutes. Goes right to voicemail. Why won't she answer?"

"Because it's dead. Look," he said, pointing to an outlet near the floor. "She left her charger—again. She does it all the time."

Rosie nodded. "I tried to find this guy on that website, but there are so many of them! And they use screen names . . . and I can't get into her account unless I have the password, but I can't change the password without access to her email. . . . I've tried everything—her birthday, initials . . . and there's nothing in all this stuff—just work. Christ, Joe—I even tried 'Deer Hill Lane.'"

"She would never use that . . . not after what happened there."

"I know! I'm losing my mind. . . ."

Joe walked to the table where Rosie was working. She looked up at him, afraid to let him see her and what was going on in her head.

"I don't know what to think. What to believe."

"Listen to me. Your sister is lying in a bed, trapped beneath some old dude's hairy arm. She's got a wicked hangover and she's desperate to sneak out of there without having to fuck him, because that's what he'll want if he wakes up. You'll see."

Joe reached out and stroked her hair, waiting for a smile. But she couldn't comply.

"Did you find any evidence suggesting that my theory is wrong?"

"There is something strange," Rosie said. "Look . . ." Rosie typed the name *Jonathan Fields* into a search engine. "There's no divorce record, at least not in Connecticut."

Joe sat down on the edge of the bed next to the table and turned the laptop to face him. "So maybe he got divorced in New York or New Jersey, or anywhere. Did Laura say where he lived?"

"I assumed he was local. . . ."

Joe shook his head quickly. "No, no . . . see that's what I'm saying—he could be from anywhere in driving distance."

"Then we'll never find him!"

Mason crawled into his father's lap, rolled over, and hung upside down across his legs.

"Take a deep breath. It's still early—at least take a shower and have some coffee. You look deranged right now."

"Thanks. That was the look I was going for."

Joe tickled his son's belly. Mason laughed.

"Come here, baby." Mason found his mother's arms. She pulled him close and tried to smile.

It was unconvincing.

"I'll take a shower."

Joe got up, Mason back in his arms. "I'll make coffee and feed this guy. I can go in late today."

Seven turned to eight. Eight turned to nine.

By nine thirty, Rosie was inconsolable.

And obsessed with Jonathan Fields.

She was in the kitchen now, with Laura's laptop open on the table. She stared at the screen as she scrolled through images of men with the same name on Google. But the name was so common, there was no way she would ever find him.

Joe stood with Gabe at the center island, holding Mason in one arm and Rosie's bag in the other.

Gabe had come the second they'd called him.

"So what's the plan here?" Gabe asked.

"I'm gonna drive around, look for the car. Mason can watch shows on the iPad."

"Richmond—also the garage on Main . . ."

"Yeah, and the harbor. But she only left fifteen minutes to get where she was going, so downtown's a better bet."

Rosie heard them. She heard every word. She heard the silence that followed and felt their eyes on her back. But she couldn't turn away from the images.

Joe started to move. Two steps and he was standing behind her. He kissed the top of her head.

"I'm going now," he said.

Rosie reached her hand back, finding his face. Joe pressed her hand to his cheek, then kissed her palm.

"I'll call if I find something. You do the same."

She couldn't turn around. She didn't want to see the worry that had crept behind his eyes. This guy, whoever he was, supposedly had a job that he would now be at if nothing had gone wrong last night.

Gabe answered for both of them. "You got it."

Rosie heard the door to the garage open and close. Gabe pulled up a chair beside her.

"Hey," he said.

"Hey."

"You hanging in there?"

Rosie shook her head. *No.*

"We'll find her."

She managed a nod, but Gabe didn't let it go.

"Hey . . . listen to me now."

Rosie turned to face him.

"There are a hundred scenarios between Laura nursing a hangover in this guy's bed and whatever it is you're thinking. Most of them fall within the Laura Being Laura category. She's been wound up pretty tight since she got back."

Rosie nodded.

"No police?" he asked.

"No—you know I can't do that unless this is real. Jesus. *Laura Lochner back ten years later—reported missing—with a man she didn't even know. . . .*"

Gabe sat back and held out his hands. "Okay—I got it. No police until we know for sure."

"You think it's a mistake? Not calling them?"

"That's not my decision."

No, Rosie thought. This fell on her shoulders. She'd thought about calling the police since the moment she'd found that empty bed. But what if she was wrong? What if *they* were wrong? What if this was just Laura Being Laura? They all knew what would happen. The past would come screaming out of the shadows. It would be big news in this small town.

The computer screen went back to the photograph in the woods, down by the creek. It caught Gabe's eye.

"Oh my God. Look at us. . . ."

He smiled then, and in a way that brought back memories. They had each played a role in their shared childhood story. Joe, their strong, handsome leader. Rosie, the pretty girl looking on as Laura, the reckless tomboy, found some kind of trouble. And then there was Gabe—the brains of the operation.

That was what she needed now. Someone whose mind could focus through the storm. Someone to think and figure this out. Gabe worked in IT. Sometimes he worked for clients who needed access to things that others didn't want them to find.

"What can we do?" Rosie asked him, pulling him back from his own memories.

He slid the laptop closer and woke up the screen.

"These dating sites, the ones with the complicated profiles and rules, they're actually easier to manipulate. To create a false identity. Men can find women, make their dates, and stay hidden to certain people—a wife or girlfriend who's come on to find them. Can't do that on the phone apps. Those feed off Facebook. Most people can't be bothered to make a fake Facebook account—and even when they do, they look fake."

"Can we get into Laura's account? See the men she's contacted?" Rosie asked.

"Not without a password or access to her email. You said you've been searching the site?"

Rosie clicked on the icon that held her search. "I kept it within twenty miles of here. Look—it could be any of these guys. We've got no photo and no screen name, so I can't narrow it down."

Gabe studied the pages, the faces of the men who might be Jonathan Fields. Then he began to type.

"I'm going to widen the search to thirty miles. . . . Can you print these pages?"

"Okay—but why?"

Gabe was already on his phone. "I have a contact at Verizon. I can get the location of where her phone is, or at least the last place it was live. We'll see what's around there and bring the photos. Maybe we'll get lucky."

"That's it?" Rosie asked. "Can't we hack into her email or get her call record? I know she was in touch with him to make their plan for the date."

"The police can," Gabe said. He looked up from the screen again, his phone pressed to his ear.

"With a warrant. Same for this website. They don't like to betray their clients. Doesn't help business."

Rosie watched and listened as Gabe made his call. It sounded like a woman on the other end of the line. He made small talk, let out a quick laugh. When he asked for the favor, his voice grew more serious.

Please let her be okay. . . .

Rosie's phone rang. She picked it up from the table. Gabe's eyes followed her as she moved across the room. It was Joe.

"Hey," Rosie whispered.

Joe was yelling over the sound of the street noise. But his words came through loud and clear.

"I found the car! It's on Richmond. I found it!"

Thank God!

"Is she there? Is anything there, inside?"

Gabe's expression grew curious.

Joe sounded breathless. "Just her other purse. There's nothing in it but junk. She got a parking ticket at seven forty-five p.m. and another at ten this morning—they're on the windshield. It's been here all night. What do you want to do?"

Rosie didn't answer. She held the phone away from her ear and looked at Gabe, shaking her head. He seemed to understand.

"Rosie?" Joe said again.

"Gabe may have something. . . ."

Rosie's phone went silent just as Gabe got his answer. He stood up and started pacing as he listened.

"Are you sure?" he asked the woman on the other line.

Joe was speaking again into Rosie's ear. "What did he find?"

"Hold on," she said. Then, to Gabe: "What did they say?"

"The phone is offline. Last place it was live was down by the water—just after eleven."

"But that's miles from Richmond Street—Joe just found the car there," Rosie said. None of this made any sense.

"Rosie?" Joe was yelling now. She yelled back, into the phone, "Just hold on . . . she's not there . . . she's not on Richmond . . . she went to the harbor! Oh God! What the hell is going on here?"

Gabe walked to where Rosie was standing, and took the phone from her hand.

He was close to her now, in his navy suit with his serious face. He and Joe exchanged a few words. They would meet at the car. Joe had the spare key and would drive the car home. Rosie would take his car and follow Gabe to the harbor, where they would look for Laura. They had suddenly resumed their roles in the story. Gabe making the plan, Joe leading the charge.

"What do we do?" Rosie felt helpless as she waited for instructions.

"We need those photos. Where's the printer?"

Rosie pointed to the stairs. "The attic—Laura's room."

She watched him leave.

Suddenly her throat tightened, choking her. This was real. This was happening. Laura was missing, and the worry had gone from her tangled thoughts to her husband, and now to Gabe.

Laura . . .

She hadn't looked like a reckless tomboy last night. In that dress and those shoes. Her hair down, flowing around her shoulders.

Laura . . .

But that picture from their past—the sadness. The longing. And those little bloody fists.

Gabe came back into the room and stopped in front of her. His arms pulled her in.

"It's going to be okay. I promise you," he said.

But when she felt his shirt dampen against her cheek, the tears breaking free, she was no longer that helpless girl. And she was the only one among them who knew that he was wrong.

SEVEN

Laura. Session Number Two.
Four Months Ago. New York City.

Dr. Brody: Why did you punch your fists through that wall? You were only six. . . .

Laura: It was probably nothing. My parents used to say I made mountains out of molehills. If someone gave me a rainbow of colors, I would mix them up to make black.

Dr. Brody: Look . . . your hand . . . your knuckles are turning white. . . .

Laura: Sorry . . . sometimes I still smell the plaster. Feel the bones bruising.

Dr. Brody: Children develop sharpened skills of perception if they're always in danger. Sometimes they're right about what they see, and sometimes they're wrong. But they see everything.

Laura: I didn't exactly grow up in the jungle.

Dr. Brody: Emotional danger—emotional neglect—those will do the trick.

Laura: You've lost me. How was I neglected?

Dr. Brody: I don't know. You were the one who was there.

EIGHT

Laura. The Night Before. Thursday,
8 p.m. Branston, CT.

There is something all wrong about Jonathan Fields's car. Yes, it's a Toyota and not a BMW, but there's something else.

"Do you like music?" he asks as we stop at a light. Then he laughs, at himself I think. "That was stupid. Of course you like music. I meant to ask what kind of music. I can find something on the radio."

That's it. This car has a radio. An actual radio with knobs and buttons. The knob for the volume twists right and left. The one for the channels pushes up or down. Large white arrows lead the way. It has AM and FM. No satellite service. No iPhone connector, Bluetooth, or hardwire. And yet it's not old. It smells new. Brand-new.

Jonathan hits a button to search for a channel. It stops on something with Top 40 stuff, and I feel like I'm in fourth grade again, riding with my grandmother.

"This okay?" he asks. He glances at me and smiles. The light changes. He makes a right from Schaffer Boulevard onto Grand Street.

I hesitate, but then I can't help myself. Grand Street is way out of the way if we're going to the waterfront, and let's just say it's not exactly a scenic route. It's the part of town that's suffered most at every economic downturn.

"Do you know a secret shortcut?" I ask. It's not the best way to ask the question, but it's better than saying, *What the hell are you doing?* Which is what I'm thinking and what I want to say.

Now he seems unnerved.

"No," he says. He answers with the intonation of a question.

So I give him my answer.

"It's just—Schaffer goes all the way down. Under the train and highway." I'm pointing back toward the right direction, from which we have just departed.

"I go this way to avoid the lights," he says. He's very clever. Only, there are lights this way as well, and you have to drive slower because the forgotten teenagers who line the streets at night will walk right out in front of you and not give a shit. This is their neighborhood and they do what they want. We used to come here to buy pot, and from the looks of it, nothing has changed. There's no reason to be here unless you live here or want to score weed.

Maybe that's it, I think. Maybe he just smokes a lot of weed and so he made this turn out of habit. I can live with that.

Adele comes on the radio, and I find myself looking again at the dashboard. It's not just the radio. The entire console is old-school. Analog. Red and white. Buttons and knobs to twist and push—not just for the radio, but the heat and the wipers and the odometer reset. It makes my sister's minivan look like a spaceship. The seats are blue-speckled fabric. The armrests cheap plastic. No way this guy drives this car by choice. Not Jonathan Fields.

We make awkward small talk. It's actually painful, reminding me of the distance we will have to travel to be more than strangers. And then I'm reminded of how desperately I need to make that journey, with someone, anyone. And it all feels hopeless.

Maybe it's just Adele. *Damn it, Adele, what will it take to make you happy?* I hit the search button to silence her.

"You said you just moved back here," he says.

"Uh-huh."

"From the city?"

I already told him this on the phone.

"Uh-huh." I know this is immature. This is old me talking, and new me tells her to shut the hell up along with Adele and her desperation coming through the radio and make nice conversation. I tell myself I can make that long journey if I just follow the instructions, the rules, one at a time, starting with a normal answer to his question.

"I was a research analyst. Tired of going to the office. I can do what I did at home, and there's a market for independent research now."

He pretends to be interested.

"I follow one industry—chemicals—and the companies in it. But also other industries that impact that one, and the economy and trade policy and currencies. . . . God, I'm boring you, aren't I?"

"No, not at all. I mean, I do similar work looking at investments," he says. "I used to commute into the city. But my firm opened an office here, so it made more sense, you know, when I was married and we thought we'd have a family."

"And now you're stuck here? They won't let you transfer back to the city?" That's an obvious question, right? This is not easy for me.

"I hadn't thought about it. Just trying to get back on my feet, you know?"

I nod, look sympathetic. But, really, he's been divorced for over a year. No kids. I wonder if he's still in love with his wife. His *ex*-wife.

"Your sister still lives here—it's not so bad," he says.

"Rosie could be happy anywhere," I quip. Rosie was happy with Joe because we grew up together and, well, he's Joe. She was happy to follow him to UConn. Happy to come back and be an administrative assistant (aka secretary) and help pay for his law degree. Now happy to be home with Mason. She's been this way all of our lives.

Sometimes I wish I were Rosie. I wish I had her magic potion for being happy.

I wish there was a recipe for it. But then again, I would be the one person to measure wrong.

Jonathan Fields makes a left and eventually we go under the bridges for the train and the highway. Now we have to turn left again to get back to Schaffer, where we started. We've just driven in a large rectangle. But I say nothing. He's not driving like he knows his way around—like he's lived downtown for a year. He's driving like he just moved here.

We park on the street four blocks from the string of bars and restaurants that abut the apartments along the water. It's an inlet from the Long Island Sound, so not exactly the ocean. More like a river. But there are boats and sunsets and all of that. The smell of the ocean. The sound of the waves. And it's as far away from the part of town where people like my sister live, so it attracts the young, single crowd.

And every divorced dad in the county looking to get laid.

Maybe it's a good thing he doesn't know the fastest way here. Maybe if he did, I would worry more.

Jonathan Fields wears dark tailored jeans and a loose button-down shirt tucked in with a belt. Loafers. Dress socks. Two buttons are undone at the top of the shirt, just enough to reveal a small tuft of chest hair. No jewelry. *Thank God.*

I am a fan of chest hair. It's masculine. Manly. I don't understand all the waxing and laser removal. I like manly men. It makes me feel that it's safe to lay down my sword and shield—that I won't get ambushed in the night because someone else is watching the perimeter. It's nice to be part of an army, even if it's a small one.

Asshole had chest hair. I used to weave my fingers through it. And suddenly I miss him more than I can bear. I think his name, his real name, and feel his embrace. I feel his skin against my skin, arms and legs weaving, torsos locked together. Warm breath on my neck as his mouth finds its way to mine. A deep kiss. A sigh.

He said the words as we lay still. *I love you.*

And I believed him. For once, I let myself believe.

I got it wrong. It won't happen again.

And now . . . I have to start over, make another long journey from strangers to lovers. I'm so tired and we haven't even begun, *Jonathan Fields.*

He pulls the key out of the ignition and looks at me with a smile. He says something corny like *Shall we?* and my brain feels like a circuit's been tripped by the conflicting information. The car. The *Shall we?* But then the jeans and the chest hair. I feel confused, so I smile and open the car door. I need air.

"Where should we go?" I ask. I haven't actually eaten here

before. I come here with Rosie and Mason to watch the boats. There's a huge playground and it's a long drive from her house— all the makings of an outing. And Rosie loves her outings. I feel a surge of warmth wash over me as I think about Rosie and Mason and Joe, and my work and the future. There is so much that is good.

I hear Mason call my name. *Lala!*

I hear Rosie in my head. *You don't need a man.*

And I think, as I watch Jonathan Fields walk, *But I want one.*

"I know a place," Jonathan says. He waits for me to walk ahead of him and I feel his hand on the small of my back as he gently guides me into a bar, sending that shiver. But this one is prickly and uncomfortable, replacing the warmth. It's not the way someone touches someone before they've had a decent conversation. Or a drink, at least. Or maybe they do and this is just me not knowing what the *fuck* I'm doing. . . .

There's a table in the back corner, and I sit facing the wall because he takes the other seat, facing the crowd. I've been told that's what a gentleman does. Something about keeping watch— watching our backs. But, really, let's be honest. We're at a bar with a whole mess of attractive young people. I can think of other reasons he might want to sit facing the crowd.

Maybe he wants to keep a lookout for women who might recognize him and call his name and chase after us as we scurry to the door.

He leaves to get us drinks and I need one the way a fish needs water.

I used to think that I think too much. That I search for answers when there are no questions, find solutions that have no problems. That I *make mountains out of molehills*, as my dear mother used to say. My mother and Dick. They both used to say it.

And then I stopped thinking too much and guess what happened. I slammed right into the side of a mountain.

Seriously. Just give me a magic pill to make it all go away.

Or a cocktail, which is exactly what appears before me.

"Thanks," I say to Jonathan Fields as he sits down. I glance up inconspicuously as I swallow a large portion of my drink, just waiting for his eyes to find someone younger or hotter or sexier. But he doesn't. He looks at me and only at me.

And suddenly I want to be the woman I think he wants. *New me.*

"Okay," he says, leaning back in his chair. He's comfortable now, not like he was in the car or even at the first bar. It's like he's just come home from a long day at the office and kicked off his shoes.

"Let's start over. I'm so bad with first dates. I never know what to talk about. What to ask about. It's like walking in a field of land mines."

And just like that—bull's-eye. I kick off my shoes as well.

"I know," I say to him with as much relief as I can possibly display in one facial expression. "It's so horrible, right?"

He shakes his head with enthusiasm and leans forward. "You know, it's like the worst of everything, meeting online. If you go out with someone you know from work or someplace, there's a starting point. A familiarity. And if you meet someone in a bar, then it's just like flirting and all of that—there's a rule book for it. Or a handbook—you know what I mean, right?"

"Yes!" I say. "This is my first time doing this. And it's awful! I mean, not you . . . That didn't come out right. You're not awful. It's just hard to find a place to start." It's just like you said, Jonathan Fields. Only not exactly, because I have never known any of this to be easy. Not. Ever. Not even with Asshole.

I kept the last text message he sent me. The one saying it was over and to never contact him again. I read it sometimes to remind myself about the mountains.

"Okay," he says again. He likes that word a lot. "So just ask me anything. What do you want to know?"

"Honestly?" I ask.

"Yes. Anything!" He leans back again. He reaches for his beer, and this time his eyes do a quick scan of the room. It's perfectly normal, I remind myself. He's facing out. He's protecting me from wild animals that could pounce at any moment. His eyes do not stop and linger on anyone, but return to me and my question.

"Okay," I begin, because if Jonathan likes that word, new me likes it too. People are always more comfortable when you acclimate to them, to their style and their language. It's why people often look like their dogs. I learned this in a psychology class.

"What I really want to know about is your divorce. How you met your wife. Why you got married. What went wrong. Is that too personal? It's fine if it is. But that is, honestly, what I most want to know."

This is a lie, of course. What I most want to know is what happened to his BMW, or why he told me he had one when he doesn't. And even if he did lie to impress me and lure me out, there's just no way he chose that car without a gun to his head.

And that woman from the first bar calling out his name . . . and the way we got here, to the harbor . . .

"Okay." He begins his answer with his favorite word. "We met in college. Swarthmore. Senior year. But it's not what you think. We didn't just stay together and then get married. We actually broke up after graduation. I moved to Boston—that's where I'm from. Sad to say, I lived with my parents for about a year while I was looking for a job. She came here, or to New York, rather. Then a few years later, when we were about twenty-eight, we reconnected on Facebook!"

He says this like it's a miracle, so I light up my whole face.

"No way!" I say. *It's a miracle!!!!!*

"Yup. And we started talking and then I came to see her and she came up to see me, and then we lived in Boston for a while and then back here. We really thought we would start a family."

Now he seems sad, so I become a gray sky. "I'm sorry," I say. "Can I ask what happened?"

He goes on for a solid ten minutes, talking about all of their fertility treatments and how his wife has endometriosis, etc., etc., and TMI. I remind myself that we are trying to travel a long distance at the speed of light. I am sympathetic. I am. I truly am.

But I want to know about that car. And why he didn't move back to New York.

It's not fair to Jonathan Fields that I feel annoyed. He's just answering the question I asked.

He finally stops. He gets us another round. I watch him walk away and think that I like the way he walks and that he is a nice man. He loved his wife. He wanted to have children. He has parents who loved him enough to let him live in their basement after college. He is a good man, and I will try to find a way to let him in.

Then I think this. I think about my sister and how if I met her today, I would not make her a friend. I wouldn't dislike her, but we are too different and we would annoy each other. She would judge me and I would judge her and we would get in a girl fight and that would be that. But she is family, blood, and so I will never leave her. Not in a million years. The things about her that might annoy me I find endearing. I don't know if she feels this way about me, but I think she does. Even if I move away again, part of me will always be hers and part of her will always be mine.

She is the first person I call when the shit really hits the fan. Like it just did not two months ago. And she came running as fast as lightning.

So what is it about love between strangers? What makes two people who are not family, not blood, stay and not leave? Do they just decide to do it? Do they swallow down their misery at being together when they want to be apart? Staying with Rosie is not a choice. Loving Rosie is not a choice.

Then I think about Jonathan Fields and his wife and all those years they spent together. And then she just decided to leave? Just like that. Or maybe not. Maybe I don't know the whole story. Still, I wonder.

"Okay," he says. "Now my turn." He sets down the new drinks. I smile sheepishly. "Okay. Shoot."

"Was that guy in New York, the one you mentioned on the phone—was that a serious thing? Was it a hard breakup?"

I try to decide what he's asking me, really. Is it whether I am capable of a long-term relationship? Is it whether I'm still in love with someone else? Or is he still trying to find out why I came back home?

And from there, why I left.

"Yes and no," I begin. "It wasn't that long that we dated. But I did have feelings for him. And, yes, it was hard when he ended things. I guess we're in a similar type of boat—obviously mine is much smaller."

He studies me carefully. "You said on the phone that he sent you one text ending things and then just disappeared. Stopped calling and texting you. Did you try to find out why?"

I shake my head. "No. I mean, if someone dumps you in a text and then disappears like that, I think that's a sign. What would prevent him from doing that again? Walking away is a bad habit, but it is a habit and it's hard to break."

I expect him to pontificate on this rather introspective observation. But instead he dwells on my behavior.

"But you didn't at least reach out? Even on social media? Ask one of his friends?"

Now I feel cornered. I can't answer this without revealing the fact that I don't use social media, and that I didn't really know his friends. We spent our time together alone. It was new. New and perfect.

I shrug and that's all I give him.

"Okay, you know what?" he says. "It doesn't matter. We've both moved on in our boats and now here we are and that's a good thing. I know that sounds trite, but I really believe that. Everything that matters is here right now, or coming tomorrow. And what I see here right now is an incredibly beautiful, smart woman, and I am lucky that guy was a total prick because now you're here and not there."

He says this with total sincerity. Not even my finely tuned skills of perception can detect an iota of BS.

It comes again, the surge of warmth like I felt before. He's found a wormhole.

We talk more about this. About life and about mistakes and how hard it is to look forward or live in the present moment. He speaks also of his family in Boston. His mother who just died a year ago. His father who was married to her for forty-four years. He speaks of a sister and her family who moved to Colorado and I speak of my sister Joe and Mason. He doesn't ask me if I want children, so I don't have to lie, and the conversation keeps flowing like the water just outside, flowing into an ocean—of what, I have no idea. But I like it. I like it all.

His eyes stay on me the whole time. I can smell his skin when he leans forward to sip his beer. And then I smell the beer when he leans back. And all of it mixes together with the vodka I've been drinking into a brilliant cocktail of attraction.

I fight to keep it. I fight against the little things that enter my brain and go on the list of concerns I will use to build my mountain of a molehill—things I am perceiving that don't add up. The timeline of his story between college and moving back here. His company, which doesn't sound like any of the companies that have stayed out here in Connecticut. He says it was a hedge fund, but the larger ones have moved out of Branston. I know this because his business is my business.

There are more wrong things that I have been gathering: facial expressions, sideways questions about my past, my childhood. I can't decide if these things are normal, because I'm not normal. My sense of perception. My mountains from molehills. My fists for hands.

I drove my parents crazy. I know I did. They told me I did. I was hard to love. Maybe impossible. Maybe I still am.

I shove this all aside. Jonathan Fields is a nice man and he leans forward for his beer but really because he wants to be closer to me. I can feel it. These thoughts are wrong. These concerns are meaningless. I gather them so I can push away nice men like Jonathan Fields who want to love me. And I do this so I can keep finding the wrong men who won't love me.

I want to cry. I feel tears coming, but I hold them back.

Knowledge is power, right? I will stop this from happening. This is why I came home. This is my job now. To stop old me from ruining my life.

I go to the bathroom. I splash cold water on my face. I get my shit together and return to the table.

Jonathan Fields gives me a huge smile. Then he opens his mouth to start a new conversation. Only it's not new. It's the same one he's been trying to have all night.

"Okay," he says. "So why is it you haven't been back home sooner?"

What is going on here?

Why is he so interested in my past?

He seems to know about my list of concerns. Maybe he's trying to stop me from making it any longer. But that's exactly what he's doing.

"You know what?" he says. "Let's get out of here—go for a walk by the river."

I tell myself it's nothing. A molehill. Not a mountain. There are no instincts I can trust. No skills I can rely upon. Just determination.

My mouth opens and out comes the word he likes so much.

"Okay."

NINE

Rosie. Present Day. Friday, 11 a.m.
Branston, CT.

Another hour passed quickly. Rosie and Gabe drove in his car to meet Joe on Richmond Street. There was a frenzied discussion about what to do next and, again, whether they should call the police. Gabe didn't weigh in. This was their call. And, in the end, Rosie's. It was her sister who would have to live with the consequences, one way or the other.

Joe didn't have to say it—the impact it could have on Laura, on her emotional stability, if they dredged up her past and forced her out of the shadow of anonymity she had created.

Gabe was the only one of them who was not reeling with fear, and on his face Rosie could see something even worse—resignation. Time felt precious, but that's all it was. A feeling. An urgency fed by the panic of not knowing. If something bad had happened, it was over. They were already too late.

Rosie made the decision, though without the conviction she'd had even an hour before when they were standing in her kitchen. They would wait.

Joe took her minivan back to the house and she took his car and followed Gabe to the waterfront, where Laura's phone had last sent a signal. The exact location was a parking lot between an office building and a gym. But that meant nothing—people coming to the restaurants and bars parked in all of the lots, and along the streets as well.

So they walked the streets and the paths between them, stopping in apartment buildings, asking people if they recognized any of the men from findlove.com. They had narrowed the thumbnail photos down to twenty-seven. Laura had said enough about him to rule out the rest. Full head of hair, clean-shaven, fit. Still, it was a needle in a haystack, and they landed back at the street where they'd parked their cars, with nothing helpful.

Gabe laid the sheets of photos on his hood, studying the faces.

"Do you recognize any of them?" Rosie asked. Gabe sometimes talked about his cases. Most of what he did was more mundane—working out glitches in corporate computer systems. But for his other work—using IT to investigate spouses—it was, invariably, women who hired him. And it always made Rosie think of her mother.

"Funny you should say that," Gabe answered. "The last case where I needed to sort through this shitty website was Melissa's. Her husband was trolling for younger women under a fake profile."

"Sorry . . ." Rosie said. Gabe and Melissa liked to forget this little fact about how they met.

"No, don't be. You know, it's okay to sleep with your client as long as you marry her." Gabe gave her a wink and Rosie managed a smile. But the levity slipped away quickly.

"Some of these guys have been on here for years. This

one"—Gabe pointed to a man with a seductive smile, holding a fish at the end of a line—"he was on here two, three years ago—before Melissa's case. I remember this stupid fish."

Rosie looked at the picture. "We should cross him off the list. Laura would have mentioned the fish. She would have found it ridiculous."

Gabe took out a pen and put an X through the photo.

"Yeah," he agreed. "She would have psychoanalyzed the hell out of it—a pathetic attempt to convey success, manliness, dominion."

"It's a curse and a blessing—how she sees through everything and everyone."

Gabe's face returned to resignation. "Except herself," he said. "She never understood why she did the things she did."

Rosie began pacing the sidewalk, arms folded around herself, squinting from the sun, which was almost directly overhead. She checked her phone. It was eleven.

"The restaurants should be open now," Gabe said. "Most of them serve lunch. The staff will be setting up."

Gabe had read her mind.

Rosie stopped talking and looked at the massive complex lining the water. "I've only been to the park. Mason doesn't have the patience to sit at a restaurant."

Gabe pointed to a street off to their right.

"We've been down here. Melissa and I. Young crowd—younger than we are. Except for the divorced men. They come here to shop at these places—like kids in a candy store. They're all pretty much on one block. There—two streets down."

Gabe started walking. "We should get started."

They went to three places before getting a lead. It was at a bar that served food, very bad bar food—but enough to keep people from leaving when they got drunk and hungry. The atmosphere was dark and it smelled of stale beer. They spoke to the bartender, who had just opened up.

He glanced at the photos, reluctantly at first, until Rosie told him that her sister was missing. His eyes focused harder then, returning to each photo to study the men.

Then a smile came and left in an instant.

"Yup," he said, pointing at one of the men. "This guy—he's a regular."

The photo was attached to the screen name here4you.

"Why did you smile when you saw him? What's funny about it?" Gabe asked.

The bartender paused, glancing at Rosie, then looking away as though he didn't want to see her expression change when he answered the question. Instead he looked only at Gabe.

"This guy . . . comes in during the week. One, maybe two times. Never on the weekend. Thursdays are his favorite."

"So he was here last night?" Rosie asked. She looked at Gabe, wide-eyed, then back to the bartender.

"*Every* Thursday."

Rosie frantically pulled out her phone and found a photo of Laura. She was in their backyard pushing Mason on the swing.

"Was he with this woman? Do you recognize her?"

The bartender leaned in close to see the picture, then shook his head. "I don't know. . . . There are so many people who come and go every night. Maybe."

Gabe was suddenly frustrated, standing taller with both hands on the bar. "How are you sure you saw this guy, then? If there are so many people coming and going?"

The bartender leaned back defensively. "I know the guy because he's a regular. Sits in the back corner. Gets the drinks at the bar. Pays cash. Leaves a shitty tip."

"Does he ever come in with a woman? A date?" Gabe asked.

"Yeah—that's what I'm saying. Comes on the weekdays. Usually with a different woman."

"A different woman each time?" Rosie asked.

The bartender nodded. "Yeah. All different ages, races, thin, not so thin, short hair, long hair. He doesn't have a type. Doesn't seem too picky, either."

Rosie gasped. "*God*, it's him! It's got to be!" she said.

"Hold on." Gabe pointed to the man's picture again. "You're sure? This man?"

"Oh yeah. See that smug smile? How it curls up more on one side? Wears it every time," he said. "Cheap son of a bitch. Never even orders as much as a french fry."

"You got a name?" Gabe asked.

"No. Like I said. Pays cash and sits in the back. But wait . . ." He scratched his head as though ushering a memory. "A few weeks ago he went to the bathroom and this chick he was with called over a waitress and bought a round with her credit card. We had a laugh about it. First time we got a decent tip from a table he was at—but only because the woman was the one who paid."

"Is she here? That waitress?" Rosie's eyes were scanning the place, but it was empty.

The bartender shook his head. "She works nights. I can try to reach her. You got a number or a card or something? If she can remember what night, what they were drinking, we might be able to find the slip. It would at least give you the name of one of his dates."

Gabe pulled a business card from his wallet. He wrote Rosie's cell phone number on the back and handed it to the bartender.

"Try us both; it doesn't matter," he said. "As soon as you hear from her."

"Will do," the bartender said. "And text me that picture of your sister. I'll get it to everyone who worked last night. I really hope you find her. If it's any consolation, he seemed harmless. Just another asshole working his game."

"Thanks, man." Gabe shook his hand, but Rosie couldn't wait. She was walking fast, back to their cars on the street. Gabe grabbed her arm and stopped her.

"Hey," he said. "This is good news. Laura was here last night. We know from her phone records. This has to be our guy. And now we can find him . . . and then find Laura."

"I know you're thinking the same thing I am," Rosie said, pulling her arm away. "It's why I haven't called the police. It's why you haven't made me."

"Rosie . . ."

"No—we have to stop. We have to think this through."

"There's nothing to think through. We found Jonathan Fields. He's a harmless womanizer."

"Gabe . . ." She looked at him with dismay. It was not possible that he was forgetting. "She didn't get back in my car. The parking tickets—one right after she got to Richmond Street. And one in the morning. There are only two things that could have happened last night. . . ."

"I know, Rosie. You think I don't know? We've stayed in touch—but it hasn't been easy having her back. Seeing the pain that's always there—and Melissa, she doesn't want me anywhere near your sister, because even she knows, just from the stories she's heard, the things that can happen around her."

Gabe was angry and it was unsettling. Rosie could count on one hand the number of times she'd seen him lose his composure.

He calmed himself before continuing. "I can almost see her last night—that look in her eyes as she falls in love with him. And I can see the rage as she finds out that he's a con artist. I know them all—every one of her faces—and I know where they lead her."

"Then you know . . ." Rosie said, pleading. "If this guy was a player, a liar, and if Laura found out, it wouldn't matter how harmless he was. . . ."

But Gabe wasn't listening. "She always said that word—'love'—as though it were an object. Something that could be held and touched. She spoke of it as though it wasn't all around her, from you and Joe and Mason—from all of us, and from all of those men who tried to love her. It isn't like that. I've tried to tell her. When I met Melissa . . . it just grew, and it took work. I tried to tell her."

Rosie wanted to scream. "So did I—a million times. How it's sometimes work. Just getting up every day and deciding that you are going to love this person even though it's not sweeping you off your feet. It's like she's been on a desperate search her whole life—it's on her face in that picture, the one on the computer. Even back then . . ."

Gabe shook off the frustration and closed his eyes tight. And for that brief moment, Rosie knew exactly what he was feeling.

"Look at what followed—what happened to her first real boyfriend," Rosie said. "What if it happened again? With this man, Jonathan Fields?"

She paused briefly before saying the rest, all of her thoughts fusing together. Becoming simple. Becoming clear.

"The thing is, Gabe, I'm not worried about what he might have done to her. I'm worried about what she might have done to him."

Gabe nodded, growing solemn again.

"Let's get back to the house," he said. "I know how to find this guy. That's all we can do now."

They got in their cars. Pulled away from the curb. And drove away from the harbor.

TEN

Laura. Session Number Seven.
Three Months Ago. New York City.

Laura: . . . maybe I've just been unlucky in love. Isn't that a song? Or in a song? There's another expression. . . . What is it? "The heart wants what it wants."

Dr. Brody: But if that heart is broken, it will want the wrong things.

Laura: Cheery . . . but . . . are you saying that's me? My heart is broken?

Dr. Brody: It's just a euphemism, Laura. Hearts don't break.

Laura: Obviously. But people do, don't they?

Dr. Brody: In a manner of speaking. When do you want to talk about it?

Laura: Talk about what? I tell you everything.

Dr. Brody: About what really happened that night in the woods . . .

ELEVEN

Laura. The Night Before. Thursday, 9 p.m. Branston, CT.

We walk on the path along the water. The air is perfect, neither hot nor cold against the skin. It smells of salt and seaweed. The smell of the ocean. It is blissful.

And it fills me with despair.

I tried to explain this to the shrink, how a perfect night provokes the longing so hard and fast that it feels as though it will explode right out of me. Perfect nights were made for lovers.

We stroll together, me and Jonathan Fields, taking in this perfect night with its air and its smells. And the desire to be past this moment, and the ones that have to follow so that maybe we will stroll as lovers and not strangers—the desire to be in love on this perfect night that is screaming out for lovers—rises all the way to my throat.

I hold my breath to keep it inside.

My cheeks flush and he notices. But we continue to stroll. I make myself exhale and take a new breath and it begins to pass.

Jonathan Fields. I like the way he strolls, his hands in his jean pockets. The button-down shirt tucked in. He's rolled up his sleeves and I can see the hair on his forearms, light brown. He's not like a bear or anything. It's that masculine thing again. I don't know why I like it so much. Rosie likes it too. That's why she fell for Joe. He was a *guy* from the day he was born. A dude. I've wondered if Dick was like that and maybe that's why we are drawn to the same men. I can't remember, not even a little bit, about whether our father had hair on his arms or his chest, and whether he strolled the way Jonathan Fields strolls now, with a little swagger and a little nonchalance. Confidence, maybe. Or, maybe, arrogance.

We walk for a while, looking at people, laughing when we see others who seem to be on a first date, as though we are better than they are because at least we recognize the absurdity of it, the awkwardness. We smell the air and take in the anticipation of where we will go next. And what we will do there. I can tell he's thinking about it. His face changes with the thoughts, though I don't think he is aware of it.

But I am. I am aware of everything.

And I have not forgotten about the car or the woman in the bar or the holes in his story. I have not forgotten that we are not lovers on this perfect night that screams out for them.

I grow quiet.

"Are you all right?" he asks.

I nod and smile.

And then he does something miraculous. He reads my mind.

"We loved the beach, my wife and I," he says.

Ex-wife, I think. But I don't correct him. It's a habit. That's all it is.

Isn't it?

"After it got so hard to have kids, we stopped going. Because all of a sudden there were kids everywhere at the beach. They were in the surf with their fathers who threw them in the air. They were building sand castles. They were chasing seagulls. I'm sure they had always been there, but after we couldn't get pregnant, the nicer the beach day was, the harder it was to stomach what was missing for us on that beach."

I've gathered myself once again. I am calmed by his story, which is just like mine. A beach without a child. A perfect night without lovers.

"I never got kids," I say. "Until my nephew was born. And even then, it wasn't until he started to know me that I could understand the power children wield."

Jonathan looks at me now, a question causing his eyes to narrow. Only I can't read his mind the way he's read mine.

"I thought you hadn't been back much?" he asks.

Again, with the questions about my past. What the fuck?

Still, I answer.

"I came home for holidays. Usually just a night or an afternoon. But my sister would bring Mason to the city. He knows me. He does."

I stop then, because he doesn't deserve to know more. How Mason learned to say *Lala* before *Dada*. *Aunt Lala*. I have a name he's given just to me. And when he sees me, his face lights up with a million colors of delight. I know where he likes to be tickled and I know how hard to toss him on my bed, into the fluffy comforter. I know how long to chase him before his laughter will give him hiccups. And I know how soft his skin feels when I kiss his cheek.

So fuck you, Jonathan Fields. My nephew knows me.

"Does it make you think about it?" he asks then. I can feel him trying to pull me back.

"What? Having kids?"

"Yeah. Of course."

I've been waiting for this question.

I shake my head. "It scares me even more," I say.

"Scares you? Why?" he asks.

"Because they're so easy to break. Rosie says this all the time. She says it scares her. So of course it scares me."

Now he grows silent and I wonder if he's picturing me picking up a child and breaking it in two. But that's not what I mean.

"It's a big responsibility to be a parent. To know what to say and what not to say. Kids are blank slates, and everything we draw on them stays forever."

He gives me a curious *huh* like he's never had this thought, like all the years he wanted a child he never thought what he would do with one after it arrived.

And I think he is normal and I am not. But then I am the one who can still read the things that were drawn on me as a child. *Fists for hands. So hard to love.* And the eyes that never looked down at me, no matter how long I held my desperate gaze.

Jonathan Fields has stopped walking. It's my mood. He can feel it rolling in and out like the current we hear in the distance.

"Something's been on your mind since we left the first bar. Hasn't it?"

Goddamn, Jonathan Fields. You really are inside my head, aren't you?

So much has been on my mind, but I know what he means from the words he's chosen—*since we left that first bar*—so I say it.

"That woman—from the bar on Richmond Street. The one who called your name as we were leaving."

He knew this was coming, so his answer leaves his mouth as smooth as silk.

"She was a woman I went out with a few weeks ago."

My heart sinks. It begins to drown. Who runs away from a woman who calls your name? A woman you dated? An asshole, that's who.

"Did you meet her on findlove?" I manage to ask. It's hard to speak when your heart is drowning.

He nods. "We went out on three dates."

"Three dates," I say. It's the magic number. The industry standard. Sex on the third date maintains some decorum but prevents the wasting of precious time if things aren't good enough in that department.

I've done my research.

Now he looks away, embarrassed as well. "Yeah . . . three dates. She came back to my apartment. It was really weird. I feel bad saying that, saying anything about another woman. Don't kiss and tell, right?"

I can't answer. I need him to finish.

"I told her the next day I didn't think it was a good fit."

He looks at me then, with a strange kind of earnest. The kind that I usually feel spreading when I am desperate to be understood.

"I thought it was the right thing to do. Not lead her on. Let her find someone else. Shit—it's not like there aren't a ton of other men just like me on every dating site and app and . . ."

He sighs and leans his elbows on the metal rail that lines the boardwalk, keeping people from jumping in at moments like this one.

I find words.

"So what happened?"

He shakes his head and clasps his hands together.

"She wouldn't stop texting, calling. I responded for about a week, but then I told her I was going to stop and I did. She still sends angry texts every day. I saw her after you walked in, and I knew we had to get the hell out of there."

I consider all of this information. I don't like it, but this actually makes me feel good. Maybe it's pathetic, but I feel happy that with all the things I've done chasing after love, I have never been a stalker—texts, calls, emails—nothing.

I smile and he catches me.

"What?" he asks.

I start laughing because I actually believe him and now feel relieved. My heart crawls out of the sinkhole.

"Is it terrible that I'm wondering what happened on that third date, in your apartment, that made you realize it wasn't a 'good fit'?" I make quotation marks in the air with my fingers. My mood has taken another drastic turn.

Now he laughs as well.

"Sometimes there's just no chemistry. You must have walked away from men for similar reasons."

Again, he turns the light on my past. But we are not going down that road.

"It's a giant candy store, isn't it?" I say instead. "Only, you get to try everything before you have to buy it. Take a bite. Good but not perfect. Pick up another, take a bite. Better, maybe. Or worse. Maybe the first was better."

He nods. "Exactly like that. And when it's the second time around, there's fear."

"Because you know there's a chance you'll be wrong? That what tastes good in the store won't be as good when you take it home?" I ask.

"And," he says, holding up a finger like Sherlock Holmes, "there's even more fear that you're the candy."

"Ah!" I say. "True." I look at him and try to think this. *He's the candy. I'm the one choosing the flavor.* But, no. They are just words. He knows it. Somehow men are never the candy. Never, never, never.

We start to walk again. He leads me back to the street where he's parked the car. The car that's all wrong, that's on my list of concerns. But at least I've crossed the woman from the bar off the list, because his story has convinced me.

"So, how did your sister meet her husband?" he asks now.

I'm the candy, so I try to be sweet and give him an answer.

"We all grew up together," I begin. I go on and on then, about Rosie and Joe and Gabe Wallace and the tree I used to climb and the skunk cabbage and the frog eggs. It gushes out of me, the words, the stories—no longer to please him but because they live inside me, flowing on a river of joy and sorrow. Hot lava and cold water. Wet, dirty clothes. Sunbaked skin. Laughter. Freedom. Bloody fists and tears and clear lines. Black and white. There were no shades of gray when we were young. Before we learned that everything is gray.

I stop, though. I don't tell him about my first boyfriend. And how he ended up dead.

"So your sister and her husband were friends from birth? That's a great story." He says. "I have to admit. It makes me sad, though."

"Why?" I ask.

"It reminds me of me and my wife, friends from college. There is something about meeting when you're young like that. Before you learn to hide."

We get to his car and he clicks open the locks.

He stands beside me and opens my door.

"What is it you're hiding?" I ask him. I can't help it. He opened that door as well.

Then he answers. "I could ask you the same thing."

And there is something in his voice that stops me again. He wants to know about my past. Why?

I've been fading in and out of dreams and nightmares.

I look at him, and neither of us speaks. I wonder which is real. Which is the truth. Is this a dream or a nightmare?

How long does it take, I also wonder, to know? Our mother didn't know what was in her husband's heart or mind, even after eighteen years. Sharing a bed. Sharing a bathroom. Sharing meals and vacations and births of children. I can't see behind the eyes of a man I just met, but I'm not at all sure time is the reason.

I should fear the possibility that this is a nightmare. And I should not get back in this car. This car that's all wrong.

But I can't bear to let go of the hope that this is a dream and the knowledge that no amount of time will give me the answer. We might still be strangers even after we become lovers.

"Come on," he says. "Let's head back to town."

There is a faint whisper in my brain as I get in the car.

What is it you're hiding?

He never answered.

Still, I let Jonathan Fields close the door.

TWELVE

Rosie. Present Day. Friday, 12 p.m.
Branston, CT.

Back at Rosie's house, Gabe created a new account on findlove .com. The screen name was here4you2. The photo was the screenshot of Jonathan Fields—the man the bartender identified. The profile was live by noon.

They selected women like Laura. Mid-twenties to early thirties. Never been married. No children. Living within ten miles of Branston. And pretty. They sent emails to over sixty profiles. The subject line read: *DO YOU KNOW THIS MAN?*

The body of the email contained a plea from one woman to another. *I met this guy online and I'm worried something's not right about him. Did he ever contact you?* Gabe left his cell number, and Rosie's.

"One in a hundred profiles on this site is fake. Avatars—fake pictures and enticing information. It's almost always women who do it. They use an avatar to contact the guys they're seeing. Or sometimes their husbands, boyfriends. Then they wait to see if he responds, if he wants to meet. That confirms he's cheating or lying. You get the idea."

Rosie nodded, staving off panic. A plan was in place. They would wait for a reply. And while they waited, Gabe would comb through the papers in Laura's room again, see what he could find that might help them. Rosie would start calling the people she knew from Laura's life. There were surprisingly few, she realized, and this made her uneasy. Guilty. She had been so consumed with her own life since Mason was born.

She would start with a casual call to Laura's work colleague named Jill. And Laura's old roommate, Kathleen—the one she'd never met because she spent weekends in New Jersey. Gabe knew how to find their numbers. She would also get in touch with Asshole in New York City, if she could figure out who he was. She would be careful not to raise concerns in case this was nothing and Laura wanted to return to her life without having to explain why her crazy sister called in a panic looking for her.

She fixed a cup of coffee and placed it on the table next to her phone and Laura's computer.

It was half past two when she heard the door.

"We're home!"

Joe set Mason down and he ran to his mother. Rosie scooped him up and hugged him tight.

"How was the park, lovebug?"

She closed her eyes. Breathed him in. Tried to pull herself back from the urgency of the situation. She knew he could feel it.

He squirmed from her arms and ran to the corner where they kept his toys. That left Joe, standing with her in the kitchen, his eyes shifting from her to Mason and out to the street where Gabe's car was parked.

"No luck?" Joe asked.

Rosie told him about Jonathan Fields and the bar where Laura's phone had been. They had his picture and his screen name. And how there might be another woman who went on a date with him, who used a credit card. Maybe they could find her. Maybe she would know more about him.

Joe looked quickly at the clock above the sink.

"It's almost three."

"I know."

"We should call. . . ."

Footsteps pounded the stairs. Gabe walked in, empty-handed.

"I have her social security number. That's all I found. It was on a reimbursement form."

Rosie got up from the table and joined them at the island.

"I think we need to call the police," Joe said again, filling the brief silence.

But then something new came across Gabe's face. Something she didn't recognize. It looked like guilt, or shame maybe. And it didn't suit him.

"I need to tell you both something. I don't know that it matters."

"Jesus, Gabe, what?" Rosie had her phone in her hand. Joe was right. It was time. And now this?

"Maybe it's nothing. Maybe I'm just pulling together memories to make sense of things—I hadn't thought about any of this for years, but it's been playing in my head since you called this morning."

"A memory? Of what? When we were kids? What are you talking about?" Joe asked.

Gabe closed his eyes. Hung his head. Jesus—was he trying to

see it more clearly, this memory from the past, or not wanting to see them when he finally said the words? Rosie was losing patience.

"Just tell us, Gabe! What do you know?"

"It has to do with my brother."

Joe was quick to respond. "Rick?"

"Yeah. Before he left home."

"For the military school? But that was so long ago—Laura was, what, eleven?" Rosie remembered Gabe's brother. Rick had been a troublemaker. Two years older than Gabe. Four years older than Laura. But he had never been their friend. Rick Wallace was the vicious dog whose house you ran past, hoping he wouldn't see you. Joe had gotten into it with him more than once. Fists flying, even as young boys. Mrs. Wallace cried about him to their mother. How she couldn't control him. How they had to send him away.

Joe was alarmed. "What happened with Rick?"

Gabe began the story.

"Do you remember when Laura would see Lionel Casey. In the woods?"

"Fuck, Gabe—why would you bring up Lionel Casey?" Joe was looking at Rosie when he said it. She was thinking the same thing. Of all the people, and under these circumstances . . . first Rick and then Lionel Casey—the homeless man who lived in the nature preserve. The man who was eventually found inside the car of Laura's dead boyfriend, and who'd spent his life in a mental facility as a result.

"Listen," Gabe continued. "I know it's hard to hear the name. But do you remember when we were little, when he used to wear that cape and walk the stone wall at the end of the pond? Laura said he looked like a vampire."

Rosie nodded reluctantly. The stories about the old hermit who lived in the deep woods of the nature preserve would have been funny now, as grown-ups, had things not ended the way they did, with Lionel Casey implicated in the death of Laura's boyfriend.

"Of course we remember," Rosie said. Laura always made them run back to the house to get garlic and crosses. She loved tracking him, thinking she saw his footprints in the soil. "He stopped doing that long before . . ."

"I know. But one time it was just the two of us. Me and Laura. I don't know why, or where the other kids were, where you two were. But she came running over, in the house to my room, banging on the door. She said he was out there again, with that cape, walking the wall at the end of the pond. God, I must have been thirteen then. It was the last thing I wanted to do. We were getting older. Teenagers, you know? But Laura was still a kid, still wanting to have her adventures."

"I remember," Rosie said. "She used to beg us to play with her. She didn't like that things were changing. She felt like she was getting left behind."

"That's why I went with her. We walked the path to the pond, but there was no one on the wall. She said we should split up. That I should go one way and she would go another, both of us walking around the perimeter of the pond until we met up again. I started to wonder if she'd been making it up, about Lionel Casey being out there that day. But I went along with it. I told her after we'd searched the perimeter, I was going home.

"She agreed and I started walking. I made it halfway around and didn't see her. I thought maybe I'd been faster, so I kept walking in the same direction, until I was back where we started. With no sign of Laura. It was so quiet that day. The trees were still bare. I called her name, then listened. I called it again. Still, no answer. I didn't know where to start looking for her. I remember hearing nothing but my feet on the dead leaves. I thought maybe he'd been there. Maybe he wasn't just a harmless old hermit after all."

Gabe stopped and the room was as quiet as the woods he'd just described. Lionel Casey had not been a harmless old hermit, and all those years they'd gone into the woods, he'd been there. Hundreds of times. Together, in pairs. Sometimes alone if one of them left before the others. Never aware of the danger.

"I went to the places I thought she would go—the field, the overlook. And then, finally, the fort. Remember that fort we built? One piece of plywood lodged between the trees?"

"We remember Gabe. Please—just tell us what happened," Joe said. Rosie couldn't speak, or move. She could barely breathe thinking about her sister out in those woods with Lionel Casey.

"She was there, in the fort. But not with Casey. She was there with Rick. And he had a knife to her throat."

Rosie gasped, hands to her mouth.

"What?" Joe said, his voice raised with anger.

"It was just his stupid pocketknife. But still, he was holding her by the hair with the knife . . . and I just fucking lost it. My brother had been a pain in the ass, but this was beyond anything he'd done before. Seeing Laura like that . . . it was too much. We got into a fight, rolling on the ground, kicking and punching each other. And then all of sudden, he was off me. Lying on the ground, holding his head."

Gabe placed his hand on his head as though acting out the scene. All of them were picturing this moment—knowing what was coming.

"I looked back," he continued, "and there was Laura, holding this stick with both hands. White-knuckled, hair clinging to the sides of her face that was wet with mud and tears. She was a wild animal. She came at him again and I got up and grabbed the end of the stick. I got it away from her. My brother stood, cursing at both of us, but he ran. Back to the house. Of course, I told my mother what he'd been doing to Laura with that knife. He said he was just trying to scare her because she thought she was so tough. But that's when he left."

"Before the year was up," Rosie said. "I always wondered why your parents didn't wait until the end of the term. Jesus Christ, Gabe. What are you saying? What do you think this story means?"

"I don't know. It's just a story. But I have this image in my head. Of Laura, like a wild animal. Holding that stick. Swinging it at my brother's head. If I hadn't stopped her . . ."

"That's enough." Joe held up his hand. "Enough. Was this the only time it happened? Did your crazy-ass brother hurt her again?"

"I don't know. Honestly. Rick wasn't about to tell me, and Laura never wanted to talk about it. But, God, I think about how angry she always was and I have to wonder if my brother was the cause of it."

"No!" Rosie wouldn't hear any more. "I don't believe it. If it had been more than that one incident, she would have said something. She would have done something about it."

"Maybe," Gabe said. "I hope you're right. The thing is, we're at a crossroads right here and right now. You already said, Rosie, that one of two things happened last night. And if it's the one I think it is, maybe we give her some time."

"Time for what?" Joe asked. "What have you two been discussing?"

Rosie looked at Gabe but didn't answer.

"You think she hurt this guy and now we should give her time to get away? Like some criminal? Seriously?"

Gabe was about to answer when they heard the sound. The *ping* on Laura's laptop.

Rosie rushed back to the table and stared at the screen. Joe was right behind her.

"No!"

Joe grabbed her by the shoulders, but he had no words to calm her.

The message was from a woman with the screen name second-chance. It was short. One word. All caps.

DO YOU KNOW THIS MAN? Had been the question.

The answer was brief.

RUN.

THIRTEEN

Laura. Session Number Nine.
Two Months Ago. New York City.

Dr. Brody: I'm sorry, Laura. It must be very hard to carry such a heavy burden.

Laura: Which one? I've always felt burdened by something.

Dr. Brody: The guilt.

Laura: Ah, right. That one.

FOURTEEN

Laura. The Night Before. Thursday,
9:30 p.m. Branston, CT.

We don't make it far.

He takes the same way back, and we are stopped at a light on Grand Street. A bodega is on the right, young men with their pants halfway down their asses crowd around the entrance. Yes, they still do that in downtown Branston. They haven't gotten the memo.

On the left, two old women sit on the stoop of a dilapidated town house, their knees spread wide even though they wear skirts. There's nothing to see but white granny panties, and they couldn't give a shit.

Jonathan plays music again. He hasn't spoken since we got in the car down by the water.

Finally he does.

"I have a confession," he says.

"Oh yeah?"

"Yeah."

"So what is it?"

Do we really need to go through all of this? Just spit it out.

He sighs. He says, "Okay." *Of course.*

Then he tells me. "I Googled you."

I shrug. "I Googled you. I thought that was normal."

"What did you find?"

How is this now about me? I don't have a confession. Not one I'm willing to make.

Still, I answer, seeing as we are playing a little game.

"Nothing, actually. No Jonathan Fields matched your picture. But I didn't try very hard, to be honest. There are a lot of you."

He sighs again. He says, "Okay." Again. "My last name isn't Fields."

Fuck.

"What is it then?"

"Fielding."

"And you lied because . . . ?" My heart bangs against the walls of my chest.

"That woman—the one from the bar—she found my ex-wife using my last name. She tried to friend her on social media. Facebook and LinkedIn. Followed her on Instagram. We don't speak much, so I didn't know. I couldn't warn her. They started messaging each other."

"That's crazy," I say. And it is.

"It was benign at first, but then she started asking questions about me, and when my wife—sorry, my ex-wife—got suspicious and cut her off, she started saying all this stuff about what an asshole I was and how could she have married me and what kind of an idiot was she because I probably cheated on her the whole time. Stuff like that."

I think about this as the light turns.

"So why are you telling me now?"

"What do you mean?" He doesn't glance at me because he's driving again.

My heart slows, the volume clicked down to a tolerable level. This all sounds reasonable in the world of online dating.

Not that I would know. But that doesn't stop me from accepting his explanation.

"She didn't flip out on you until you slept with her on the third date and then ended things. Which, I have to admit, still has me curious about what happened in that bedroom that you found strange but turned her into a strung-out addict for more of you and whatever it is you had going on that night."

This gets me a smile. Or maybe a snicker.

"Don't you think you should have waited to tell me? You haven't even given me a fighting chance to go psycho on you yet."

Another smile. Another light. This time we have an empty street corner on one side, and a deserted park on the other. He takes the opportunity to look at me.

"It's the first time I've lied about my name. It feels wrong. Like if we ended up seeing each other again, it would be too late to tell you and then I would have messed things up."

Sweet. Jesus. Christ.

He might want to see me again. *Happy.*

Lying will mean the end. *Sad.*

Confusion sets in. I'm not good with confusion.

"So," I say, struggling now. "Is that your confession?"

Light turns. Car doesn't move. He doesn't see the light because he's looking into his lap with his eyes closed.

"No," he says.

Now I'm worried. What's so bad that he can't even drive the car?

A pimped-out pickup truck pulls up behind us, lights blinding as they pour into the Toyota. Then a honk. Jonathan Fields—*scratch that*—Fielding—drives through the light and pulls over at the curb.

"I Googled you," he says again.

"I know. You said that."

"I found you."

The engine hums as it sits idling. We are beside the park, which has a fence running along the side of the road. Not a soul in sight now that the wifebeaters have driven past. I consider my options. They aren't good.

Did he stop here on purpose to tell me that he's found me?

I play it cool.

"Okay," I say.

"I mean *you*. The real *you*. Not Laura *Heart*. Laura *Lochner*."

"So we both lied about our last names? Is that what you mean?"

He shakes his head. I knew he would. I was just buying time. *Think. Think.* There's the door handle. The street. The deserted street and the fence and the bodega two blocks away.

"I get it," he says. "I mean, I would use a different name too. . . ."

I stop him right there. "How did you find my real name?"

The best defense is a good offense.

"There were no Laura Hearts who matched your photo. But Heart is your middle name so an image came up with all three. Names, that is. All three names. *Laura Heart Lochner*."

I don't know if I believe him. I've been so careful. I Googled myself before I started this misadventure, and I didn't see any images of me with all three names. But then again, I didn't look at every image. Maybe he has more patience. Maybe he's more careful because of that woman. Or maybe he's more careful for other reasons.

Or maybe he already knew.

"Okay," I say again, only this time with resignation. I'm cornered.

"Look," he says. "I read all of it. Every article I could find about what happened, and obviously I still came to meet you . . . so . . ."

I don't let him finish. "Are you a reporter or something?"

He gets offended, but I can't tell if it's rehearsed. Reporters can be sneaky as hell.

"No!" he insists. "I told you. I just wanted to make sure I knew what I was getting myself into."

"I could say the same." I pull out my phone, prepared to Google Jonathan Fielding. But my phone is dead. I don't know when it died, but it's dead.

He hands me his phone. "Do you want to check? It's only fair."

I push his hand away. "No," I say. What am I going to find that could even come close?

I face the executioner straight on. I feel him hang my hope first so I can watch it die before my eyes. That's what they used to do to exact the maximum punishment—hang the coconspirators one at a time, making them watch.

"So what do you want to know? Everything is right there—in the articles you read. It was eleven years ago, so there's plenty of them."

He tries to find my eyes, but I can't bear it.

"It's okay," he says. Suddenly I can't stand that word. "Look, I just wanted you to know that I knew. Like with my last name. I like you and I don't want to start out with lies."

I close my eyes. Count to five, then six, then seven. I'm still counting when he speaks again.

"Something happened to me when I was a teenager. Something traumatic like that. I mean, not just like that, but similar in that it stayed with me. Hung over me for years. I think it still does."

He waits for me to engage, but I'm still counting numbers, looking straight ahead. My hand is on the handle of the door.

I can't stand this conversation. I can't go back there. To that night. I was an idiot to come home and think the past wouldn't be here waiting for me.

He keeps talking.

"I was at the beach with some friends. We used to go there to drink and hang out. It's a small town, where I grew up. Cops turned a blind eye. Anyway, we saw this old guy out there, in the ocean; he was swimming laps. Back and forth, in the moonlight. We didn't pay any attention after we realized what he was doing—you know, just swimming."

I try to listen. I try to focus on Jonathan's story. But the woods are pulling me back.

"Then all of a sudden he stopped—like he was too tired or something. He waved an arm and called out to us. I took off my shoes and started running toward the edge of the water. A girl was on her phone calling 911. The other kids were like, *What are you doing? He could drown you!* And I knew they were right. But it just seemed wrong not to try to help him."

He pauses and I realize I should be having a reaction, an *Oh my God, what did you do?* or a *What happened next?* But I haven't been listening closely enough. Something about the beach and a man swimming . . .

He continues without me.

"By the time the police came, he'd gone under. Just like that. I will never forget that sight. Watching his head disappear and then, the very last thing to go under the black water—the hand that was waving for help."

I say it then. "So what happened?"

"He drowned, that's what happened. Right in front of my eyes, and I did nothing to help him. I didn't even try."

I find more words. "What could you have done?"

He shakes his head like he's heard this a thousand times, and I wonder if he tells this same story to every woman from findlove .com. I wonder if he told it to that crazy woman who stalked his ex-wife. I wonder if it's even true.

"Nothing—I know. He was too far away for me to have gotten to him, and I didn't have any training or anything. He could have grabbed me and pulled us both down. I know all of that. Still, the sight of it haunts me. That hand, just disappearing."

Long pause. Heavy sigh. He's waiting for my confession now. I don't give it.

Instead . . .

"I'm sorry. That must be very hard. To carry such a burden." I got that line from the shrink.

"Anyway . . ." says Jonathan Fielding. This is his second favorite word, and I hate that I am finding things not to like. Things I can use later, after it ends badly, to convince myself he was all wrong—*anyway*.

"So when I read about what happened when you were in high school, I understood a little bit about how these things can happen and then affect you for the rest of your life."

I smile. It comes over my face like a mask.

"I read everything I could find. One of the articles said that they'd found the car abandoned at the other end of the preserve. Deep in the woods. And some homeless man sleeping inside it."

"Lionel Casey," I say, finally. Might as well.

"Right. Lionel Casey," he repeats after me. "He never went to trial, because he was found mentally incompetent. He died in an institution still claiming to be innocent."

I shake my head. "Yes," I say.

Long pause. And then . . .

"Do people still think you did it? Is that why you don't use your real name?"

I look at him now and I don't know what I see. My mind has gone there, back to those woods, back to that car, back to that night, and he has become part of it now, this burden of all burdens. My hand squeezes the handle, and before I can stop myself, I am out of the car, running alongside the fence to the park.

I hear him call my name. "Laura!"

I hear another car door shut and my name, louder this time. "Laura! Stop!"

I run and run until I find the entrance and then I am in the park, the dark, littered park, that I pray will swallow me up.

Jonathan Fielding is fast. Faster than I am in my high heels, and I have a new theory on why men invented them. I feel his hand grab hold of my arm and yank me back so that I fall into him and we are both on the ground.

"Jesus Christ!" he says, standing up, brushing himself off. "What's the matter with you?"

I don't get up or brush myself off or do anything except stare at this stranger whose name I don't even know.

"I'm sorry," he says. "I shouldn't have asked you that—if people thought you killed that boy. Please . . ."

He reaches his hand out, but I don't take it.

"I wasn't implying that you . . . I just, I was just trying to relate. To understand what you might be going through being back here, where it all happened."

I'm listening again. He pulls me back with what sounds like reason.

Then he looks around us.

The park is silent but ominous somehow, like we have silenced it. Like it's waiting to come back to life and feast on us. People have been murdered in this park over car keys and wallets.

"We shouldn't be here. Let me drive you back to town at least. Please, Laura."

He reaches out his hand again, and this time I take it and pull myself up to stand. I brush the dirt from Rosie's dress. We walk, quickly, back toward the entrance. He doesn't stop talking. Explaining.

"People said things about me too. About all of us who were at the beach that night. They asked us why we didn't try to save him."

It's not the same. Not even close. But I let him continue.

We get to the car. He opens my door and I get inside.

Again, for the third time, I get in his car.

"I really just didn't want there to be any lies between us so early on—that's all. That's why I wanted to tell you I knew and tell you that I understood, so you wouldn't think that I thought badly of you. . . . God, I'm making it worse, aren't I?"

Jonathan Fielding is a talker now. He knows just what to say, because I believe every word. I have crawled deep inside our story, the story of me and Jonathan, and I only see what is right in front of me. I don't see that two days ago I had never heard of him and he had never heard of me. I don't see that our story is now chapters long, filled with questions and explanations and secret investigations into the lives we were not ready to reveal. That woman in the bar. That night in the woods. The holes in his story.

Am I doing it again? Am I constructing him? Writing our story to fit my desires?

I can ask all I want. There is no one there to answer. I'm alone with my defective mind.

Alone. The story of my life. And in spite of everything I know but can't see, that's the only story I want to end.

FIFTEEN

Rosie. Present Day. Friday, 2:45 p.m. Branston, CT.

A second email arrived soon after the first. The same woman from findlove.com who had sent the first email. The one that said, simply, *RUN!*

And now the second one—*HE'S NOT WHO HE SAYS HE IS*.

Gabe responded, asking for more information. He didn't tell her about Laura missing. He didn't want to scare the woman off. He said it was important. *I need to know if this is the same guy— what name did he give you? Did you get his phone number or an address?* That was all they needed—something to ID the guy. They waited for over two hours, but there was no further reply. Gabe went home, beckoned by his jealous, needy wife, leaving Rosie and Joe to take turns watching the screen.

Rosie paced the room, Mason in her arms. He was looking for attention now. He could sense something was wrong. Very wrong.

"Where did she go?" Rosie asked. "Seriously—why would she tell us those things but then disappear?"

Joe shrugged. "We don't know what she even means by any of this. Maybe she just got burned. Maybe she's just pissed and wants us to think things about him. And now she's changed her mind. . . ."

Rosie kept walking around the kitchen island, her eyes darting between Joe and the computer and the door—still hoping to see Laura burst through it as though nothing was wrong. Joe kept talking.

"It's after five, Rosie. I know what Gabe was saying, but . . ."

"It's crazy. That story about Rick and Laura."

They'd both been saying it, reeling in the chaos Gabe had left in their kitchen.

"I can't believe we didn't know. That she didn't tell us. That he didn't tell us—and you know Mrs. Wallace told your mother, or something close to it. She told your mother everything. And then your mother never said a word."

"You're right. We should call the police," Rosie said, thinking out loud.

Joe came to her side and wrapped his arms around her and their son.

"Okay . . . and I'm going to call a sitter—he likes Zoe the best, right?"

Rosie nodded and stroked Mason's soft hair. Then she looked to her phone and dialed 911.

She gave them the address, told them the situation. A unit was dispatched.

"Fuck," Joe said when she was done. "Here we go."

He got up from the table and took Mason from her arms. He called the sitter and begged for her to come, even just to take Mason to the park for an hour. He put him in a booster seat and turned on cartoons. He gave him some cookies and milk to distract him. Then he refreshed the computer screen. Still, nothing more. No more messages.

Rosie stood at the window in the family room, watching the street.

"Do you think Rick Wallace did something to her? Is that what Gabe was trying to tell us?" She was talking to herself now.

Joe remained in the kitchen, watching her stare at nothing.

"I don't know, Rosie."

The car appeared—no lights, no siren. It pulled to the curb and stopped. Doors opened, then closed. Rosie was waiting for them on the front walk.

"My sister didn't come home last night." She explained it all in the kitchen.

"I'll take Mason upstairs until Zoe comes. Maybe he'll nap. Maybe I can see if I can find anything else in Laura's things." Joe made excuses to leave the room. Mason knew cops only came when there was trouble.

The officers sat at the table, taking notes. Findlove.com, Jonathan Fields, the bartender, the woman they'd found using a fake profile. Those three letters—*R–U–N*.

Rosie gave her name—Rosie Ferro. Then her sister's name and description. She pulled up a photo for them to see.

Age, last address, height, weight, the color of her eyes.

Rosie hadn't spoken to the police since that night eleven years before.

What if she was wrong? That night was upon her now as she described her sister.

"Can you spell your sister's last name?"

The letters stuck in her mouth as she searched for a sign of recognition. *L-o-c* . . .

The younger of the two was a woman, Officer Pearson. She looked to be twenty-five, maybe thirty. She would have been a teenager herself that night Rosie heard Laura scream.

The older one was a man. Officer Conway. He was closer to forty. Wedding ring around his finger and some extra pounds around his waist. He would have been on the force back then.

"What time did she leave the house?"

Rosie pulled herself back. "I'm sorry—what was that?"

"The time," Officer Pearson asked again. "That your sister left the house?"

She gave them the time, as well as Laura's phone number and email address.

"A friend of ours was able to get the location where her phone died. He has a contact at the carrier, but that was all he could get. It's been dead since then."

Officer Conway flipped his notepad back a few pages. Pretended to read something. "So that's how you found this bar—where someone recognized a photo from possible men on this website?"

Rosie nodded. "That was our first lead. Now we have a woman on the site who knows him."

Now Pearson. "But you don't know for certain that your sister was with him last night. Or that this photo belongs to the man she was communicating with. Is that right?"

"Nothing is certain. That's why we need her phone records and emails, and access to her account on the website. She spoke to him on the phone. I know that for a fact. His number will be there!"

Now Conway. "You know because she told you?"

"Yes. Because she told me. She got dressed up for a date. She brought nothing with her but a purse. She was going to meet this man, Jonathan Fields. His number will be there!"

Rosie could see the doubt creeping in. Laura hadn't been gone a day yet.

"You need warrants, right? Can you get them or not?" Rosie asked.

Pearson and Conway exchanged a look.

"It's up to a judge, but most likely not until morning. We can put out a locate on your car," Pearson said.

Rosie pounded her fist on the table. "No! I told you—we found the car. It was parked on Richmond. We drove it home! It's right there—in the driveway!"

Conway now. "So the car isn't missing. Just your sister?"

"Yes!"

Two heavy sighs, then the officers stood up.

"We have her social security number," Rosie said, handing a piece of paper to Conway. "What happens now?"

"We'll file a report. Likely not much happens until tomorrow, unless there's more that surfaces between now and then to indicate a crime has occurred. Most of these cases, the person shows up." Conway tried to sound sympathetic but it came off as patronizing.

Rosie stood, helpless, as both officers walked to the door. "And it doesn't matter that we know she wouldn't do this?" she asked, following behind them.

Pearson answered without stopping. "Like my partner said, they usually turn up."

There'd been no promises. No sense of urgency. They didn't seem to recognize the name, but that would happen the minute they put it in the system. *Laura Lochner. The girl found next to a dead body. The murder weapon in her hand.*

The decision to call them had felt monumental—as though they would find Laura in an instant even if it came at the cost of dredging up the past. But the car drove off, again with no sirens, no lights. Nothing.

Joe returned from upstairs. He checked the screen then looked up at Rosie, shaking his head. There was nothing new.

"What's happening?"

Joe came closer. He was moving slowly. Ominously. He had papers in his hand.

"What?" Rosie asked. She didn't like what she saw on his face.

He handed her the papers. Three of them. Typed notes.

"I found these in her room. In the pockets of her coats."

"Just like she used to do," Rosie said. When she was a teenager, Laura would hide things from their mother in her coat pockets—coats worn in a different season, shoved into the back of the closet. It could be anything—cigarettes, condoms, her phone. Not that their mother ever bothered to look.

Rosie opened the first note.

I know what you did.

Then the second one.

You should never have come back.

And the third.

You will pay.

Rosie stared at the notes, reading them over and over. Joe stood beside her, holding her by the arms.

She looked at him hard, trying to gauge the amount of fear in his eyes. "Did you know about these?"

It wasn't the same as hers, her fear at seeing these notes. It changed everything.

Joe was indignant. "What are you asking me?"

"Did Laura tell you about these? Where they came from? Who might have sent them?"

He let go of her and walked away, then turned back. "I can't believe you would ask me that. Don't you think I would have told you? If not right away, then certainly this morning when she didn't come home?"

Rosie couldn't answer him because she didn't know what to think anymore. There had been so many conversations that seemed to hush when they heard Rosie coming down the stairs or around the corner—Laura and Gabe and Joe, sometimes just Laura and Joe.

Maybe she told him about the notes. Maybe she told him other things as well.

"Do you know?" Rosie asked, finally.

"Know what?"

She couldn't say the words. She'd never said them. Never asked the question. Not in eleven years.

"What, Rosie? Just say it already!"

And then they came, escaping from her mouth before she could catch them. The words, the question she didn't want answered.

"Did she tell you she killed him?"

It had always been there, this question. Hanging over all of them since that night.

All they ever knew was what Laura told the police. She was in the car with her boyfriend. The door opened from the driver's side. A man dragged him out. Laura heard the crack of wood against bones. Then a cry. She crawled out the other side and hid in the brush by the side of the road. The man swung the bat twice more, then got in the car and drove away.

They held her for twenty-four hours until the car was found, deserted in another part of the reserve, deep in the woods. Lionel Casey had made it his new home.

Laura was never charged. Still, the question lingered—why was she found standing over the body? The bat in her hands? Blood on her clothing?

Rosie asked it again.

"Did she tell you she killed that boy?"

Joe shook his head. "No."

Then she stood in the silence, wondering things about her husband. Wondering things about her sister. What she had done all those years ago to a boy in the woods. Her first love. A boy named Mitch Adler.

And what she might have done last night to a man named Jonathan Fields.

SIXTEEN

Laura. Session Number Eight.
Three Months Ago. New York City.

Dr. Brody: Can't you see his cruelty?

Laura: Who, Mitch Adler? Cruelty is a harsh word. He was just a high school jerk-off playing his options.

Dr. Brody: He knew he was causing you pain. It wasn't incidental to his selfish actions. It was intentional. And that is cruelty.

Laura: He seemed troubled to me, and I was drawn to him because of it. Like I could make it better if I just broke through. If I loved him enough.

Dr. Brody: You thought you could fix him and then he would be able to love you?

Laura: I know that sounds ridiculous. I see that now. He was never going to love me.

Dr. Brody: Does that remind you of someone else? Someone from your childhood?

Laura: I don't think so. What are you getting at?

Dr. Brody: Sometimes we try to fix the past by fixing the present.

Laura: Well, that's stupid.

Dr. Brody: It's how our brains work. It's subconscious. And it's not stupid.

Laura: But it's dangerous.

Dr. Brody: Yes. It can be very dangerous.

SEVENTEEN

Laura. The Night Before. Thursday, 10 p.m. Branston, CT.

I know what you did.
You should never have come back.
You will pay.

The notes came at different times and in different places. The first was folded under the windshield wiper of Rosie's minivan when I took it to the track to run. Round and round in circles I ran, the car parked just up a small hill in the lot of the public high school of the town next door—a town that has schools with good facilities and no guards at the gate because why would they? That's why people pay millions of dollars for a house there. I wonder what they would think if they knew their poor security let in people like me. People who may have killed someone.

I run each lap in two minutes. Whoever left that note was watching me, waiting for me to make a turn around the bend away from the lot.

The second came in a package from Amazon. It was slipped between the openings where the box hadn't been taped. It was a box with pajamas, which I had ordered online and had shipped to Rosie's house.

The third, I found under my pillow.

They were typed. On white paper, cut off after the words, then folded several times like origami.

Why don't you lock your doors? I asked Rosie the day I found the third note. *Aren't you worried someone might steal something?*

Rosie gave me her classic Rosie look of *Are you kidding?* We were in the kitchen. She swept her arms out in front of her with a great deal of drama. *I wish they would! Half this stuff is crap from our old house and Joe's old house—everything is old. Take it! Take it all—just not the wine.*

Haha. I laughed with her, then went upstairs and sat on the bed in the attic, staring at the door and the window and the closet where I'd just hidden the last note. Or the latest note. That was two days ago. Maybe there were more coming. Or maybe something else.

I should be worried about the notes and not this stranger who sits beside me. Maybe I am. Maybe that's why I haven't slept more than two hours at a stretch since the first one arrived. Exhaustion in my bones. In my brain. The thick fog is not helping me as the stranger and I pull into the underground garage.

I've been talking about that night to this stranger. Jonathan Fielding. The night of the party in the woods. I don't stop.

His name was Mitch Adler. He went to the public high school, and I'd met him at a party six months earlier.

He was not a nice boy. He was not a good boyfriend. But I

told myself there were reasons, and that I was the only person who could fix him.

"You probably read that he came to the party with a girl," I say.

Jonathan nods. He doesn't want to cause another freak-out where he has to risk his life chasing me through a dangerous park.

Then he says, "His parents said it was the girl he'd been seeing all year, bringing her to the house for dinners. They said they thought she was his girlfriend."

And he continues, "And they said they had never met you or heard your name until that night."

Jonathan Fielding, you have done your homework.

I add to his research. "Her name was Britney. Blond hair. Blue eyes. Turns out she *had* been his real girlfriend for over a year. I had no idea. I thought I was his girlfriend. He had sex with her in his car before they went into the woods to join the party," I say. That's the truth. "The car was there. It was parked up the road from the others."

"Why?" he asks.

"Why what?"

"Why did he leave the car so far up the road?"

I shrug. "I don't know. Maybe he thought he would get lucky again."

Then he looks at me. "But not with that same girl? Britney— the one he'd already had sex with? But with you—two girls in one night?"

Fuck you, Jonathan Fielding. But, yes.

The car is off. We sit in the darkness of the windowless garage and, now, my mood.

"I don't know what he was thinking."

He says nothing more, but I know what *he's* thinking. All of the facts are there for anyone to find, and I'm sure he's found them.

I feel defensive. I'm back at the police station eleven years ago, blood on my clothes. Splinters in my hand from holding on to that bat so tight.

Tears streaming down my dirty face. My dirty soul.

"I wasn't going to have sex with him in that car. I let him think that, but I wasn't going to have my first time be like that—in the backseat of a car with a jerk who brought someone else to a party. Someone else named Britney who happened to be his real girl-friend."

Jonathan looks at me and smiles. It's not a warm smile.

"What did you think was going to happen?" he asks. But it isn't really a question.

"I don't know what you mean." But I do know.

"How were you going to fend him off? That seems dangerous." He touches my arm and I see a glimpse of reassurance. "I'm not judging you. I just don't understand why you would leave with him. Go to his car. Get inside."

I wipe away every trace of an expression.

"That was harsh." He backs off. Now I see sympathy. "So what did happen?"

It does not get past me that he never mentions the bat. He is not sold on my story the way the police were after they found the car and Lionel Casey.

"I'd been dating the guy. He was a shit. He asked me to do something. An ultimatum. A condition to keep him. And I was desperate. I thought if we were alone, if he saw how much I loved him, he would stop being a shit. I didn't know about Britney, how he'd been with her for an entire year. I only knew he came and went in my life for months and it was torture. I never knew when he would be there. I never knew when he would disappear. But when he did come back—it was intoxicating. Nothing else could touch that feeling. Didn't you ever run into a woman who made you feel that way?"

He thinks for a moment, but not really. The shrink was right. Normal people don't fall into traps like that. Only the broken ones.

"I'm sure I would have if I hadn't met my wife so early," he says, lying—and I realize from this lie that he has the ability to be kind. Because that's what that was—kindness. I was a broken hot mess. I was that friend who everyone tries to help but who won't listen to reason.

Then he eases into another question. "Why were you so drawn to him? To this shithead who only fed you scraps?"

I have an answer. It's a lie.

"Our father left when I was twelve. Left us for another family. That probably has something to do with it. That's when it all started. It took me years to understand myself. What pieces were broken and why. It was such a relief when I finally sorted it out."

This is a good lie—that Dick leaving was the start of my problems. My anger. The truth is that I was broken long before Dick left us.

But Jonathan buys it and moves on.

"So then what happened with that guy in New York? The one who disappeared?"

It's a good question, Jonathan Fielding.

"I don't know. Honestly. He was the first man I thought was actually good," I say. Then I shrug and look sad. *Truth. Truth. Truth.* All of it true, even the sadness.

"So this must be hard for you," he says. "Getting back into dating. You must be analyzing everything—even what I'm saying right now."

I wave my hand in circles like a magician. "If only I had magical powers to see what's going on inside there." I smile. Try to sound playful.

Our story turns a page. A new chapter begins.

"Well," he says. "It's not easy for me, either, if that makes you feel better."

Yes, it does. Misery loves company. Misery beats empathy every time.

"How so?" I ask. I want it to be bad. I want to hear how he's suffered so I don't feel so alone in my own suffering. I've been around Rosie and Joe and their marital bliss for too long.

"I told you my mother died last year, right?"

I nod. He did. I almost forgot because I can be selfish that way, hearing only the part about how much his parents loved him and feeling the fury of envy from it.

Exhaustion caused by chronic insomnia can make a person selfish.

"It came soon after the divorce. Maybe a month. My wife was at the funeral. Sorry—my ex-wife. I don't know why I keep doing that."

Neither do I.

"That must have been hard," I say. Both of us, we keep saying this. And I wonder if he was a patient of the same therapist. Haha.

"When they lowered her casket into the ground, and I looked at my ex-wife, across the grave, not beside me—it was just like watching all the love in my life go into the ground with her. It hasn't left me. That feeling I had, like it's all so fragile. The very thing that makes life worth living can be gone in an instant and there's not a thing you can do about it."

Holy. Shit.

I stare at him because he's closed his eyes and can't see me stare.

And because he's crying. Not like a waterfall. Just two or three drippy little tears.

He blinks them away, opens his eyes again, and catches me staring.

I look away.

"I'm sorry," I say. "I didn't mean to stare. You just caught me off guard."

He smiles and shakes his head. "All this talk about the meaning of life, and these horrible events from our past and bad breakups . . . I guess these things don't come up that often in conversation, so I push them aside. Get up. Go to work . . ."

"Check your likes and winks on findlove.com."

"Exactly."

I exhale loudly so he knows I'm running alongside him on this emotional obstacle course.

"It's been a lot. I'm sorry. I've been in a very reflective place since I've come home. This is all my fault."

"You know what's funny, though?" he asks.

I have no idea. "What?"

"It feels good in a way. Cathartic."

He knows how to turn the pages. I'm right there with him.

"I know. I haven't had one conversation since I've been home that's transcended mommy gossip, sports, and funny stories from our childhood. Always the funny stories. Never the other ones."

"Same here. Even when I visit my father or my sister. We don't ever talk about my mother, except to remember how she used to like this thing or that thing, or what she would have said about something happening in the news. None of us talks about the hole in our lives, or how it shines this bright light on death and loss. It's lonely sometimes."

Jonathan Fielding, you have no idea how lonely it is. Or maybe you do. Maybe you know in a different way, having had such incredible love from a parent and now having it gone. Maybe that's worse than spending a lifetime yearning for it. Maybe the hole that's left is just as big and the urge to fill it with other things just as strong.

I want to reach across the cheap plastic console of this car that's all wrong and put my arms around him. I want to bury my face in the nape of his neck and smell his skin and feel the warmth of him. This man who knows. This man who understands.

I can hear Rosie scorning me. *Can't you see how these men are like a drug for you? Don't you get it? They can't fill the hole. They just make it bigger.*

I'll quit tomorrow, Rosie. I promise. *Just one more.*

I have to see if maybe this one's not wrong. His words. His tears. How can I still not know the difference? I learned not to turn them away, the right ones. I learned how to see through the wrong ones, not construct them into more than they are. Didn't I?

Is it wrong that I see Asshole across from me now?

Jonathan Fielding reads my mind again.

"What was his name?" he asks.

"Who?"

"The man in New York. The one who left you. Who disappeared."

Asshole, I'm about to say. But that's probably not the best answer.

"Kevin," I say. True. But the word is bitter on my tongue.

There's a pause. A long one, and he stares at me now. Payback's a bitch. Then I feel a line slowly drawn down my cheek. Just one. It curls around my chin and stays there until I wipe it away.

"Jesus—now I'm sorry!" he says. His hand reaches across the

cheap plastic console of this car that's all wrong and wipes my cheek. Erases the line with smooth, soft skin.

"Both of us crying—I don't know what that says about this date."

I don't even try to smile this time.

"He hurt you pretty bad, huh?"

"Apparently," I manage to get out as the muscles around my mouth tremble. "I don't know why. It only lasted a few months."

We're still in this car. Half an hour later and we're still sitting here in the darkness. I feel trapped, suddenly, like I'm in a cell with no way out. But there is a way out. It's a door handle, then an exit sign, then a street, then Rosie's car, the way home, the driveway, front door, unlocked of course, lingering garlic, up the creaky stairs, down the narrow hall to the attic and my bed where I will fall into the fluffy comforter that smells like my nephew and I will lie there awake all night. . . .

It's just another cell. This is what I realize as I sit in the car that's all wrong with this stranger and this hope and these tears. It's a cell where I stare at the ceiling in a state of fear about who is writing me ugly notes and why did Kevin leave me without a trace and when will I ever turn off this mind that is killing me in a million small ways every day?

Which cell is worse?

I decide to stay.

"Was he the first one you thought you got right?" Jonathan asks. "After figuring out your issues with your father?"

I move my head up and down. *Yes.*

I hear Kevin's words in my ear. *I love you.* I feel his skin on my skin and his hands in my hair and his breath so warm against my cheek. He said those words even though I had told him everything—about that horrible night. About my fists for hands and my father who left and my mother with her men. Rosie and Joe. And Mitch Adler. He said the words in spite of everything.

"He broke it off in a text message," I say. "I don't know why." It makes me sound pathetic.

"Just like that?" Jonathan asks. Even though I already told him this.

"Just like that." I guess I have to keep saying it to convince him.

Jonathan Fielding shakes his head with wide eyes like I've just told him something unbelievable. But he doesn't know my past, how many wrong men I'd managed to find in the haystack, and how they treated women. Or me, I suppose. Maybe it was just me.

"That's just wrong. Breaking up with a text. I don't care what day and age it is. I sure hope it works out between us because I don't know if I can handle the modern world."

"You've already been stalked. You got through that. I think you'll be okay," I say, trying to move away from this story. I can't bear it. Not tonight. I'm so tired.

Jonathan pulls the keys from the ignition and grabs his wallet from the cheap plastic console. He opens his door and the dome light turns on, making both of us squint.

"Why don't you come up for a drink? I feel like I want to keep talking to you, but it's silly to be sitting in the car in a garage. I have a decent view. . . ."

Hell. No. I know better than that.

"We could go back to the bar on Richmond. Maybe the stalker is gone," I suggest like a nice church girl.

He gets out of the car. He walks to my side and opens my door. He gives me his hand.

"Come on," he says. Something comes over him then. It's unbridled. It's strong and manly and it sweeps me away like the ocean at the harbor.

I give him my hand and leave the car. Close the door. Stand beside him.

He looks me in the eye. The tears gone. The questions answered.

"Come on," he says again. "You're safe. It's not the third date yet."

Another page. A new chapter. This one has a title I'm familiar with. *Mischief.* It's a title I like, that old me likes, and I cannot refuse her. Not after everything I've just put her through.

Old me rushes out the back door like a dog who's been stuck inside all day. Running free on the lawn. Sun shining on her face.

"I may be safe," I tell him. "But you may not be."

Haha.

EIGHTEEN

Rosie. Present Day. Friday, 11 p.m. Branston, CT.

The house was quiet. This time, it was Joe in the bed with Mason beside him. They didn't even bother putting him down in his own room. Even after an hour at the park with Zoe, Mason could feel things weren't right in the house. Kids are like animals that way, sensing the storm before even one cloud appears in the sky.

Joe was in the bed, but he was not asleep. He was on his laptop, quietly searching for men named Jonathan Fields.

Back in the kitchen, at the table with Laura's laptop open, Rosie stared at the message inbox for their fake findlove.com account. There was nothing new—not from secondchance or anyone else they'd contacted. Sometime between seeing those notes and this moment, the cells in her body had shifted. The shock and terror at the thought of Laura being gone, maybe forever, and in some horrible way, had morphed into something else. Not quite resignation like she'd seen on Gabe's face. Not the feigned concern of the police. It was a mosaic of pain and sadness, fear and anger. She could taste them all as her thoughts shifted through scenarios.

Laura missing, never found. Laura found, hurt or worse. She couldn't even think the other word. The tragedy was starting to take hold, progressing through stages. She suddenly had a window into the aftermath for parents whose children go missing—every day wondering. Every day, hoping. Every day, mourning. That could be her life now. The thought was unbearable.

She rested her head in her palms, elbows propped on the table. How did people learn to go on after something like this?

She thought about the parents of Mitch Adler, how they had learned to live with the loss of their son—their only son in between two daughters, a giant hole ripped into their family. That teenage boy, barely a man, whom Rosie could still see clearly in her memories, just gone. He was not a nice boy. Chances were, he would not have grown into a nice man. Still, whatever his life held, that life was ended on a gravel road. A crushed skull. Blood pooling around it. And Laura, standing there.

They didn't stay long, his family. They had relatives in Colorado and were gone before Christmas. Rosie searched for them and couldn't find any trace back in Connecticut. Still, they had friends here. Mitch had friends as well, many of whom had likely stayed or returned. Any one of them might have seen Laura in town. Any one of them could have sent those notes.

Rosie thought about what she might do if it had been Laura lying on the ground instead. If she might hunt down the person she thought was responsible. It was far less satisfying to believe that the killing was at the hands of a mentally ill hermit—a man who could not be held accountable. Justice must have felt very hollow to the Adler family.

She heard her phone ring on the counter by the sink and she was there in an instant.

"Gabe? What's happened? Tell me . . ."

Gabe's voice sounded tired. "The waitress called—the one from the harbor bar who waited on Jonathan Fields and one of his dates," he said. "She found the credit card slip."

"The date who bought drinks with her own credit card?"

"It was three weeks ago, like the bartender said. Her name is Sylvia Emmett."

Rosie's hand pressed into her chest.

"Rosie?"

"Yeah. I'm here. I want to speak to her. Can you get a number?"

"I did. I left a message. I gave her both of our numbers. She could be in bed already. It's late."

Rosie was walking now, around the island. "What if we go there. Or the police! They could go. We can't wait all night. My God, Gabe—"

He interrupted her. "The police? You called them?"

Rosie stopped walking. "I did. It was time. . . ."

"What did they say? Did they . . ."

"Nothing—they didn't seem to know who she was and they weren't too concerned, either. They said they would try to get the phone records by morning."

The line was silent for a long moment. Then: "It's good you called, Rosie. You're right. It was time."

Another abrupt shift swept through her. She didn't want to be right. She wanted Gabe to tell her she was overreacting. Tell her she should have waited. Tell her she was wrong.

Then she remembered the notes Joe had found in Laura's coat pockets. The threats. Gabe didn't know about those, either.

"There's something else . . ." she started to say. But another call was coming through.

"Rosie?" Gabe was waiting for her to finish.

"Hold on—there's another call. Maybe it's that woman. . . ."

"Go! Pick it up!"

Rosie answered the second call. "Hello?"

"This is Sylvia Emmett." The woman said it in a whisper. She said it like she didn't want to be on the other end of the call.

Rosie took Joe's car to the west side of town. The streets were quiet, empty. There was nothing there but industrial buildings—warehouses and car dealerships. She passed a furniture outlet and saw the neon lights of a diner. She turned in and parked, walked inside, and sat across from a woman with dark brown hair pulled up in a ponytail. She was young, like Laura. And pretty.

"Are you Sylvia?" Rosie asked.

The woman motioned for her to sit down. "Yeah," she said.

Rosie slid onto the bench, the table between them. "I'm Rosie. Thank you for calling back. You have no idea—"

"I have a boyfriend," the woman blurted out. "He can't know. . . ."

The waitress was upon them. Sylvia ordered coffee.

"I'll have the same," Rosie said. Then, to the woman, "My sister went on a date with a man last night. She never came home."

Sylvia sat back, wide-eyed. "What does that have to do with me?"

"Her phone was last online near a bar by the harbor. The bartender recognized this man. . . ." Rosie pulled the picture from her purse and laid it on the table. She pointed at Jonathan Fields and stared at his smug smile.

"My sister went on a date with a man from this site. The profile matches—the age, description. And he was at the bar where her phone was last online."

Rosie watched the woman process the information, part of her hoping that she was about to say something that sent them on a new course, a course where this man, this player, was not the man her sister met. She couldn't decide if that would be better or worse.

But it didn't matter. That hope was quickly dispelled as Sylvia's face changed from shock to recognition.

"He loved that place. It was always crowded. Easy to get lost."

"He said his name was Jonathan Fields," Rosie said.

Sylvia shook her head with disgust. "He lies about his name. I met him at a different bar. Not through any dating site. I was out with some friends and he was there—alone. Trolling, it turns out. He was relentless, but cute. First he told me he was Billy Larson. But on our first actual date—which was at that bar by the harbor—he told me he had lied about that, and that his name was Buck Larkin. He covers his lies with more lies. After he told me he'd lied about his name, I thought that was it—that was the thing he was hiding. He said he didn't like women looking for him on social media. He said he was worried they might tell his ex-wife and that it would hurt her feelings. Ridiculous, right? I didn't think it at the time. Not with handsome Billy, or Buck, or whatever his name really is, sitting across from me and two glasses of wine . . ."

The waitress returned and set down the coffee. Sylvia took hers in both hands, spun the cup around in the saucer. Her mind was on this man, Jonathan Fields. Billy Larson. Buck Larkin. The liar.

Rosie didn't speak. She didn't want to interrupt the story for fear that it would end before it could lead her to her sister. And Sylvia seemed anxious to tell it all as quickly as she could.

"We went on three dates in total, if you count the night we met," Sylvia continued. "The first two times, he was a perfect gentleman. Paid for the drinks. Paid for dinner the second night. Opened doors for me, listened to me. He was the reason I had doubts about my boyfriend—you know? He was everything Dan isn't. But when I look back on it, I can see how he paid careful attention to everything I said, and, yes, I lied about still being with Dan. But we're not married. We don't live together. I don't know. Maybe I'm just as bad as he is."

She stopped, took a sip of coffee. It felt like forever.

"So what happened?" Rosie asked finally. "Why did you agree to meet me in the middle of the night?"

Sylvia looked up, suddenly hesitant.

"Please," Rosie said. "I need to know what might have happened last night."

"Look, I don't know if this is going to help you find your sister. It's hard to talk about it. It's humiliating."

"I don't think any of us get through life without doing something humiliating."

Sylvia smiled softly. Exhaled. Looked into her coffee.

"I just wanted to be sure, you know? About Dan. Before we got married or had kids. I'd never thought about it until I met Buck at that bar. He was so attentive, you know? And Dan, well . . . he's not exactly a talker. It made me wonder if I was rushing into things. I had feelings for this guy instantly. He was emotional and intelligent. He even cried when he told me about his divorce."

"So Jonathan Fields . . ." Rosie said, thinking out loud. "I mean Buck, or whoever he is. This man"—she pointed again at his picture—"he liked to talk?"

"You have no idea how good he is. It was as though he could read my mind. Everything I brought up, he had something clever or insightful to say about it. He never looked bored or antsy. Intellectual, well-read, you know? I honestly thought I was falling in love with him right then and there, by the end of the third date. That night, we met at a place downtown. . . ."

"On Richmond?" Rosie asked.

"Near there. On Main—one block over."

"The car my sister was driving was found on Richmond! Did you go to his apartment?"

Sylvia shook her head. "No. But he asked me to go there—all three times I saw him. We talked for hours. I told him it was too soon for me to go to his place—maybe next time. This whole thing about sex on the third date—it's ridiculous, and I wasn't falling for it. So he suggested we go for a walk. He wasn't put off at all— or so it seemed. And I was really attracted to him. It filled me with so much confusion and guilt, but also this passion I hadn't felt for so long. He was inside my head. I don't know how else to describe it.

"We went down this side street. He said he wanted to show me something. It was some kind of gallery. It was closed, of course, and the street was empty. It was after midnight. He showed me this painting in the window. He said his friend painted it. Total bullshit, I found out—the artist was dead. But that's not the point."

Sylvia leaned in close, lowered her voice. Her eyes scanned the small dining room, which was still as empty as it had been when Rosie had arrived.

"There was an alley between the art gallery and the next building. That was why he'd brought me there. He grabbed my hand and pulled me just inside, between the buildings. Just a little bit— so little that I still felt visible from the street. He said he couldn't stand not kissing me for one more second. And then he did—he kissed me. And it was just like the way he got into my head and took over my thoughts—he did that to the rest of me in that alley.

To my body. It was all so gradual, so natural and perfect that I didn't even know what was happening really until my face was pressed against the side of that building and he was inside me. . . ."

She stopped then. Closed her eyes and shook her head quickly, as though trying to erase the memory that was before her now.

When she opened her eyes again, she blinked away tears.

"I want to be clear, though. He didn't assault me. There was no force. Just brilliant seduction. He made me want him. He clearly expected sex on the third date and he got it."

Rosie reached across the table and took her hand. "I'm so sorry." She meant it, but still, this couldn't be the end. This couldn't just be about seduction and regret. Unless her fears were right. Unless Laura's regret had turned to rage.

"Can I ask you what happened after that? If you saw him again?"

Sylvia slid her hand away and folded it into her lap.

"Everything changed. As soon as he had my face pressed against that wall, everything tender and loving about him turned ugly. He started saying things to me, in my ear. Dirty talk, they call it, but I had never heard it that dirty. That filthy and degrading. He bit down on my earlobe until it bled. And he was so rough and crude. When it was over, he couldn't wait to get rid of me. He barely waited for me to straighten my clothes—he zipped up his pants and started walking. I had to run to catch up to him."

"Jesus," Rosie said, imagining the scene.

"Look—I'm not naïve. And it's not the first time I've been in a situation that wasn't—you know—a relationship. I'm not the girl who thinks every guy she sleeps with wants to marry her."

Sylvia pressed her hand on the man's picture. "But this man is sick. He walked ahead of me the whole way back to the restaurant. He said something like *thanks*. And then he walked away.

Just like that. He didn't walk me to my car. He didn't kiss me good night. He was making a point of it. Like he wanted to make sure he made me feel as used as he possibly could. I don't think it was about the sex. He wanted to hurt me. But that's not all. . . ."

She laughed then, a maniacal burst that came from deep inside her.

"I waited two days before texting him. The worst two days of my life. The facts were all there, and the feeling in my gut as well, but I clung to this shred of hope that I was wrong. That he was just awkward or kinky or something, but that the rest of it, the conversation and the way he looked at me and made me feel, was genuine. Because if I was that wrong about him . . . if I could be so easily manipulated . . . then the world felt like it was turned upside down. Like nothing was real."

Rosie didn't know what to say, so she said nothing. She was picturing Laura with this man, wondering if she would be able to see through it. She was so good at that, at seeing people. Unless they were men offering the hope of love.

"You probably think I'm just an idiot," Sylvia said after a short while.

"No!" Rosie said. "That's not what I was thinking. We can't live our lives never trusting anyone. That would be miserable."

"Well, maybe so. But when I finally texted him, the number was unrecognizable. It was gone. Some kind of burner phone. TracFone. Disposable. His names were all fakes. He was done with me and he made sure I had no way to find him. I tried. Google. Facebook, other social apps. He was gone. And I was left with my guilt and shame, but also, you know what?"

"What?" Rosie asked.

"Gratitude. For Dan. For that boring guy who sits on the couch watching football and doesn't hear a word I say, but loves me and is honest and loyal and doesn't call me a cunt when we're making love. That man, Billy or Buck, or Jonathan or whoever the hell he is—he's sick and he's a liar. He's never who he says he is. But I try now to think of him as a gift. Because he showed me what kind of monsters are out there.

"Promise me," she said then, taking hold of Rosie's arm this time. "Promise me that you will never tell anyone about this. I can't lose what I have. Not over this. Please."

"Of course," Rosie reassured her. "I won't say a word. But can you just sit with me a little longer? Tell me more things about him, the stories he told, things he said about his past, anything—it might help me find him. And then find my sister."

Sylvia nodded. "Okay," she said. "But then you have to promise me another thing."

"Name it."

"I'm not a vengeful person. Or a violent person. But if you do find him, I want to know who he is," she said. "And somehow, I want him to pay."

NINETEEN

Laura. Session Number Eleven.
Two Months Ago. New York City.

Dr. Brody: It can become confused in the mind. Intimacy and sex. Power and sex.

Laura: You sound like an article in *Cosmo*.

Dr. Brody: I know. It's cliché. Do you remember when it changed? You used to find power through other things—chasing vampires and climbing trees. Even school and sports.

Laura: Jumping through hoops.

Dr. Brody: Maybe. But it changed, didn't it? What brought that change?

Laura: It'll sound absurd to you.

Dr. Brody: Try me.

Laura: It was a kiss. Everything changed with one kiss.

TWENTY

Laura. The Night Before. Thursday, 10:30 p.m. Branston, CT.

Jonathan Fielding lives in a nice building, with navy blue carpeting in the hallways and beige wallpaper. All of the trim is gold, so it looks elegant and fancy. Maybe a bit old-fashioned, but that's normal for this town.

We don't speak in the elevator. We don't speak as we walk down the hall to his door. Or when he finds the key and puts it in the lock, turns the knob, and lets us in.

"Here it is," he says, finally. "Home sweet home."

Only it's not sweet at all. And it doesn't feel like anybody's home. It's close to empty.

He deciphers my expression and makes a preemptive excuse.

"I know, I know." His hands are held up in front of him, head bowed like he's making an apology. Humble. Contrite. "I haven't had time to get it properly furnished."

That's an understatement.

I walk in and look wall to wall. On the left is the kitchen. It's very white and clean, as though it rarely gets used. There is nothing on the counter except take-out menus and plastic silverware. Not even a saltshaker. Not even a dirty glass he didn't have time to put in the dishwasher.

Dead center is the living room. There's a small sofa against the wall. It's black leather and has no pillows. It faces the opposing wall where a very large television sits on the floor, propped up on a temporary stand. It's waiting to be hung. Beside it is a cable box and some wires going into the wall.

There is nothing else. Not a coffee table. Not a painting or a picture or a rug. Absolutely. Nothing.

"Okay," I say skeptically as I gather this information along with the other things he's told me over the past three hours.

He said he's been divorced for a year. He said he lived here even before that and worked here as well. He said he only commuted to the city a few times a month.

More things to add to my list of concerns—with the car and the woman (yes, I add her back on the list now) and the fact that he's stayed here voluntarily, in this small town where he has to get dates on a website.

I begin my inquisition.

"So tell me you moonlight for the CIA."

He laughs nervously. Throws his keys on the bare kitchen counter. They make a loud noise as they slide across it. There's nothing on the counter to stop them.

"What?" he asks.

"You've been here a year and all you have is one sofa? Didn't you get anything from your old house? I thought people divided things up when they got divorced."

Eyebrows raised, tilted head. Wry smile. That crooked smile. Is it endearing? Or was I wrong before? Is it smug?

"I know. I just . . . I didn't want any of it. It all reminded me

of her and our life together. It's not like I still love her or anything. But it is the death of a dream, right? The dream I had of a
family and all that."

Hmmm . . . Jonathan Fielding, you can do better than that.
Can't you?

"But then you didn't just make a run to IKEA and load up?
Do you even have any dishes?"

Jonathan Fielding opens a cupboard and points proudly to a
set of white plates and glass tumblers.

"You want a drink?" he asks, changing the subject.

"Sure," I say. But I return to the subject. "Seriously. You've
really been here for a year? Living like this?"

He has a bottle of scotch and he pours two glasses.

"I know. It's pathetic. Maybe we can go to IKEA on our next
date . . . assuming you still want to have one. I do. I know that
much."

He hands me the scotch and leads me to the sofa in the otherwise empty room.

We sit on opposite ends. Still, it's small and when he pulls one
knee up onto the cushions, he's one lean away from me.

"Tell me more about the fun things. The good things," he says.
"It sounds like you have great memories of your childhood—with
your sister and her husband and the other kids in the neighborhood. It must have been incredible to grow up next to all those
woods."

Well, when you put it that way . . .

"I guess it was happy in some ways." I say this and I somehow
even believe it. Yet the word "happy" is not quite right. I try to
clarify.

"It's strange, though. I can pick out certain moments that, in
my mind, right now, play back as joyful. Like—oh my God! How

we used to tightrope across this enormous fallen tree. And right below it was the nastiest pool of mud and skunk cabbage you can imagine. I nearly fell in it once, but I dug my nails into the bark of that tree so hard that I was able to hang on and shinny to the other side. . . ."

Joy.

"But then other times, I remember this unrest that was always there, casting a shadow on everything."

Anger.

"Well, that was your father, right? Your mother knowing he was cheating. Crying in the kitchen to your neighbor—what was her name?"

"Mrs. Wallace. Gabe's mother."

"Right—of course you were unsettled. Your very foundation was like quicksand."

I nod solemnly. It was all Dick's fault. So neat and tidy.

I change back to the joy.

"I had my first kiss in those woods."

"Really!" he says, and I feel him shift a little closer. I didn't mean to be provocative. But now it's too late.

"It was nothing romantic—believe me! There were seven or eight of us. We were playing spin the bottle by this fort we'd made with a piece of plywood."

"Very high-tech."

"Yes. Very," I say, smiling now. "Rosie and Joe weren't there. I'd brought two friends home from school. Gabe was there. His brother, Rick, but only because of this girl, Noelle, who also lived on our street at the time and was in Rick's grade. I think she had a friend as well."

Jonathan Fielding adjusts himself with nonchalance, but manages to move a little closer.

"How old were you?"

"Fourteen, maybe. Joe and Rosie were together by then, so they were sixteen and seventeen. Gabe was sixteen as well. His brother was about eighteen. I don't know—we were all teenagers."

"A giant pool of raging hormones."

"Ugh . . ." I cringe at the image he's put before me. "Anyway—there were three boys there. One of them I didn't even know and I can't remember his name—can you believe that? The first boy I ever kissed and I don't even know his name."

"That always seemed strange to me, that game. Kissing friends in front of other people, then watching them kiss other friends."

"I only played that one time, but I didn't like any of the boys that way and thank God the bottle never landed on Gabe. He was my best friend, so that would have been awkward."

This was not entirely true. I would come to like one of those boys after that day. If like and desire are one and the same.

"I'm just saying—as a guy—that it would have been more than weird. He would never have looked at you the same way."

"He was like my big brother, so I don't think he would have even done it. It would be like kissing Joe. Can you imagine if he'd been there? Jesus."

A little closer now, with a shift of his leg, a move of his elbow.

"It sounds a little incestuous—your neighborhood. Growing up together like that, and then Rosie and Joe getting married. They know everything about each other. Sometimes I think it's good to have some things you keep to yourself, or only share with people you aren't involved with. People who can be objective."

"And who won't use your past to win arguments over who has to take out the garbage."

"Exactly!"

Awkward silence. I drink more scotch. Thank God for scotch.

He takes my glass. He gets up and goes to the kitchen. I hear ice cubes. I hear them crack when the liquor hits them.

"So you kissed that one guy whose name you don't remember. But not Gabe. And the other boy who was there—Gabe's brother?"

He returns, hands me the drink. Sits noticeably closer and I realize he got us refills for this sole purpose. There have been many kisses since that first kiss. I know what's what.

"Yeah—Rick. He was a bad kid. Down to his bones. He spent nine months a year at military school in Virginia, but he came home for a few summers. His mother used to cry about him to my mother in our kitchen. She was actually relieved when he joined the army."

"And you had to kiss this guy?"

"Yeah. Kind of killed the whole *first kiss* thing—the guy I didn't know and the guy I wished I didn't know. But it was really short—he was a little scared of me, to be honest."

"Scared of you? Why?"

"A few years before I . . ." Heart pounds. Wave of adrenaline. Fight-or-flight reaction surges in an instant. The human body in top form.

I can't tell this story, but now I've started it. I go for a modification.

". . . I used to tell on him when he was mean to us. I think I'm the reason he got sent away to military school."

"Oh shit—he must have hated you."

"I don't care. He used to pick fights with everyone all the time—even his brother. One was pretty bad. I saw him fighting with Gabe by the fort and I started yelling that I would tell their mother. Rick threw one last punch then ran off. Told me to go fuck myself first, which was nice since I was only eleven."

"And then a few years later you kissed him."

I pretend that wasn't really a question and move on.

"Okay," I say with the most engaging smile I know how to make. "Your turn. First kiss?"

Jonathan Fielding starts to tell a sweet story about some crush he had in ninth grade. It's a script from an after-school special. But my mind is reeling, so his words bounce away.

Rick Wallace. *The bottle spins, starts to slow.* I see it turn past Gabe and the nameless guy and I cannot believe what is in my heart. I hate Rick Wallace. I hate how he used to terrorize us. *It slows more as it passes Noelle.* I remember the look on his face when I hit him with that stick. When he felt the power of my rage.

It stops. It points to Rick Wallace. Gabe starts to get up, but there is no time for him to stop it. We move to the center of the circle. Rick grabs the back of my head and kisses me with more than his mouth. He kisses me with years of his own hatred. With fantasies of vengeance. I can feel it all in the heat of his breath. But then I feel something else— his body responding to my mouth. My breath. Telling the hatred it will have to wait.

That day when I was fourteen, I felt, for the very first time, the power of sexual desire. Until then, until that moment, I had been the girl who acted like a boy. Who had fists for hands. Who climbed trees that swung over our house and punched holes in walls and swore like a truck driver, horrible obscenities flying from my little pink lips. Shock and awe. I had an arsenal of weapons to use against anyone who dared be my enemy. To use against the enemy inside myself. The unrest. The longing.

But nothing as powerful as this one.

I left the fort. Left the woods. Left Rick Wallace. And I ran home as fast as my legs would carry me.

But I did not outrun it. That night I dreamed about Rick

Wallace. About his mouth on my mouth and his hands on my body. I dreamed of his body releasing the hatred. The hatred relinquishing its power in the face of this greater force, this desire. And what was left in its place was the one thing I craved.

Love.

Jonathan Fielding's voice has left the room. The story ended.

"That's a nicer story than mine," I say even though I haven't heard one word of it. Still, it's a pretty safe bet.

Silence. Longing stare.

"I want to kiss you," Jonathan Fielding says.

I don't say yes. I don't say no.

He leans across the sofa. He only has one hand free because he's holding his drink. It pushes against the drink in my hand and scotch spills on the black leather. He takes my glass in his other hand and he places our glasses on the bare floor.

With both hands now, he gently takes my head like it's a baby bird and pulls me to him. He closes his eyes but mine stay open.

His breath touches my cheek. His mouth is on my mouth. His hands hold my face.

And it all rushes over me. A tidal wave. A mud slide.

I've been kissed a million times. I've been through it a million times. Still, it washes me away.

We move through the stages. I know them well. Lips pressed together. Soft, almost still. A breath taken and released. Heat. We come together again, this time lips part. A breath shared. A hand moves from my face to the back of my head. Fingers in my hair. Palm closing, taking hold of me. Desire pounding at the door as his tongue sweeps over mine. This gentle kiss growing furious with passion.

Love. Evasive love. Always running away. But now a kiss, full of promise.

I close my eyes and feel the surge of power, the intoxication. It's so familiar.

I think of Rick Wallace, lying on the ground.

I think of Mitch Adler, lying on the ground.

Jonathan Fielding. What to do with this kiss? With the promises it makes? I don't even know you. It's too soon for promises.

I know I have no right.

But I hate you now for making them.

TWENTY-ONE

Rosie. Present Day. Saturday, 2 a.m. Branston, CT.

What would Laura do?

Rosie thought about the story as she drove home. The seduction. The *brilliant* seduction. The hours of talking, getting inside Sylvia Emmett's head. He made her feel something for him just so he could viciously take it away. So he could make her hate herself more than she hated him.

Laura would have been a moth to a flame. Talking and talking. Interpreting his words in a way that satisfied some fantasy of him.

And then a kiss. That's how it always began.

Why can't you just leave it at that? See what happens. See if he's worth it.

It was easy to give advice, stand on higher moral ground. And it was easy to judge. Laura and her wolves.

She pulled into the driveway and turned off the car. Then she sat, thinking.

What would Laura feel?

A kiss that got inside her, that found the need. She would be hopeful. She would lose herself to it.

And if he walked away, indifferent, making sure she knew that he had deceived her?

What would Rosie do if Joe walked away after a lifetime of friendship? After they'd become lovers? If one night they made love and then he told her he didn't care? If he told her he didn't want to be with her?

She tried to imagine it. Joe had been devoted from the first moment she'd held his eyes a second longer than she ever had before. In the hallway of their school. Talking like they always had, in a circle of friends. She'd caught him looking at her and she'd known. It had been so easy. She'd looked back and held his eyes. It had made him blush, and that night he had kissed her for the first time.

But what if that had not been the case? What would she have done? What if there was another scenario?

She would have turned to that boy in her history class who was always flirting with her. She would have flirted back and maybe even gone out with him just to make Joe see that she had options, that she had moved on. That's what people do, right?

Laura would need something different. If she didn't turn to violence, she would walk away, filled with pride. She would not let this stranger, this old divorced man from a website think he'd hurt her. But then, when he was gone and she had no way to find him again, the anger would build and she would need a target. Someone else who'd hurt her and hadn't paid.

The man in New York. *Asshole.* Laura had left with no resolution. No answer. But unlike Jonathan Fields, she knew where to find this one.

Rosie rushed inside, to her computer this time, at a small desk in the corner of the kitchen.

She knew his first name. *Kevin*. But nothing more. They'd tried to find him earlier with no luck. The two friends she'd called—Jill from work and the roommate, Kathleen—hadn't known either.

But now she had a thought. She went into her emails and searched for him. Seven old messages came on the screen. All from Laura. She knew which one she was looking for—it was from May—at the start of things. She was with him at a hotel across the street from his office. She'd told Rosie the name.

And there it was.

Laura: Guess where I am.

Rosie: Work? It's Tuesday at 3.

Laura: I'm drinking champagne at the West Hotel. Kevin only had an hour.

Rosie: I thought you said he was good in bed. ☺

Laura: Haha. He works across the street, so we had the WHOLE hour.

Rosie: Jealous ☹

She hadn't been jealous. She'd been worried. Laura was on a high. Emailing and texting with details about her adventures with this new man. Kevin. She kept saying that he was different. That he was good to her. That he loved her. But she seemed manic. Anxious. Her words were different, but her mood was the same as with all the others.

Rosie logged into the findlove.com account and clicked on the search they'd used to get those pictures—the ones with Jonathan Fields. *Divorced. Thirty-five to forty. Income $150,000+.* She hadn't noticed it earlier, but she could see it now. Jonathan Fields was the best looking man on the page. He looked younger than forty. And there was something about him—the smug smile, the way his head tilted. It was arrogance.

He reminded her of all the others. Most of all, the last one Rosie had known. The one from Laura's junior year. Mitch Adler. He'd tortured Laura all summer, casting her down a long, winding roller coaster that hadn't stopped until the night of the party. That night in the woods. Rosie had seen it unfolding. He'd come with another girl. A sophomore from the public high school—his school. He'd made sure Laura saw them together. Rosie had been on the other side of the fire with her friends, with the older kids who were in college. She'd glanced over now and again to check on Laura, the way she always had. She'd seen Mitch walking up the path, this new girl right behind him. Laura had pretended not to see. She'd found some friends near a cooler of beer.

When Rosie had looked again, Laura was gone. So was Mitch, but the new girl was by the fire, forlorn. There had been a game playing out and Rosie had known it wouldn't end well. But she had been so tired of it. Tired of being Laura's babysitter. She had not looked across the fire again until she'd heard the scream.

Rosie checked the time. It was four a.m. The room was still. Outside, nothing but darkness. The world was asleep, but time was not. She heard the clock tick above the sink, relentlessly. Every second that passed felt like another step deeper into a life where Laura was never found.

She got up. Grabbed her keys, her purse, and headed back to the car.

. . .

The West Hotel was on Ninth Avenue between West Twenty-third and West Twenty-second. Rosie was there by five thirty.

She parked on the next side street, then walked back to the front of the building. She looked up at the windows and imagined Laura looking out from one of them, sipping champagne. Watching for her new love to step outside his office and make his way to her.

Kevin. She didn't even have a last name. She turned to face the buildings across the street. A cab drove by. Then a delivery truck, the metal ladder pinned to the side clanking as the truck hit a pothole. The sky was orange with the morning sun. Time was slipping away.

She started at the top of the block, reading the names on the sides of the buildings that had offices. How was it possible that she hadn't asked what he did or how they'd met? Just like that night at the fire, she had grown tired of looking after her sister.

There could easily be two hundred people who worked on this block. Dental offices. A deli. She didn't care how long it took. Or how crazy she felt. Exhaustion was spinning her thoughts. Apartments. A doughnut shop. She went inside and got a coffee.

"Have you seen this woman?" she asked the man at the counter, showing him Laura's picture from her phone. He shook his head.

"How about a man named Kevin who works on this block?"

Nothing. She didn't have a picture. Why would she? She hadn't bothered to ask for one. Hadn't wanted to know. She had not wanted to see the train go off the tracks.

She took a long sip of the coffee, then snapped on the lid.

Back outside. A print shop. More apartments. A dry cleaner.

She heard herself asking the questions—*Do you know a man named Kevin? Do you know this woman?* Some faces reflected the absurdity. Others mirrored her concern and asked if she was all right. Others, still, answered quickly then fled. She could be anyone. She could be dangerous.

Each doorway, each building—some reaching into the sky with dozens of offices on each floor. She stopped and asked anyone she could find. She was careful not to miss anything. An hour passed. Then another. The sky was light. She'd expanded her search two blocks both north and south. So many buildings were still closed.

On the verge of starting down a new block, she looked back up the street and spotted a woman opening a building that had been closed when she'd passed it. She ran to the doorway and slipped inside before it could close again.

The building was right in the middle of the block, right across the street from the hotel, like Laura had said. Rosie searched a directory that hung by the elevators, searching the names. Searching for one name—*Kevin.* They were health-care offices. All different kinds, from massage therapists to orthopedists. And then, there it was! The name she'd been looking for all morning. *Dr. Kevin Brody. Ph.D. Clinical Psychology.*

Christ, Laura. She had been expecting a banker or lawyer. Someone Laura would cross paths with at her job. But a doctor? A shrink?

And then a worse thought—*her* shrink?

She rang the buzzer, knowing before she did that no one would answer. It was barely coming up on eight a.m. And it was Saturday. But the hotel . . .

She rushed across the street and through the revolving door.

A young man was at the desk just inside.

"Have you seen this woman? I think she stayed here a few times over the summer," Rosie asked. She held her phone up with Laura's picture.

The man took the phone and looked closely.

"I don't know. Maybe. I work the night shift and it's really quiet. I rarely see any of the guests."

"She might have come in late Thursday night."

"Definitely not then. I worked that night and I would have remembered. She's really pretty. Is she in trouble?"

Rosie looked back to the street and the building where Dr. Kevin Brody worked. She could see her reflection in the glass right beside it. Sweatpants, T-shirt. She hadn't brushed her hair or showered for almost two days. But it was the anguish on her face that was shocking.

"She might be. She's missing," Rosie said. "I think her boyfriend worked across the street."

"Do you have his picture?" the man asked.

Rosie grabbed her phone and Googled *Dr. Kevin Brody NYC*. An image popped up from a professional website. She was about to enlarge it and show it to the man at the desk. But then she saw something else. An article just beneath it from the *Post*.

Local Doctor Killed in Robbery

Rosie's hand clenched her mouth. She clicked on the article and scanned the contents. It was one paragraph. He was assaulted outside his gym. His wallet and phone were stolen, as well as his gym bag. He died of *injuries sustained during the attack*.

And then the last sentence, striking Rosie right in the gut.

The beloved doctor *leaves behind a wife and two small children*.

TWENTY-TWO

Laura. Session Number Thirteen.
Two Months Ago. New York City.

Dr. Brody: Change begins with understanding your blind spots. It begins with recognition that something's wrong even if you're drawn to it.

Laura: You mean to them, don't you? The men I'm drawn to? Starting with Mitch Adler.

Dr. Brody: Think about what he asked you to do, how he treated you. It was about power, and you kept giving it to him. You didn't see that it was insatiable. That he was never going to give you what you wanted.

Laura: But I thought he would.

Dr. Brody: Because he fed you just enough to make you believe. And when he did, it made you feel powerful. You said it felt intoxicating, like a drug. Can you see the pattern?

Laura: And what about now, Kevin? Am I doing it again?

Dr. Brody: We need to be careful, Laura. The lines are starting to blur.

TWENTY-THREE

Laura. The Night Before. Thursday, 11 p.m. Branston, CT.

"Stop." I don't know that this word has ever left my mouth before.

We lie on the black leather sofa that smells of scotch, bodies pressed together as we make this treacherous journey from strangers to lovers.

I push him away and sit up. I try to straighten my hair, but my fingers get caught in a tangled mess.

"What's wrong?" he asks.

"I shouldn't have come here."

Now he is sitting beside me. He thinks he understands what's happening as he reaches for the glasses on the floor.

"Okay," he says. "Here . . ." He hands me a drink. I take a sip.

"I shouldn't have posted those things about myself."

"What things?" Now he gets nervous.

"Just . . . everything. And the pictures and tonight. I shouldn't have worn this dress and these shoes. I never wear red lipstick."

"But you look nice. I'm not sure what you're saying. I get that you don't always look like this. Made-up, dressed up. I was married for six years," he says.

This makes me look at him.

"And what about you? What are you hiding?" I ask.

He shrugs and smiles that smile that caught my eye. "There's really not much I can do. I shaved. Put on a nice shirt."

"That's not what I meant."

"I know."

Then he gets up, walks to the kitchen. He grabs his keys from the counter.

"Come on," he says. "I'll walk you to your car. I don't want you to be here if you don't feel comfortable."

I don't move. Not one single muscle. I don't want to leave.

Rosie never understood. I can hear the same conversation looping over and over. It's the one where she tells me it's not that complicated. You go on a date. You talk about superficial things. You meet again. You talk some more. Reveal some more. Little by little, you ease into the water, making sure it's not too hot or too cold or too deep or too muddy.

There's nothing that time won't reveal, she said.

But she is wrong about that.

The day Dick left us, he came to our rooms to say good-bye. He came to me first. He stood at the doorway while I sat on my bed.

Has your mother told you that I'm moving out?

I nodded. Our mother told us through tears. Through desperate words and despair that our hugs could not calm. Four arms wrapped around her as she stood in the hallway, suitcases piled beside her.

I'll see you on the weekends.

I nodded again. I knew it was a lie. He couldn't leave my room fast enough.

He went next to Rosie. I heard him knock on her door. I heard it open and then close and when it did, I ran from my room and pressed my ear against the hollow wood. Rosie was crying and he was comforting her, making those sounds people make to babies. *Shhh.* He told her about the weekends and how everything was for the best.

Rosie yelled at him then. I couldn't believe it. Sweet, obedient, Rosie—yelling at Dick.

Why do you have to live with that woman?

Dick opened his stupid mouth and said his stupid words.

Because I love her. Someday you'll love someone and you'll understand.

Stupid, selfish Dick. Rosie cried again. Dick said *shhh* again. But then he said something else, something unexpected.

Your mother is no saint.

Rosie stopped crying and I heard footsteps. I ran back to my room and closed the door. Dick left Rosie on her bed with her red eyes and wet face. He walked down the hallway and down the stairs. We both came out of our rooms, Rosie and I. We stood together in that hallway listening to the last sounds our father would ever make in our house. And to the final pleas of our mother.

Don't go. . . . Don't leave us!

I know Rosie felt it then the same way I did when we heard our mother. Nails on a chalkboard.

I never asked Rosie what Dick meant about our mother not being a saint, and she never asked me. Now we are adults. We've known our mother all our lives. What good has time done to reveal the truth? About our father? About our mother?

About any of us?

Nothing, that's what.

"I don't want to leave," I say.

He's frustrated with me. I can see how he's tensed up and I want to change it. I want to make it stop.

It begins with recognition.

But I don't care why I feel this way, how broken I am. How wrong I am. I can't go back to Rosie's attic and wait for a call from this man who's standing in front of me right here and right now.

I think about the last time I saw Kevin. I feel the words *I love you* sink into my bones, transforming me cell by cell. Hands releasing fists. Peace visible on the horizon of what has been a restless life. I went home that night and conned myself into believing it was here to stay.

And then it was all torn out of me.

I can't go home and wait for it to come again. Not again.

So I give him what he wants. Or maybe the runner-up. I give him my darkest secret.

"That night that you read about—the night that boy was killed. It was my fault."

Frustration: gone.

"Okay," he says. He sets down his keys and grabs the bottle of scotch. Then he returns to the empty living room and sits beside me.

"I'd been dating him, Mitch Adler. He wasn't a good guy, but that made me fight even harder," I begin. My hands are shaking. He steadies them as he refills my glass.

"One of the wolves?" he asks, smiling because he remembers my story about Catholic school. I'd forgotten telling him. I've told him so many things. Three hours is a long time to talk to a stranger.

"I think I found the leader of the pack with that one. It was stupid high school head games. I can see that now. But at the time, it had me in knots."

"I had a friend who always fell for guys like that. We were in college then, so don't feel so bad."

Everyone has a *friend like that*. Most of them learn from their mistakes.

"I went to the party that night knowing he'd be there. He hadn't called me for weeks. He hadn't returned any of my messages."

"And you didn't assume it was over?"

I look away and don't answer.

"It sounds ridiculous to tell this story now. As a grown woman. I'm hearing the words in my head and I don't want to say them."

He swirls his glass, takes a drink. "I get it. We were all in high school once. Just tell me what happened."

I cringe, but then say these ridiculous words.

"He came to the party with his girlfriend—the one I didn't know about until that night. Britney. I already told you that part."

"You must have been upset," he says, trying to move things along. He's been wanting to hear this story all night and I don't care why. I don't care about my list, which now includes this empty apartment. There is something about him that has reached me, and I want to hold on to it.

"I was devastated. I wouldn't show it, of course. I pretended not to see him. I went to get another beer. But then I felt a hand on my arm."

"Ah—so the silent treatment worked."

"It was part of our script. He asked me how the rest of my summer was and I said it was great. I turned away, pretended to be part of a conversation going on next to us. Then I felt him push my hair away from the back of my neck. He leaned in close, whispered in my ear that he needed to see me alone. I thought maybe that girl was just a friend. That I had overreacted. We went behind some trees. Kissed, laughed. He said he'd missed me."

This is where I should need to stop, because the memory of that night is too painful. Because it tortures me to go back there.

But a wall has grown around this story. I didn't ask for it. But it's there now. It stands on its own. It never asks for maintenance or permission to be there. And I like it just fine.

I don't need to stop. So I continue with only feigned emotion.

"He took a step back then. He smiled and folded his arms and soaked up the love that was radiating from my body. It was like he just turned the valve a little to the left and it started to flow right out of me. I thought his smile was from being happy—happy that I loved him and that we were sharing this moment. But then he started to tell me about the girl he'd walked in with."

This is the part where I do pause. One hand squeezes the glass. The other begins to close, fingers bending in perfect unison until they reach the palm.

The smell of the fire. The damp brush of the deep woods. We steal a kiss behind a tree. He breaks away. He looks at me with tenderness, and I have a moment where I believe that I have finally done it. I have given enough, been enough. He opens his mouth to speak. I think the words before he says them.

But he didn't say the words old me was waiting for. The small child tugging on a sleeve, wide eyes. Pleading eyes. And the words that he did say filled me with a bigger rage than I had ever known.

Jonathan has guessed it.

"He told you she was his girlfriend," he says.

I nod. "He said he needed to get back to her. And the thing is, I was not the kind of girl who would cry and beg and plead. That was my mother, so I knew it was useless—and besides that, it repulsed me, violently, to show any sign of weakness, even if I was weak. So instead I just shrugged. I told him he'd better go, then, before she got mad at him."

I see us now, in my glass of scotch. I see Mitch and remember the swirling together of warm, lusty bliss and red-hot rage. Danger waking me from the illusion of safety. My hands in fists at my sides, but a smile on my face because I knew how to win that fight. Or, at least, I thought I did.

"Then he said, changing course, *I could send her home.* He was a worthy opponent that way. When I didn't try to stop him, he brought out bigger guns. I said he should do what he wants. And he said that he had a dilemma."

I hear his words. I'm back in those woods.

I have a dilemma. . . .

What dilemma . . . ?

I know she loves me. But I don't think you do.

"He said I needed to prove it to him."

"What the hell did he mean by that?" Jonathan asks. He seems genuinely pissed off on my behalf.

"He meant exactly what you think he meant," I say. "He wanted me to sleep with him."

"Well, I hope you realized what was going on!" Jonathan is so sweet to be concerned for me eleven years after the fact.

Of course I realized what was going on. The boy I loved wanted me to have sex with him as a condition to staying with me. To *loving* me. Not exactly earth-shattering stuff.

"So what did you do?" Jonathan asks. His eyes are wide, his brow furrowed.

"I laughed like it was no big deal. I told him I'd been with someone else all summer, so he missed his chance to be my first. I told him I was worried he wouldn't measure up, but I was happy to find out. *Let's go,* I said. Honestly, this story should make you go back to the kitchen and grab your keys and walk me straight to my car."

Jonathan places a hand on my shoulder. "Why? Because you were young and in love and couldn't make the best decision?"

"It's more than that. Most girls would have run away in tears, cried to their friends. Got shit-faced, puked, then gotten on with their lives. That's what Rosie would have done."

I'm not digging for sympathy, or for one more person to let me off the hook for my self-destructive behavior. I hate this part of me, then, now, and at every moment in between. She is undeserving of sympathy.

I look at Jonathan Fielding and wonder if it's this part of me that has drawn me to him. That let him inside my head, which is the straightest path to my heart.

I've paused to drink and ponder. Jonathan is eager for the end. He says nothing, but stares at me with that serious expression.

"But I'm not like those other girls. Not like my sister. I rattled off things I could do with him—using as many obscenities as possible—and then I asked him if he knew what he was doing because I didn't want to waste the night on him if he didn't."

"Jesus," Jonathan says. He smiles. "Ballsy move."

"It was some strange game we were playing then. I was waiting for him to blink. He was waiting for me. Neither of us did."

"Did he answer the question?"

"No. He just smiled and said something slick like *Don't worry; you'll enjoy it.*"

"So that's why you went to his car? He called your bluff?"

Jonathan treads carefully. He wants the end of this story. And I want the end of our story. Me and Jonathan Fielding. I want the journey to be over. I'm so tired. And now my head spins from the scotch.

"You don't have to tell me the rest," he says.

But he doesn't mean it. I am so close to opening my mouth and rendering my confession. I don't want to break the spell of intimacy that pulls us together.

I smile sadly and look away. I think suddenly about the notes. The threats. If someone wanted me to pay for that night, why am I still here? Why am I not in jail or lying in a hospital bed? Why am I not dead and buried? What are they waiting for? To torture me?

"Laura," he says, his hand on my cheek now, turning my head to face him. So gently. "I don't care about that night. I can see that it still upsets you."

Liar, I think. He would have to be an idiot not to care about that night. And Jonathan Fielding is no idiot.

Notes, notes, notes.

I've been home for five weeks. I've received three notes. And now I'm on a date with a stranger who's been asking me about that night in the woods.

I stand up from the couch. My head spins and spins. Scotch and confusion.

"What's wrong?" he asks.

I don't answer because I don't know. Except, perhaps, one small thing.

"Laura? Tell me what's wrong. . . ." He grabs my hand as I turn to walk away.

I stare at him and think *something. Something is very wrong.*

TWENTY-FOUR

Rosie. Present Day. Saturday, 8:30 a.m. New York City.

Rosie sat at a small table, a fresh cup of coffee in front of her.

"Do you take milk?"

Laura's roommate, Kathleen, worked as a graphic designer for a marketing firm downtown. Laura had found her through an advertisement. They had not been friends, but there had been no complaints, either. They shared a two-bedroom walk-up on Jane Street. Laura worked long hours. She rarely ate at home. Kathleen had a boyfriend in New Jersey and was gone most weekends. That was all Laura had said about it. Rosie had been there a few times before when she'd come to visit her sister, and every time her roommate had been gone.

"Yes, thanks," Rosie answered.

"I'm sorry I didn't get back to you yesterday. It didn't sound urgent—your message," Kathleen said apologetically as she walked back into the kitchen.

"I didn't know what was happening. I wasn't sure . . . and I didn't know how close you were to my sister. That seems strange now—that I didn't know. You were never here when we came to visit her."

Rosie could see Laura's room through the small living space next to the kitchen. The door was open. The room bare.

"Did she take everything when she left?" Rosie asked. The day she'd picked Laura up, the boxes had already been packed and moved to the street.

Kathleen returned with a pint of milk and she sat down. Her eyes followed Rosie's through the adjacent room to the open door.

"She did," Kathleen answered. "That's how I knew she wasn't coming back. The furniture is mine. Just a bed and a desk. The closet has built-ins so she didn't need a dresser. You can look if you want, but I went through it after a few days. I've been showing it again."

"If you don't mind—I might just walk through."

Rosie's hand was shaking when she picked up the coffee. She set it back down, drew her hands to her face.

Kathleen looked at her with caution, as though she didn't want to be pulled into the storm. "So what's happened, exactly?"

"I don't know what's happened. That's the problem. She went on a date with a man she met online and she never came home."

"How long has it been?" Kathleen asked. "She used to leave for days at a time. I never knew when she would be here, when she was coming home. She worked long hours. And she traveled. She was covering industrial chemicals, she said. Took the train to Pennsylvania, Upstate New York. Sometimes she flew. She wasn't one to . . ." Kathleen couldn't find the right words, so Rosie finished the thought.

"I know—she wasn't one to be considerate of other people in her life. People who might worry about her or wonder where she was."

Kathleen looked at Rosie and nodded. "I got used to it. I never worried about her."

"It's different," Rosie said. "She had my car. She knew I would worry if she didn't come home, or call, at least."

"You're right," Kathleen said. "I didn't mean to imply that she was inconsiderate. It wasn't like that. If she thought I worried about her when she was gone, she would have let me know where she was. Things I cared about, like dishes in the sink or taking out the recycling—she never forgot those things. We were friendly, but not friends, if that makes any sense."

It did. It made perfect sense. Laura wasn't used to people worrying about her. Caring about her enough to worry.

"Did you know her boyfriend? The one she had right before she left?"

"Not really," she said.

But Rosie could tell she had an opinion.

"Did she tell you what happened? Why she left New York? Left her job?"

"She just said she needed a change." Kathleen looked back toward Laura's room. "I came home one Sunday night and found her in there. She was sitting on her bed, staring out the window. She was sitting in the dark—no lights on anywhere in the apartment. It took me by surprise when I saw her. It was so quiet. So dark. I went to the edge of the door and knocked on the wall just outside. I didn't want to bother her if she wanted to be alone. She had a glass of something in her hand, resting on her knee. Both feet were on the floor. Her hair was falling around her face. It was hard to tell, but I think she'd been crying."

"I asked her what was wrong, and she just said that it was over with the guy. She never told me his name. I asked her if I could help, if she wanted to talk. She thanked me, politely, but then said she would be fine. She just needed a little time. I asked her if she wanted the door open or closed and she said closed. So I closed her door, turned on the lights, took a shower, made some food. She never came out. I thought she'd gone to bed. But she must have started packing, because the next afternoon, she was gone. The room was cleared out. She left me a check for two months' rent and a note saying she was moving home for a while. That was it."

Rosie stared at Laura's roommate, picturing this scene. It was so familiar. Rosie had found her like that countless times when they were still living on Deer Hill Lane. Laura, sitting on the edge of her bed, in the dark, staring out a window.

"I tried to call her," Kathleen said eagerly. "She didn't answer and didn't return the call. Like I said, we weren't friends, so I didn't think it was my place to do more than that."

Rosie smiled sadly. "No—don't feel bad. You couldn't have done anything."

"Still," Kathleen said. "Now she's missing. I wish I'd found out more that night. Maybe it would be helpful."

Rosie got up. "Can I look in the room?" she asked.

"Of course."

They walked from the kitchen to the living room, then to the doorway of Laura's room. Kathleen walked past her and turned on the light.

"This is it," she said. "Just the bed and desk."

Rosie stood still for a moment. The room had been so full of life the last time she'd been there—before the day she moved out. It was in the spring and the windows were open. Jane Street was lined with trees and the smell of blooming leaves had been coming through on a cool gust of air. Laura had a bright orange quilt that Mason had found irresistible.

"My son was here last spring—jumping on that bed." Rosie walked to the window and looked out at the street below. "It was May. Before she'd met him."

Rosie tried to remember that day. "I would have remembered if she had. Laura was always different when she had a new man in her life."

"I couldn't say one way or another. I'm sorry. She mentioned him in passing over the summer. She wanted to bring him here for the weekend and asked me if I minded. I was leaving anyway, so I said it was fine."

"He was married," Rosie blurted out. "He had kids."

"Oh," Kathleen said. She was visibly surprised. "I had no idea. But that doesn't seem like Laura. The few times we spoke about more than the apartment, she was very earnest—maybe that's not the right word. But that does surprise me. Did she know?"

"What? About the wife and kids?"

"Yeah."

"How could she not?"

"If it wasn't on the Internet. If he was a good liar. I've heard a lot of stories."

"But after *months*, wouldn't she wonder why he hadn't taken her to his apartment?"

Kathleen considered this. "Maybe he had another apartment. It just doesn't seem like Laura, from what I could tell about her. She made some comments about your father, about his affairs—I don't know the whole story, but wasn't she estranged from him because of it?"

Rosie sat on the bed and looked at Kathleen. "She was. I've only seen him a few times over the years. He hasn't even met my son. But honestly, I don't know if that would be enough to stop her. If he said the right things, told her stories about his unhappy marriage. If he told her he loved her . . ."

"Yeah. I suppose that would get to any of us under the right circumstances." Kathleen looked out the window as though she wanted to fly right out of it, away from this conversation. Away from the trouble of Laura Lochner. Rosie had already delayed her in leaving the city to visit her boyfriend.

But, like it or not, there was more to tell. "It doesn't even matter anymore. Something happened to him. To Kevin Brody. He was killed."

She waited for the appropriate response. Shock. Silence. Apprehension.

"It was a robbery outside his gym. Laura never said anything. She said he'd broken it off with one text and then ghosted her—you know? No calls, texts."

"My God . . . when was he killed?"

Rosie pulled out her phone and found the article from the *Post*.

"Mid-August. Early morning." Then she had a thought. She turned abruptly and looked at Kathleen. "When did you find her here, in the room crying?"

"I don't know. It was on a Sunday night, as I said."

"He was killed on a Wednesday. I wonder if it was before or after you saw her. If her despair was new or days old."

"What are you saying? That Laura might have done something?" Kathleen was stunned.

Rosie caught hold of herself. "No, of course not. It just means that maybe she didn't know. Maybe it explains why he stopped returning her calls."

"And she thought he'd ghosted her after the breakup! God, how horrible."

Yes, Rosie thought. But not nearly as horrible as the alternative.

Rosie got up and walked to the small desk on the other side of the room. She checked the drawers, felt beneath the surface. She opened the closet and did the same. Then under the bed. There was nothing.

"Did she have any friends who might know something? I've called her office—the woman named Jill she spoke about. But I didn't know any of her friends here, and even from college."

Kathleen shook her head. "I wouldn't know. But—wait . . . there was a man. I heard her talking to him when I came home one night. She was cooking and he was on the speaker. She offered to pick it up, but I could see she needed two hands and I was going to my room anyway. . . ."

Rosie stopped her search and looked at Kathleen. "A man? Did you hear what they were saying? Was it her boyfriend?"

"No. I don't think so. They were talking about the boyfriend. Laura was saying something about him to the man on the phone. Hold on, I'll remember his name."

Rosie stood before her impatiently.

"And I think he was here, actually. Outside the apartment. I was working from home that day, so she left without her keys, which she couldn't find. I heard the buzzer and looked out the window. It was Laura. and she was there with a man. He was wearing a suit—he had his jacket draped over his arm. It was hot as hell that day. I was surprised she was home so soon—she never left work early. I don't think she took one sick day the whole time she was living here."

"What did he look like?" Rosie asked.

"Wait—I remember his name!" Kathleen said, her eyes lit up. "It was Joe."

Rosie stared at the woman, unable to speak, or move, her husband's name now ringing in her ears.

"Are you all right?" Kathleen asked.

But Rosie didn't answer.

Joe. That was all she could hear. The sound of her husband's name.

TWENTY-FIVE

Laura. Session Number Fourteen. Seven Weeks Ago. New York City.

Dr. Brody: This isn't a good idea, having more sessions. Things have become complicated. We never should have started . . .

Laura: No—please. I'm so close. I can feel everything shifting.

Dr. Brody: Laura . . . all right. Close your eyes. . . . Can you see yourself as someone else? Another woman there in the woods with Mitch Adler?

Laura: I think so.

Dr. Brody: He pulls her behind a tree, kisses her. She can feel his desire and it makes her believe that she's finally done it. She's finally made him feel safe enough to love her. There's a rush. Euphoria. You know what it's made of. You've told me.

Laura: Power. It's the rush of power. . . .

Dr. Brody: What do you want to say to her? That girl in the woods?

Laura: That it's just an illusion? He'll never love you?

Dr. Brody: Don't ask me. Tell me. You're the one who has to see it.

Laura: Okay. Fine. I would tell her that he'll never love you, so stop trying.

Dr. Brody: Right. Exactly. He is never going to love her. The power is an illusion.

Laura: I would tell her to walk away. But I know she won't. She never will. Why is that?

Dr. Brody: That's because you can't forgive her for trying. And you want her to suffer for it.

TWENTY-SIX

Laura. The Night Before. Thursday, 11:30 p.m. Branston, CT.

I find my purse in the kitchen. I search for my phone.

"Laura . . ." Jonathan Fielding stands behind me. I feel his hand on my shoulder. And I stop. I stop looking for my phone. I stop looking for a way to leave.

My body moves back until it touches his. It is disconnected now. It doesn't listen as I remind it of the things that are wrong.

"Shhh . . ." he whispers. "It's all right. Catch your breath. Your phone is dead, remember?"

A chill races through me. His voice is soft, but his words . . . are they ominous? Is he trying to remind me that I am helpless now, trapped between the counter and his body? The door on the other side. Another hand touches another shoulder and suddenly no part of me is free.

We have different phones. Different chargers. It's already been discussed and acknowledged that I can't do anything until I get back to Rosie's. The chill morphs into a heat wave.

And I like the heat.

"Do you want me to get you home?" he says then, but he might as well ask a child to put down an ice cream cone.

"It was a black Chevy Impala," I say. Suddenly I need to finish the story. I need to know why he's been asking me to tell it, and if he knows the ending, maybe the truth will reveal itself. He'll have no further need to pull it out of me.

I have to know what this is. From ignorance comes insanity. And he seems so real to me, this man. I have been observing him. Listening with such care, making my list, those little things that seem wrong. But there are so many things that seem right.

"I used to tease him about his car because it was an old man's car. His father gave it to him when he upgraded to a Lexus, so it was, actually just that. An old man's car."

Jonathan's arms grow tighter around me, locking together in front of my chest. I can feel every inch of him now. The metal buckle of his belt against the small of my back. The front of his thighs pressing into the back of mine. His chest running up my back, so warm and strong.

He whispers again. "You don't have to do this."

But I don't stop.

"I'd been there with him before—in the back of that car. Many times. And many times he had asked me. Many times he'd pulled me just a little closer to that point they warned us about in school."

I laugh then, and when I do, I realize I've been crying. The tears that come find old tracks down my face.

"Sex Ed . . ." he says, laughing as well. "*The point of no return.*" He says this in a deep, mocking voice and I feel his body move with the laughter that rolls from his belly.

"Exactly," I say. I don't know why I'm laughing as hard as I am. It's not funny. A few more words and a boy will be dead. But the sadness seeps out of every seam.

"I remember being scared. And I remember being excited. I was seventeen. Already late to the party. No one would have cared and at least it would have been over, you know? All the anxiety and anticipation . . . I think the only reason I waited that long was because of him. It was all I had left that I hadn't given him."

I think carefully about what to say next. The words that line up are not the ones I want him to hear. *It felt like this . . . just like this.*

There is heat between us. Tension. One hand strays until it reaches my stomach. His lips find my neck.

I feel him melting.

"And then we were there, in the car, and everything else—the other girl, the way he'd been all summer, my sister's warnings— it was all on the outside. All the noise, shut out of our world. I remember the quiet when the door closed. Just the sound of us."

I quiet myself then, and listen to the same sound. *The sound of us.* Breathe in. Breathe out. A hand over silk. Another hand over starched cotton. A sigh.

"You really don't have to tell me. . . ."

"My intentions were good. I was going to test him—see if he would really go through with it, our first time together in that car, at a party we both wanted to get back to, and with that girl waiting for him. And if he didn't stop, then I would be the one to pull away, to tell him he was an asshole and end things for good."

I rest the back of my head against Jonathan's chest and close my eyes.

"I think maybe it was just an excuse. Permission I gave myself to be in that car with him, to let things go too far. Part of me wasn't ready to let go. Part of me still believed that I could . . . I don't know, break through, maybe. It made no sense to me, why he would keep coming back if he really felt nothing."

The memories spring from hiding, the months of analyzing his every move, his every word. Rationalizations. Justifications. Advice from my friends. *Maybe this, maybe that.* I wish I'd met Dr. Brody sooner. I wish someone had told me the truth.

It's an illusion. He's never going to love you.

But then I also wish I had never met Dr. Brody. I wish I still had my illusions. Nothing has filled the empty space they left behind.

Jonathan slips his arms away. He takes a step back, leans against the refrigerator door. I turn around to face him.

"What?" I ask.

"I don't want to get carried away. I'm very attracted to you, but we've just met."

My mind twists with this new information. It would have been so easy. But he's pulled back.

"I'm not seventeen anymore," I say.

"I know that. I'm just trying to be respectful. It sounds like you've had some bad experiences and I don't want to be one of them."

Holy. Shit. Does this man know me. Already—he knows how to get inside.

"So what happened in that car?" he asks, and I am reminded about the part that comes next. The part about the dead boy.

"I never got to find out which one of us might have stopped. If he would have done what you just did. Or if I would have followed my plan. Or if I would have stopped caring about anything but getting more from him, any small piece, no matter how destructive.

"I remember the sound of footsteps outside the car. The road was gravel—the kind with small stones that kick up when you walk over them."

"Is that why they didn't find footprints?" he asks.

"You really do know a lot about this." *Yes, you do, Jonathan Fielding.*

"It was in one of the articles. That homeless man, Lionel Casey, his lawyer made a big deal about that—the absence of any evidence that he was at the scene."

"But then they found him in the car, didn't they?"

Jonathan nods. "Yes, they did."

"He was crazy, you know. And dangerous. People came forward after they heard. People who'd seen him in the woods and been scared. He chased a girl half a mile, screaming that he would send her to Hell. He used to dress up in a vampire cape. . . ."

"Laura—I know. I'm not saying he wasn't there. But all of these details from the scene, they all played a role in how you were treated. Or mistreated, I should say."

Mistreated. That was not a word I had ever thought to use about that night. It was not a word anyone had ever used to describe what had happened to me.

"I guess I'm still defensive," I try to explain. "I still feel responsible."

"I don't see why you would."

I look at my bare feet. At my naked toes. And I think about the moment I put on the shoes I later took off at his door. It wasn't more than a few hours ago that I was in Rosie's attic, getting ready to meet this man. *What am I doing?*

"Mitch was there because of me," I say.

"No—you were there because of him."

"You should have been a lawyer." And then I think, *Maybe he is a lawyer.* It's funny that he could be and I would never know. But then it's not, really.

"Seriously—I don't get how you feel responsible or guilty. He could have killed you as well."

I wonder if it's really possible that he is the only person who has ever said this to me. That I was mistreated in the aftermath. That I could have been a victim myself.

You can't forgive her. . . . You want her to suffer.

"There was no time," I continue with the story. "The footsteps on the gravel—we both heard them and looked up. They stopped when we did, and we both saw the same thing—a figure looking into the front seat on the driver's side. He had his hand over his eyes like he was trying to block what little light there was that night. The keys were in the ignition. Mitch had turned on the radio. I was confused; I thought it was someone from the party or a cop, maybe, so I stayed very still. Mitch must have thought the same thing, because he didn't move either. Then I heard the door handle click, metal on metal. He wasn't trying to be quiet, to sneak up on us. He just saw us and we were in the way of him and this car. Mitch was lying on top of me, his feet close to the door, and Lionel Casey just grabbed him by the ankles and pulled him out."

Silence descends upon Jonathan's bare kitchen. I can see he's horrified by this image, but I stay hidden behind my wall. Even as I recall the exact feeling of Mitch's body being dragged over mine, his hands grabbing hold of anything they could find, instinct taking over. I had scratches down my face and neck, and the sides of my torso because my shirt was pulled up. They found my skin under his nails, and fabric from my jeans. One of my shoes was found on the gravel because that was the last thing his hands found as they tried, desperately, to keep from leaving the safety of the car.

"I didn't see him—Lionel Casey. The figure looking through the window was just that, a figure. A shadow. I think he was wearing a hoodie or a jacket with a hood, because I couldn't make out the shape of his head. But I wouldn't swear to that. And when Mitch was dragged out of the car, I couldn't see beyond his face. I was lying on my back, kicking against the seat to move away from the open door. I never saw beyond Mitch as he was pulled outside. And when I felt his hand release from my foot, taking my shoe with him, I kicked myself up and away to the other door, opened it, and ran outside. I ran until I was deep in the bushes that lined the road and then I crouched down, hiding and listening."

"My God," Jonathan says. And I can see that what really surprises him the most is that I can tell this story without flinching. Without crying. Without anything at all.

"I heard him plead. *No! Stop! Please!* It was breathless, like the fear had paralyzed his voice. I didn't hear the bat hit his body. People said I did, but that's because what I heard were breaks in his pleas, changes to them that anyone would know was from some kind of strike to his body that knocked the wind out. And then they said that I only heard three blows, and yet there were four to his body. Four swings of the bat. But I never said I heard three blows. I said I heard three breaks to his pleading."

Jonathan stares now, wide-eyed. "The fourth blow might have come after he was already dead. Or unconscious. That's why you only heard three breaks."

I nod *Yes*. That *might* be how it happened.

"I heard the car door close and the engine rev. The headlights never came on, but I also heard the car peel away on the gravel. I didn't wait after that. I crept out of the bushes to where I could see. I didn't know if Mitch had gotten away and left this person in the road, waiting to get me next. Or if this person had stolen Mitch's car. So I was quiet and cautious. Until I could see.

"And then I did. I did see—Mitch on the ground. His body still. That's when I screamed and ran toward him. I stood over his body. Blood was coming from his head and his mouth. It pooled but it also sprayed. I screamed and screamed, spun around in circles, looking for this madman. It wasn't rational, because the car was gone. But I just felt this wave of panic and fear, so I kept scanning the woods, waiting for someone to come and help. I saw the bat a few yards away, and what went through my mind was that it was a weapon I could use to protect myself. I wasn't thinking about fingerprints or evidence. I was afraid for my life, even though it doesn't make sense since I knew the man was gone. The fear had not left with him—it was right there, all around me. I felt like I was prey out in the open, looking everywhere, in front, behind, near, far, frantically. Each time I turned my head, new fear came about what might be jumping from the shadows in the place I turned from. I remember that part so well—the terror and the desperation to be safe.

"Finally they came, my sister and others from the party. They came seeping from the woods, their hands covering their mouths in horror as they saw Mitch bleeding on the ground. And saw me standing over him, holding the bat and screaming like a lunatic. Every last one of them, including my sister, came to the same conclusion—I knew right then and there, because they didn't run to me, or to Mitch, to try to help us. To calm me down or stop the bleeding. They just stood and stared the way people do when they stumble upon a crime scene. I was surrounded by people—friends, and even family—and yet I was completely, painfully, alone."

Jonathan stares now too. Scrunched brow. Open mouth. I know this look well. I seem to bring it out in people.

But I can't stand seeing it. Not now—not on Jonathan Fielding.

I turn around so I don't have to bear witness. I see my purse and pull it toward me. One hand reaches in, looking again for the phone and possibly a charger hidden, perhaps, among the debris I shoved in there from my other bag.

"Laura . . ." His voice is deep and soft. He stands behind me again, like he'd done before I finished my story. He wraps his strong arms around me. Just like before. He kisses the top of my head, not like Rosie does with Mason—a quick peck as he races off. His lips linger long enough for me to feel his breath.

"I'm so sorry that happened to you," he whispers. And then I feel his cheek pressing against mine.

I close my eyes and let my hand rest inside the purse. I am the one who begins to melt now.

His pulse quickens. He kisses my neck.

Melting. Melting.

I am a woman on fire.

"Tell me to stop and I will. . . ." His hands run down the sides of my waist. Slow but firm. One of them finds the front of a thigh. The other finds the back.

"Tell me. . . ." he says again. He almost pleads. I am pulling him to that treacherous place. *The point of no return.*

Walk away. . . . It's just an illusion. I know that now, and yet I am still helpless.

I feel the rush. The power over this man.

I am an invincible woman.

I am a helpless child, tugging on a sleeve, watching as the head begins to look down. Eyes from above are about to turn, about to see me.

I am so close, I can feel it in my bones.

My hand is still inside the purse, but it no longer feels for a charger. It wants to touch him, this man. Jonathan Fielding. I pull my hand from the bag and feel the metal zipper scratch against my knuckles. But my fingertips, they brush against something cool and stiff. A piece of paper, and a horrible thought rushes through me. *A note?*

He grabs my hips and spins me around. His mouth finds mine. I suddenly know nothing of the paper in the purse or the scrape from the zipper, as my hand is now free, reaching beneath his shirt to touch his body.

Both hands find his shoulders, then his head, sweeping through his hair.

Walk away, I try to tell that woman. But she won't listen. She never listens.

She deserves what's coming.

TWENTY-SEVEN

Rosie. Present Day. Saturday, 10 a.m. Branston, CT.

Gabe sat across from Rosie at the same diner where she'd met the woman from the bar. She'd sent Joe a quick text: *Still in NY. Call if you hear anything.* Then she'd turned off her phone.

She showed Gabe the notes and told him about New York. He was with her every step, not missing a beat.

"So the boyfriend was the shrink—the one she said she'd been seeing?" Gabe asked. He looked as tired as Rosie felt, cradling a ceramic coffee mug between two palms.

"It would be just like her to seduce her therapist," Rosie said, then wished she could take it back. "God, that's horrible, isn't it? How can I say things about her when she's in this much trouble?"

Gabe reached over and grabbed her hand. His skin was warm, comforting, and it suddenly occurred to her that she and Joe never held hands anymore.

"Rosie—nothing you do or say right now is going to be judged. Not by me, at least. It *is* like Laura to do something like that. She always went for the highest climb—the guys who seemed impossible to conquer, even if it was just because they were assholes."

"Like Mitch Adler," Rosie blurted out.

Gabe didn't flinch even though she expected it. "Yes. Like Mitch Adler. And this man, Kevin Brody, he was off-limits for every possible reason. He was older. He was married. He had kids. And he was her shrink. That's Mount Everest right there."

"Christ, Gabe. I can see her, you know? Sitting in his office, being vulnerable but clever. She probably cried."

"I know. I can see it too. Walking past him a little too close. Brushing his shoulder as she passed by, looking up with soft eyes."

Rosie thought about that picture on her computer. Somewhere along the way, Laura had learned that sadness and longing didn't get her what she needed. So she'd become sexual. Irresistible.

"She doesn't know she's doing it," Gabe said. "I truly believe that. It just kicks in like a car shifting gears."

"And now he's dead." Rosie pressed her hands to her face.

Gabe leaned closer, lowering his voice. "Wait a minute—you don't think she had anything to do with that, do you? It was a robbery. . . ." He grabbed his phone and pulled up the article Rosie had sent him. "Okay . . . here—he was struck with something from behind. Knocked to the ground, where he hit his head a second time against the cement. It took over an hour for him to die."

"Struck with something . . . knocked to the ground. Is it really that crazy? You're the one who told us about that story with your brother—at the fort, remember? How she hit him with a stick? Looked like a wild animal?"

"Rosie . . ." Gabe stopped himself. Rosie could see that he knew—he couldn't deny any of it. Laura had a history of violence going back to her early childhood.

"She could be more psychotic than we know, Gabe. I love her, but sometimes you can love someone, think you know them, and then suddenly you find something out and your eyes open to a different world."

His name was Joe. Rosie could still hear Kathleen saying those words.

"Let's just back up," Gabe said. "Step one—find Laura. That's it. That's all we have to do. Then we can figure out what's been going on with her."

"Okay," Rosie said, pulling herself back. She wanted to tell Gabe about Laura and Joe, but she didn't even know what there was to tell. Was it an affair? A flirtation? Why the hell was her husband calling her sister? Why had he gone to her apartment weeks before she'd come back home? If it was anything other than an affair, if Joe was helping her, counseling her somehow, maybe for the murder of her boyfriend, he would have told Rosie. Nothing would have been worth the fallout if he kept it from her—the fallout that was now upon them.

"The way I see it," Gabe began, "we now have three possibilities. First, Laura found out about this guy being a player and can't face whatever it is she did that night. Second, something went wrong when she found out and one of them got hurt. But there's a third one now. And it has to do with those notes."

"I've thought of that," Rosie said, thankful Gabe didn't use the word "dead." Even though they both knew that was a possibility.

"If this guy is more than just a womanizer—if he's a professional con man—then it's possible he targeted Laura in connection with Mitch Adler's murder."

"But why now, Gabe? I mean, she lived an hour away in New York. It's not as though she's been in hiding. And who would have gone to all this trouble? Who would even know she was on a dating website?"

"It could be anyone affected by the murder—a family member, a friend—and what about Lionel Casey? Maybe he had family and maybe they have a vendetta because he spent his life in a mental facility against his will. If they were all just going about their business, and then one day someone saw Laura in town—it could have broken the dam."

"Or . . ." Rosie's eyes opened wider. "Gabe—what if she was on this date last night and that's when someone saw her—someone close to Mitch Adler or Lionel Casey who believed she was responsible for the death? What if this has nothing to do with Jonathan Fields or Laura finding out about him and freaking out? What if we're chasing the wrong lead?"

Gabe agreed all of that was possible.

"We should tell the police, Rosie. About those notes, about the connection to the past. They can find people faster than we can."

Rosie wasn't sure. That would mean bringing everyone back to that night in the woods. She hadn't heard from the two officers since yesterday evening. She'd assumed that they hadn't put the pieces together about Laura Lochner, past and present, because if they had, they would have called her. Telling them about the notes would make that inescapable.

"Rosie," Gabe said, "why didn't Joe show them to the police when they were at the house?"

Rosie shrugged. "I think he didn't want them to focus on the past. To not take it seriously—finding Laura."

"Okay," Gabe said, nodding a little too hard. She could tell he wasn't buying it.

And Rosie had no patience for guessing. "What? Do you think it's something else?"

"No . . . I just . . . Look—don't take this the wrong way. But sometimes when I'm at your house, and you've gone upstairs with Mason, we all keep drinking and talking. And then sometimes I leave, and they pour another round."

"What are you saying?"

"That sometimes they stay up talking. Alone. I have no idea what it's about. But maybe Laura confided in him about something. Maybe about the notes or something else. Maybe Joe's afraid to expose her to the police."

His name was Joe.

First Kathleen, and now Gabe, telling her things about her husband and sister. This could not be happening. Not to her own family. Was there no end to the trouble? Would it follow them forever?

"He went to see her, Gabe," Rosie blurted out then. She couldn't be alone in this.

"What do you mean?" Gabe looked surprised. Shocked, even. And something else—territorial, protective. His alliance had always been with Laura, and Rosie was now putting the pieces together. That story about his brother. That had to have stayed with him. Made him feel responsible for her and whatever damage Rick Wallace had caused.

"Laura's roommate heard them on the phone, and saw Joe with her at the apartment in New York. Before she moved. Before the breakup with the shrink—if there even was a boyfriend. Maybe that was all a ruse. A distraction."

"That doesn't make any sense," Gabe said, thinking. "You don't believe . . ."

"I don't know, Gabe." Rosie let the tears come now. It was too much. Too *fucking* much.

"No way!" Gabe shook his head as though he could erase the thought from both of their minds. "Not Joe. He loves you. He always has. *Always.* And Laura—she would never do that to you, even if she did have feelings for him after all these years."

Rosie wiped her eyes and gathered herself. She was in an alternate world now, where nothing was known or unknown except the facts. Joe had been seeing Laura behind her back. Joe had been having secret conversations with her at the house. Joe had found the notes, conveniently, after the police left.

And Joe had found the car.

This last fact suddenly jumped out above the rest.

"He found the car," Rosie said. "Joe—and in less than an hour."

Gabe was silent, his eyes fixed on Rosie. He took her hand again and pressed his lips against her palm. Then he squeezed it hard between his own, and she imagined that he didn't believe it. But then he also did, and now he was going to be her protector, even from his best friend. The man he'd known since childhood.

His phone buzzed on the table right beside their hands. Gabe broke away from the embrace and picked it up.

"It's a message," he said, pulling it up to the screen. "Shit! From findlove.com. From secondchance."

Rosie gasped. The woman from the website who'd gone quiet. The woman who'd told them to *RUN*.

"What did she say?"

"She gave us a phone number. She said she'll talk to us."

Rosie stared at him, eyes stinging now, from the exhaustion and the tears. She'd already heard one story about this man, this Jonathan Fields, from Sylvia Emmett, a woman he'd picked up at a bar and then lied to and mistreated. Now they had the woman from findlove.com. What story was she about to tell? Rosie was afraid to find out.

"Are you ready?" he asked her, looking at her with steadfast resolve.

It didn't matter if she was ready or not ready. They had to find Laura. Everything else would fall into place.

She opened her mouth, but it was bone-dry. So she didn't speak. She met Gabe's eyes and nodded. *Yes.*

TWENTY-EIGHT

Laura. Session Number Three.
Four Months Ago. New York City.

Dr. Brody: Do you worry when you're here? When you're with me?

Laura: No.

Dr. Brody: You don't wonder if maybe you're doing it again? With the wrong man—a man who will never love you.

Laura: Well, now I am. Thanks . . .

Dr. Brody: I'm sorry. I didn't mean to put thoughts in your head.

Laura: Isn't that your job, Kevin?

Dr. Brody: I suppose it is. Hopefully good thoughts. Or correct thoughts, I should say.

Laura: I would only be worried if I thought you were going to break my heart.

Laura: You're not going to do that, are you?

TWENTY-NINE

Laura. The Night Before. Friday, 12 a.m. Branston, CT.

It's over in minutes.

Mere minutes.

I've thought about this before. How it can take hours, days, weeks to arrive at this place. Clothes littered on the floor. Arms, legs now limp and twisted together like a pile of dead trees in a ravaged forest. I feel his heart, wild against my chest. Breath coming and going in quick bursts. Panting. Our naked skin sticks together from the drying sweat. The residue of the heat that is cooling fast.

Mere minutes. A tornado. A tsunami. So much drama before its arrival. Then it comes with a force that was fully anticipated, yet we are still unprepared. Taken by surprise. Swept away. It leaves us forever altered. The shape of our bodies, the way they respond, the way they move—these intimate details cannot be unrevealed.

Mere minutes and everything is over. I am stunned.

I press my closed eyes into the nape of his neck. I don't want to see his face.

"That was incredible," he says. And he follows it with a dramatic moan.

I think now that it was no more or less incredible than every other time. It's so predictable, and yet I never seem to learn.

Another moan, this one manufactured. I know because his heart has quieted.

Then the same hand that—moments before—clenched my ass to pull us together, harder, deeper, now lightly pats my back. Three quick pats that say, *We're done here.*

I can't bear to face this newest failure. It is bigger than the others because this time I knew. This time I understood. Dr. Brody made sure of that.

Don't invent him.

Don't fill in the blank spaces with intimacy that does not exist.

Don't mistake sex for power.

Jonathan Fielding. I made you my confidant. I made you my hero. I let you fill me with love then take it away. I clench my eyes tighter, but I cannot pretend I don't see the injury I have inflicted upon myself. It's painful. And so familiar.

Another pat on the back and this time he pulls his head away, so I have nowhere left to hide my eyes.

"Hey—I have an idea," he says. His voice is lighthearted now. "Why don't I order a pizza? I'm starving. We never got dinner."

We lie side by side on top of his black-and-gray comforter. We lie at an angle across the bed. We have barely made a ruffle. I slip my arm out from under his body, pull out a leg from between his knees. He makes adjustments for me so I can leave him quickly and without any hesitation.

"Sure," I say. "I'll be right back."

I roll off the bed, leaving him propped up on an elbow, watching. I feel his eyes on my body as I walk across the room. I enter the bathroom and don't turn around until I can hide behind the door. He's seen my ass now, in the light, and I can't get that back. But he hasn't seen the rest of me, and I guard it now with the passion of regret. Behind the door, I turn on the light and push in the lock. Then I run the water. A towel hangs on a hook and I grab it and wrap it around me like a life preserver. But I cannot be saved. I know that now.

I sit on the edge of his ceramic bathtub and let my head fall into the palms of my hands.

I try to sort out the moment it all got away from me. God help me, but I find Dr. Brody in my memory. Kevin. *Asshole.*

He used to tell me to close my eyes and see myself as another person. A woman doing the things I do. Feeling the things I feel. So I close my eyes now and picture her, that stupid woman, in Jonathan Fielding's kitchen. I hear her tell her story to this stranger and I ask her why. She makes excuses, but finally faces the truth and makes her confession. She cannot wait for this man to know her. She cannot wait to see if he will love her. She needs to know now. She needs to make it happen. So she takes out her toolbox and looks inside. The story of Mitch Adler is now a hammer. Her body, a wrench. She knows how to use them.

I see her standing by the counter, wrapped in his arms. There is still time to walk away. He's said as much. He's offered to take her home. She tells me she can feel love just below the surface. A few more strikes. A few more twists. Almost there.

Can't you just taste it?

Dr. Brody used to ask me what I would say to her if I could. I did say things. I remember them. I said them moments ago in the kitchen.

I told her the things I've learned about her, how she is repeating the past. How she knows this night will not end with love, but with sadness. I told her. She knew. She knew, but she did it anyway.

Jesus, Laura. You knew this would happen!

Kevin was not like this. Kevin saw me and he refused to let me self-destruct. I pushed and pulled and used every tool in that box, but he would not be deterred. Weeks passed before he lay down beside me, and when he did, it was not over in mere minutes. And he did not pat me on the back and order a pizza. Kevin pulled me in closer and said those words. Those words I wish didn't exist because I wanted them so much.

I love you, Kevin said. And I believed him.

Tears come hard now. The weight of my grief is before me. Jonathan Fielding has just shined a bright light square in the middle of it.

I want that back. I want to feel arms pulling me tight. I want to hear those words and know they're true.

The wanting swallows me whole.

"Are you all right in there?" I hear Jonathan say. I hear footsteps and shuffling.

"I'm fine," I call back.

He asks me something about the pizza and I answer something about the pizza. The fucking pizza.

I turn off the water. My head throbs from the scotch and the adrenaline and toxins that have been set free from the story of Mitch Adler.

This is not the time to revisit the past. I pool water from what's left in the sink as it drains and I splash it on my face. It stings, but I need it. I need to snap out of it. I look in the mirror. Run a finger beneath my eyes to clear the mascara that's smudged. Then I run all ten of them through my hair, tugging at the knots. I tuck it neatly behind my ears and try out a polite smile. First my mouth, turning up at the corners, then my eyes squinting just a little. I try a slight raise to my brow.

I have a thought to go with the smile.

Maybe the mistake isn't over. Maybe it's still happening.

Part One—choose a man who can't love you. Part Two—reconstruct him into a man who will love you. Part Three—make him love you by any means necessary. Part Four—fail and feel worthless. Repeat as necessary to stay trapped in your childhood.

And here we are.

But what if there is a Part Five? What if that part is what I'm doing now—returning to that place that is dark and lonely but also feels like home? Like where I belong. Or where I deserve to be.

And what if I was wrong about Part One? What if he's not a man who can't love me, but just a man I got drunk with and spilled my guts to and fucked on the first date?

I bring back Dr. Brody. *It begins with recognition.* I see it. I see everything.

A wave of hope rushes in and the smile becomes real. I suddenly know what to do.

I open the door and find Jonathan in the bedroom, buttoning his shirt. He turns to face me.

"You okay?" he asks again.

I smile sheepishly. "A little embarrassed . . ."

He stops buttoning. Tilts his head. "Why?"

"Isn't is obvious? This is our first date and I'm standing in your bedroom dressed in a towel."

I do not expect you to love me. But maybe you still can. Maybe I haven't ruined it.

He smiles back. He picks up a neatly folded pile of clothing from the bed—my clothing. Underwear, bra, dress. Yes—he has folded my underwear. He walks to where I stand, and holds out the pile.

"Okay," he says. "First, here are your clothes. Although I prefer the towel." He winks and I am suddenly aware that he is forty.

"Second, I've ordered a pizza, so technically it is now our second date."

"Ahhh," I say as though he's just discovered the earth is round. "I see."

"Feel better?"

Actually, I do feel better.

His hands take hold of my shoulders and he kisses me somewhere between a peck and what happened on his bed. I close my eyes and let it reach inside, this kiss of reassurance. This kiss of new promises.

"I'll dig out some plates and pour us another drink. It's either that or face the hangover that's starting."

"Okay," I say now. "I'll get dressed."

He lets me go and I retreat toward the bathroom again.

"By the way," he calls after me. "Did you notice that I have a bed? That counts as furniture."

"Yes, it does!" I say cheerfully.

But really, he has just reminded me of my list of concerns. The woman who called his name at that first bar. The car. The way he drove us to the harbor, and his job, and this empty apartment after a year of being divorced.

I close the bathroom door and reassess. No need to panic. I know there are things that seem wrong. But I also feel that last kiss on my mouth and I hear him pulling plates from a cupboard for the pizza he's ordered, so I feel better about the night. The jury is out, I decide.

It's not easy. I'm bailing water from a sinking boat.

I get dressed. I look in the mirror again. Nothing left to do. Then I feel my head pound.

I open the medicine cabinet. I don't know why I didn't think to do this before. Furniture is one thing. But a person can't live without toiletries.

Toothbrush. Toothpaste. Mouthwash. Shaving cream and a razor, though they don't seem like the kind he would use every day. Deodorant.

And one bottle of Advil.

Men aren't good with these things, I remind myself. Especially when they've been married. They buy what they need when they need it. So maybe this is all he's needed.

I open the Advil and shake the pills into my open hand. I will take two, maybe three, then put the rest back.

But I don't take any pills.

I stare into the palm of my open hand and feel the boat sink.

Among the round, auburn tablets is something else that's round.

And gold.

I stare at it for a long moment. It's unmistakable. A gold ring. I pick it up and read the inscription on the inner edge.

To Jonathan, with love forever . . .

Love.

There it is. That evasive word.

Only it's not for me. It's never for me.

My boat sunk, I drown in this realization.

But I'm not going down alone.

THIRTY

Rosie. Present Day. Saturday, 10:30 a.m. Branston, CT.

"Here we go," Rosie said. They had moved to Rosie's car, which was parked outside the diner. Gabe was right beside her.

The woman from findlove.com wouldn't give her real name, though Gabe had already found her using her cell phone. *Kimmie Taylor. Age thirty-seven.*

She picked up after one ring.

"Hi," she said. She'd been expecting their call.

"This is Rosie. The woman who emailed you. I'm here with a friend of mine. I have you on speaker."

"Okay," the woman said cautiously.

Then she was silent.

"This is the friend—Gabe. Sorry to be cryptic on the emails," Gabe said now. "We actually have a good friend who went on a date with here4you. He told her his name was Jonathan Fields, but we know he's also gone by the names Billy Larson and Buck Larkin. We haven't heard from her for a while, so we're a little worried."

Gabe played it down. He told Rosie they shouldn't say anything that might make this woman worried about the police getting involved. She could be married, or living with someone, or have a boyfriend—just like Sylvia Emmett, the woman who'd bought a round of drinks at the bar by the harbor.

"You're right to be worried," Kimmie said. "He lies about everything. He used Buck Larson with me, but his real name is none of those. His real name is Edward Rittle. Not exactly the name of a stud."

Rosie clutched her phone so tightly, her fingertips were turning white. She did her best to soften her voice.

"What can you tell us about him? Anything at all."

The woman let out one quick burst of laughter. "Where do I even begin?" she said, her voice laden with disgust. "You saw his profile, right? Said he was divorced. Said he made over $150k. Said he had no kids and worked in finance. Look—a lot of guys make shit up. They lie about everything from their weight to their height, and especially their income. Sometimes they say they're divorced when they're really just separated. I think they have secret meetings, these douchebags—to give and get advice on how to avoid being excluded from search lists. Seriously, I can hear them. . . . *Don't say you're not divorced yet! You'll never get laid that way!* Makes me want to throw up."

Gabe rolled his eyes and Rosie knew what he was thinking. She was thinking the same thing. Kimmie was one bitter veteran of online dating.

"It's horrible," Rosie said. "Don't they know that if they keep seeing a woman, she'll find out they were lying from the start?"

Kimmie laughed again. "They don't give a shit! Are you kidding me? Three dates. A fuck. And they're out of there. On to the next. It's an online free-sex buffet, that's what it is. But this one—he knows how to find just what he wants."

"So what exactly does he do? Maybe it will help us find our friend," Gabe said.

"Well, he lies on the profile. That's the first thing. Lies about his name. Lies about being divorced . . ."

"Wait—what do you mean?" Rosie asked.

"I mean he's married! Married with two kids in middle school. Living in Mamaroneck. Working as a salesman for energy-efficient windows. Can you imagine? Goes door to door performing 'energy assessments' for the electric company, but then he tries to sell people new windows for his company. It's all a scam, just like he is. Finds a way in the door and then fucks people."

"How did you find all of this out?" Gabe asked.

"It took me some time, but things weren't adding up about him. The car he was driving. How cheap he was when we went out. He didn't seem sophisticated enough for finance, you know? He seemed blue-collar to me. And eventually he let his guard down, left the room without his wallet. So I looked. It was that simple. I flipped it open and there it was—his real name and address. I went home and Googled him and whoosh—a tidal wave of bullshit came pouring out. . . ."

Rosie got the picture, but she needed to connect the dots back to Laura. "How did it start? How did he contact you, where did you meet . . . ?"

"Seemed benign at first," Kimmie said. "He calls to make sure you sound okay—no annoying accents or speech impediments. He asks if your pictures are current, but he does it in a subtle way. He asks about where you were when they were taken and then asks follow-up questions. One of mine was at my niece's graduation, so he asked where she was in college and what year was she in now. Things like that. I knew what he was doing, but I'm sure he thought he was being very slick.

"Anyway—when he meets, it's always during the week. And to his credit, he doesn't make up excuses about it. Instead he makes you wonder if he's got other women he's dating on the weekends— better women who are worthy of a Saturday night. It makes you want to be better, move up the ranks. It's human nature, you know. To compete. And for women, that means being sexier, smarter, better in bed. He knows it. He wants his women to be at the top of their games."

Rosie closed her eyes then and thought about Laura. She would fall right into that trap, and she wouldn't even know she was doing it.

I will make you see me. I will make you love me.

That face from the picture when she was a little girl. The image of her with that doctor, climbing Mount Everest . . .

"Where did he take you?" Gabe asked.

"First date—Thursday night, of course—was at that place by the harbor. The bar on the corner with the shitty food."

Gabe nodded at Rosie when she finally opened her eyes again. They had the same guy. There was no doubt now.

"The next date was on Main Street. More upscale. He got me dinner that time."

"Just like Sylvia Emmett!" Rosie said to Gabe, muting the phone. "The woman from the bar—first planned date at the harbor, last date on Main Street—dinner."

Gabe nodded silently, then looked back to the phone.

"He lives near there. Did you know that?" Kimmie asked.

Rosie released the mute button. "Another woman he dated said that as well. But she didn't know the address because she wouldn't go to his apartment."

"Well, she was smarter than I was."

"Wait—you went there? You know where he lives?" Gabe said. He reached for his phone, eyes growing wider. "What's the address?"

"Oh Christ, let me think. . . . It's in those apartments on Maple Street. There are a few buildings. His was one of the ones in the middle. Had underground parking."

"They all have underground parking. All of those buildings. There must be half a dozen." Gabe was growing impatient. "What about an apartment number or a floor? Anything at all—was there a doorman or a keypad?"

"Look," Kimmie said. "It was over a year ago, okay? I only went there a few times and it was late. I was drunk. And after I found out who he was, I wanted to forget. I wanted to forget everything about him."

Gabe was busy now, on his phone. Rosie took a long breath to slow her mind. She wanted to reach through the phone and shake the information right out of this woman, but then she remembered about Sylvia. About the cruelty. There could be other things Kimmie didn't want to remember.

"Okay," Rosie said. "Can you tell us what he was like? What it was like to be in his apartment, alone with him?"

"That's kind of personal, don't you think?" Kimmie said, suddenly indignant. Or maybe just defensive.

"Nothing like that. I just meant, was his apartment nice, inviting? Was he nice? Was he a gentleman? Did his mood ever change?"

"Was he a gentleman . . . hmmm . . . let me think." Kimmie

was now sarcastic. "Well, he took me on three dates before he expected sex. We went to his apartment, which was a total bachelor pad. Nothing in the fridge. Everything black and silver. Should have been my first clue. But he said he had just gotten divorced, like a month before, so I bought it. It made sense. God, I even offered to help him decorate. Can you believe it? I was such an idiot."

"Not at all," Rosie said. "It sounds like he was very good at what he did—conning women."

"You have no idea. He knew exactly what to say to me, exactly how to get inside my head. He talked about his dead father because my father had died when I was young. He talked about living life for the moment because you never know when it will end—again, something I was drawn to because of my father's young death. And he made me feel like I was the first woman he'd been with since his cold ex-wife, who didn't sleep with him for years. The thing is—the reason I started to wonder about him—if you can believe it, was how he was in bed. I mean, a man who's been in a shitty marriage for ten years and who hasn't had sex for a long time, and now is at the free-sex buffet—you would think he would be a little eager beaver—quick on the draw, you know what I'm saying?"

"Yes," Rosie said, imagining Joe after going four months around the time of Mason's birth. He was like a man in the desert suddenly finding an oasis. "But he wasn't like that?" Rosie asked.

"No. He has it all down to a routine. He goes for a quickie off the bat, like he's trying things out—a shark taking that first bite, getting a taste before coming back for the kill. So he made excuses for me to stay so he could go again, go in for the kill. And that's when things got strange. It started with dirty talk—really filthy stuff. And then he got demanding. Some of the things he wanted to do—well, I'm sure he found other women willing to do them to get a Saturday night date. But I wasn't into it. I left feeling disgusted, but it didn't stop me from coming back again. I came back for one last date and that was when I found out the truth. He left the bedroom to get another drink and I pulled his wallet out of his pants pocket. When he came back, I was dressed and heading for the door. I made up some story about a friend who was drunk and stranded at a bar. He didn't care a whole lot. Walked me to the door. No kiss. No nothing. He didn't get his second round, so he was disappointed. I swear to you—I sometimes wonder what would have happened if I hadn't found the wallet. If I'd stayed for the second round that time. It felt like he knew exactly what he wanted at each turn and that he was going to find a way to get it."

Gabe looked up from his phone, distracted and seemingly unaffected by a story that Rosie found horrific, and eerily similar to that of Sylvia Emmett's. "Can I text you some pictures of apartment buildings on Maple? If we drive there now, maybe you can tell us which one looks like his? Maybe you'll remember the number or the floor?"

There was a long silence.

"Hello?" Rosie said. "You still there?"

"Yeah," Kimmie said with a sigh. "I can pull up images on my computer. I can probably find it for you. Jesus, though, don't tell him we spoke, okay? I would hate for him to think that I gave him even one second of thought after I walked out that door."

"Of course," Rosie said.

"And when you find the right building, it's apartment 2L. I remember it. I remember thinking that *L* stands for 'Liar.'"

THIRTY-ONE

Laura. Session Number Ten.
Two Months Ago. New York City.

Laura: I've been thinking about what you said—about there being someone from my past I tried to fix.

Dr. Brody: Yes. I remember when I said that.

Laura: It's my father, right? The first man a girl loves.

Dr. Brody: And the one who loves her back. Who teaches her she's worthy of love.

Laura: I can see that. Only, it wasn't my father who was broken. It was my mother. He cheated on her. Left her for another woman. She was always crying. Worrying. And she didn't hide it well. She used to talk about it in the kitchen with Mrs. Wallace and anyone else she could lure inside.

Dr. Brody: Sometimes things aren't what they seem. Especially when they're things from when we were young. Our memories are not static. They're not pictures of reality.

Sometimes they're not true at all, but rather fiction that we need to believe so we can make sense of things.

Laura: So my father wasn't the bad guy? My mother wasn't the victim?

Dr. Brody: You told me a story about something you overheard. Something your father said to your sister the night he left. It's the only story that doesn't fit with that narrative, and yet it stands out enough that you told it to me.

Laura: I was listening at the door. Rosie was mad at him for leaving. Yelling at him. And he said to her—and this I know is exactly what happened—he said, "Your mother is no saint."

Dr. Brody: Something happened, Laura. Something no one told you or Rosie. But I have a feeling you knew inside even as a little girl, that your father was the one who was broken.

Laura: The one I tried to fix so he could love me? I learned all of this from my father?

Dr. Brody: It's almost always the case, Laura. With women who seek men who won't love them, and turn away the ones who can, and do.

Laura: I think I hate him even more now.

Dr. Brody: Except you don't. And you need to find out why.

THIRTY-TWO

Laura. The Night Before. Friday, 12:45 a.m. Branston, CT.

"So about that hangover situation," I say to Jonathan Fielding.

I'm dressed but still feel naked. It's Rosie's dress. I hate dresses. I hate the way the air feels against my legs. How it creeps beneath the hemline and makes its way up as far as it pleases, sometimes all the way to the sleeves. I hate my bare feet and loose hair, falling around my face and sticking to the back of my neck.

I hate a lot of things right now.

Jonathan hands me a glass of scotch from the other side of the kitchen counter. I am close to the door. My purse is right in front of me. I left my shoes in the small foyer, but they are gone now. Probably moved to a closet where I can't find them without more delay. More chances to work his way into my brain. No matter. I don't need shoes to get home.

Home, I think now. Rosie and Joe and Mason. My cozy space in the attic, hiding beneath the fluffy comforter.

Home, I think again. Only, it's not my home. It's Rosie's and

Joe's and Mason's. And the attic is where I found the last of the three notes. Not so cozy after all.

I have no home. That's the truth. But that still doesn't make *this* a place I want to stay one minute longer.

I take the drink and swallow it down.

"So what is this about the hangover?" Jonathan asks. He's smiling like we are lovers and I suppose we are, technically. The way that phrase is used. *Lovers. Home.* Just words. Stupid, meaningless words.

"Yeah . . . " I begin. I've swallowed the rage and turned it to steel. "So I thought I'd preempt it with something more medically sound than more alcohol."

"Oh?" he asks. And I see a trace of concern.

That's right, Jonathan. It's your turn to worry.

"I figured some Advil might be in order. Luckily, I found some!" My voice is cheery.

He seems relieved. "Oh, good. I'm glad. I don't have a lot of medicines in there. I don't really like to take things and I haven't been sick for a long time. God, my ex used to keep everything!"

"Funny you should mention her," I say.

"My ex? I'm sorry—I guess that is a little insensitive after the night we've had."

I study his eyes then, as he studies mine. He is looking for clues about what's inside my head. I have the upper hand because I know.

I lift up my left hand and turn it backward so the palm faces me and the bright gold ring on my finger faces him.

"Did you want to put this back on before you go home?"

Jonathan freezes. He's so still that I wonder if I should check for a pulse. He freezes like he's been dipped in liquid nitrogen.

I say nothing. I do nothing.

Rage is steel and it makes me feel strong. I haven't felt strong in a very long time, and I would be a liar if I said I didn't like it. I would be a liar just like Jonathan Fielding.

"Laura . . ." Finally he speaks. But only this one word makes it past his lips.

I pull the ring off my finger and place it on the counter.

"It's not what you think," he says. His defrosting face is forlorn but not regretful. It's not guilty, either, and this lets confusion slip past the steel gates.

"I know you've noticed a lot of things tonight. You've been polite not to bring them up. You've been trusting and forthcoming and I feel like a complete shit. . . ."

"Your car," I say, now that he's opened the door.

"Yes, the Toyota that looks like a throwback to the 1980s, only it's brand-new."

"And your job . . ."

"Right again. I don't work in Branston. What forty-year-old divorced hedge fund manager would work out here when he could be in Manhattan? Right again."

"The bare apartment, the woman from the bar . . ."

He looks away to take a long drink of scotch. He sets the glass back down on the counter. Then he picks up the ring and twists it between his fingers.

"The woman from the bar is who I said she was. A crazy stalker who bothered my ex-wife after I stopped seeing her a few weeks ago. That was the truth."

"And the . . ."

"The apartment is new. I moved in at the end of the summer."

My mind is spinning as it processes this new information. He's admitted things but given no explanations. And he's avoided the biggest one of all—the one that's moved to the top of my list. The ring. The fucking wedding ring he keeps hidden in a bottle of Advil in his empty apartment where he brings other women.

There is something about what now sits between us. Facts without a conclusion. Facts without the truth. It's a puzzle with missing pieces—the important ones that leave nothing but ambiguity in their absence. The steel begins to melt. The strength, subsiding now.

"I can't do this," I say. Tears come fast. Giant sobs follow. And the words fly out in broken pieces, cutting me like little shards of glass. "You're married!" Sob. "You lied about everything! You're lying now!" Sob. "Whatever you say, I won't know how much of a lie it is because you'll sprinkle in small truths. Little admissions that aren't fatal but instead give you credibility because why would you say them at all if they cast you in a bad light? I know how this goes!" Sob. "I've been here before. I've been with the best of them . . . better than you!"

Hysteria sets in. Jonathan's face refreezes. The rage is now liquid that seeps from my skin. I know he can see it.

"How can you do this to people? It's cruel! It's so fucking cruel!"

That word is new to me. It's a word I learned from Dr. Brody. *Can't you see his cruelty?*

He was talking about another liar. Another man I tried to make love me. A man who bled to death at my feet. Mitch Adler. Liar. Cruel, cruel liar.

I see it now, Kevin. I see the cruelty. . . .

"Hold on a minute!" Jonathan says. He moves away from the counter and leans against the refrigerator. We've been here before.

"Things moved fast tonight—faster than either of us anticipated. Yes, I told some white lies because I'm trying to meet people here, but it's far from cruel. Honestly, you're way off base."

Adrenaline now. Rage becomes fear. What the hell is this? A cover-up? Or have I done it again?

She's so hard to love with her mountains from molehills.

"Can I explain? Please, will you do me that courtesy?"

I wipe my eyes. I hold my breath. Maybe I will die if I hold it long enough.

"Okay . . . I'm going to start from the beginning. Are you good? Have your drink."

He doesn't move closer to me. I wish I could move father away.

I hold my drink. Take a sip. The adrenaline kills it the moment it hits my blood.

"I'm from Boston. You already know that."

"Is your mother really dead?" I blurt out. If we're starting from the beginning, I want to know every lie. Every single one of them.

"Yes. All of that—the man who drowned. My sister. My parents—and how I met my wife. All of it's true. And we did move to New York. And we did live out here. She kept the house. It's on Blackberry Drive—way up north and on the west side. I don't know why she wants to live there, but she does. It's not my problem anymore. I hated that house, hated the commute."

"So you did work in New York?"

"Yes! I worked in New York. The name of the firm is Klayburn Capital. It's a small hedge fund. The headquarters are in Boston, but they have offices in New York and London. When I got divorced, I didn't stay here. You were right about that. I moved back to Boston. I worked at the office there and lived with my father for a while. I was broken. Truly broken. I still loved her and I wanted the family we tried so hard to have."

"So that's the first lie—that you stayed here?"

"Yes. That's the first lie."

I finish my drink and pretend to be indignant. Ha! He's admitted to a lie! But it's so small. It's a little baby lie. And babies can't be cruel. Not intentionally.

"Okay," I say. "Go on. . . ."

He does and I can see his demeanor change. He knows he has me. He knows what's coming are just more baby lies. A cute little nursery school of lies.

"After about six months, they asked me to transfer back. They want to have an office in Branston for some of the older partners who have families here. It's a better lifestyle. They asked me to open it. One year—that's what they said. And then I can have my choice—stay here, work in New York. Or go back to Boston."

"So you just came back. That's why there's no furniture."

"Yes—I've only been back for seven weeks, which is why I don't know my way around downtown. We never went to the harbor when I lived up north. I've spent four weeks in a hotel. Three in this apartment, which I've subleased for now—off the books, so who knows how long I can keep it. I can't decide what I want to do—move to New York. Go back to Boston. And I'm working all the time. . . ."

"And the car . . ."

"A loaner. I do have a BMW. It's in the shop. They were going to charge me for one of theirs, so I just got this one for the week. I should have said that from the start, but you didn't ask and I didn't want to just blurt it out."

God . . . I need Dr. Brody. I need Kevin. How do I know what to believe? Yes, I have a heightened sense of perception, but then I never know what to do with the information. This is all so convenient. So perfect. And yet it all adds up like two plus two is four.

"The ring," he says suddenly. "The last question, right?"

"For now," I say. I try to be smug. Self-righteous. But all I've got are these baby lies.

"Everything I own is in this apartment building. I can show you the storage unit in the basement—boxes of winter clothes, some pictures and photo albums. Everything I have is from my adult life, and that involved my wife. My childhood things are at my father's house. So what to do with this . . ." He twists the ring between his fingers again, and I stare at it with remorse for my rage, and longing for what it represents.

"I couldn't leave it in the basement. I don't want it to get stolen. And I don't have a safe. I read somewhere that a pill bottle was a better place to hide valuables than socks, so that's where I put it. I wasn't expecting company—not like this. Not to the point where I caused a headache."

Now he's trying to be cute. I don't know if I like it. I can't even decide if it's real.

But something comes through loud and clear.

He wants me to stay. He wants me to believe him.

It would have been so easy to shrug and let me storm off. Maybe he's afraid he'd have another stalker on his hands. Or maybe he's afraid of losing whatever it is we've begun.

Someone tell me. Please. Someone tell me which it is before I lose my mind. The rage is turning inward, turning on me now because I am so incompetent.

"Laura," he says. And he walks back to the counter. "I know you probably want to leave. I know some of this sounds too convenient. But will you do me one favor before you go? And then I promise I will walk you to your car."

I don't say yes. I don't say no. The tears are behind my eyes again. The sobs choking my throat. So I stand there like an idiot and shake my head.

"Okay—let me get my laptop from the bedroom. We are going to Google the shit out of me and my ex-wife and my firm—I even have an email from the BMW shop. Will you do that with me? Will you let me show you?"

What is going on here? Somebody tell me. . . .

The doorbell rings then and I jump back, startled. We look at each other for a second and then his eyes light up, big and wide and bright.

"The pizza!" he says, like a little boy. He claps his hands with excitement.

He walks around the counter, behind where I stand. And opens the door.

THIRTY-THREE

Rosie. Present Day. Saturday, 11 a.m. Branston, CT.

Rosie followed Gabe to Maple Street. Kimmie Taylor had recognized the entrance from the pictures he'd sent, and the ones she'd found on the Internet. Gabe knew which building it was and she was certain of the number—2L. *L is for Liar,* she'd said.

Joe called three times along the way. But Rosie couldn't talk to him. Not yet. Not now when they were so close to finding Laura. She sent a text with a lie—*I'm stopping by the police station then coming home.* If she told him about the apartment, he'd already be here. Only, now she didn't know if he'd be here for her, or for Laura. A few hours ago, she wouldn't have minded either way. But everything had changed.

His name was Joe. . . .

She rushed from her car to catch up with Gabe. He was moving fast.

"I called the police," he said. "Told them to meet us here."

Rosie walked beside him, trying to keep up with his long strides. "What did they say?"

They got to the front door and stopped. Gabe pulled out his phone and looked at the picture, then back at the door. "This is the one," he said.

"Are they coming?" Rosie asked. "The police?"

Gabe nodded. "Yeah."

"What did they say? Did you speak to the officers who came yesterday?"

"Conway. I spoke to Conway. He said to wait outside."

Gabe looked at her then, inquisitively.

"To hell with that!" Rosie answered.

"Agreed." Gabe pulled on the door, but it was locked. A panel of black buttons was on the right side of the entrance. Gabe pushed them one at a time until a voice came out of the panel.

"Hello?" a woman said.

"UPS," he said.

"Amazon?" the woman asked.

"Yeah," Gabe answered.

Then the buzzer.

Rosie pulled the door open and rushed inside.

"That's so scary," she said to Gabe, who followed right behind.

"You have no idea. But I guess that's why people live here. So they can afford to be trusting."

Neither of them spoke as they climbed the stairs to the second floor. Then down the long hallway, following the letters on the doors. When they got to 2L, Gabe grabbed her arm, stopping her.

He pressed a finger to his lips, telling her to be quiet.

"What?" Rosie whispered.

"Take a second, okay? You haven't slept or eaten. We need to think. We should have a plan."

Rosie knew what she looked like. She'd seen herself in the

window of that hotel in New York, and again in the rearview mirror of her car. But Laura could be on the other side of that door, and nothing else mattered until she knew.

Gabe was suddenly in control, the way Joe used to be when they were children. But Joe wasn't here, so Gabe had stepped in—doing the thinking and the executing of the plan. And thank God, because Rosie didn't have the ability for either of those now. Nothing was going to stop her from getting inside that apartment and finding her sister.

Gabe laid it out.

"What if he answers and she's not there? What if he lies and says he has no idea who she is? What if he says they had a drink and she left right after?"

He spoke evenly as they stood in the hallway, but Rosie couldn't calm herself.

"I don't know, Gabe! I just need get on the other side of that door!" Rosie felt her cheeks flush. Her head was light but somehow hard to keep steady. "I have to get inside that apartment! I have to know what's happened to my sister!"

The elevator door opened then. Rosie and Gabe turned their heads when they heard the chime. Officers Pearson and Conway emerged, finding them in the hallway.

Rosie ran to meet them. She took Pearson by the arm and pulled her along.

"He's there!" she said. "The man my sister was with—he lives in that apartment!"

"Okay, Mrs. Ferro." Pearson was condescending, even just saying her name. Rosie still had her by the arm, but it was like pulling dead weight.

"It's him! His name is Edward Rittle. He lies about it—calls himself all different names. He's married and has children! He uses this apartment to be with women from that website!"

Rosie could hear herself. She knew she sounded crazy. She knew she looked crazy. She could see herself in the expressions of all of them—Pearson, Conway, and even Gabe.

And she could see Gabe waiting for her to tell them the rest of it—about the threatening notes, or how Laura had been sleeping with her therapist in New York. Also married. Also with children. And now—dead.

But she stopped herself when they reached the front of the door. She looked at Gabe to make sure he wasn't going to say a word about any of that. It would do nothing but distract them, make them worry less about her sister than this horrible man who lied and cheated and misused women any way he could.

If he hurt Laura, and if she hurt him back—God help her—but Rosie felt he deserved it.

Pearson looked at Conway for a signal.

Conway gave it. "Look—we don't have a warrant for his apartment. We don't even have probable cause for a warrant. We can knock, ask a few polite questions, but that's it."

Rosie felt her eyes widen. The air stung when it hit them. Her mouth was bone-dry. Her head throbbing. And inside her chest was the weight of a scream desperate to come out.

She took two steps to the door and pounded her fist.

"Laura!" she yelled. "Laura!"

Conway was now beside her. "That's enough," he said. He moved in front of her, blocking her from the door.

"Mr. Rittle," he said as he knocked firmly. "It's the police. We just have a few questions."

Silence descended across the hallway. Conway pressed his ear to the door, standing just beside it. He motioned for Pearson to get Rosie, which she did. And Rosie realized they were keeping clear in case someone fired a weapon from inside.

Conway knocked again.

Still, no answer. Not a sound.

"Knock it down!" Rosie said, looking back and forth between the officers and Gabe. "What is wrong with all of you? Laura could be inside!"

Conway backed away from the door. "We don't have a warrant. We aren't knocking down any doors."

Rosie looked at Gabe now, desperate for help. They never should have called the police. If they were alone, Gabe would find a way inside that door. She knew he would.

Pearson got a text. "Hold on a second," she said to them as she read it. "Okay—the apartment is leased to a company. Someone is reaching out to them to find out who lives here."

"A company? What kind of company?" Rosie asked.

"It's an LLC. Probably a real estate holding company."

They were all trying to calm Rosie down. But she didn't want to be calm. She wanted to get into that apartment.

Gabe explained it to her. "People do that all the time, Rosie. For tax reasons, to limit liability. It costs nothing to start an LLC."

"He did it to hide. I know it! He's hiding it from his wife. Can't we search the names associated with the LLC?"

"We're doing that as well," Pearson said.

Rosie looked back to the door of apartment 2L. They were trying to distract her with all of these things they were doing, but really they weren't doing anything but stalling.

"What about the manager?" Rosie asked. "Maybe he'll let us in! Wouldn't he have a key?"

"Mrs. Ferro, that's the same as breaking the door down. We

don't have probable cause to do that. Once we get the name of the party living here, and if we can verify that your sister went on a date with him Thursday night, then we can apply for a warrant."

"And how long will that take? Days? A week? My sister has been missing since Thursday!"

Pearson glanced at Conway, who nodded.

"What?" Rosie asked. They were holding something back.

"We got the phone records. They came in this morning. We called your house and told your husband. . . ."

"I've been out all morning—he didn't say anything. Why didn't you call me on my cell phone?" Rosie couldn't believe that Joe would keep that from her. But, then again, she hadn't been taking his calls.

"We assumed he would tell you. He didn't mention you were out. Where were you?" Conway asked.

Rosie tried, but she couldn't steady herself. Nothing was making sense anymore.

"I was driving around, looking for my sister," she lied. Gabe shot her a look, but she ignored it. She was doing exactly that—driving and searching for Laura. They didn't ask where. "What did you find? On her phone . . ."

"The last few calls were from a number registered to a business. A financial investment firm in New York," Pearson answered.

"Can you get the name of the employee? Jesus—don't you see the connection? The apartment is leased under an LLC. The phone is registered to a business in New York. This guy does not want to be traced. He doesn't want to be found!"

"We're now looking into both companies. Trying to find the right people to give us that information."

"Don't tell me—you have to wait until Monday, right? No need to bother anyone on the weekend. After all, it's only been a day and a half. She's probably just run off with him for the weekend, right? Too afraid to tell her crazy sister?"

Gabe was the one who answered. "Rosie—that's not true. These things take time to track down."

"What about other numbers on her phone?"

Pearson took out her phone again and pulled up the scanned record.

"Here—you tell us," Pearson said, handing her the phone.

Rosie grabbed it and started to scan the numbers. She mumbled her thoughts as she began to recognize them. *917–28 . . . that's her old work cell phone . . . 212–23 . . . that's the firm's landline . . .* Scrolling more, reading with bleary eyes . . . *203–35 . . .*

She stopped suddenly, staring at that last number. Then she began counting. Scrolling and counting the number of times she saw those digits—*203–35 . . .*

"Can you get the text messages that were written?" she asked.

"We should have them later this morning. Is there a number you recognize?" Conway asked.

All heads turned when a door opened. It was 2M, right beside Edward Rittle's.

A middle-aged woman with a small dog emerged, stopping short when she saw the police officers.

"What's going on out here?" she asked.

Conway smiled politely. "Everything's fine. Do you know the tenants in 2L?" he asked.

"Eddie? Yeah. I know him," she said, rolling her eyes. But then her face grew concerned. "Why? Is he in trouble?" she asked.

"No. We're just trying to find someone he might know."

"A woman, right?"

Rosie was about to spring into action, but Gabe held her back, grabbing both shoulders.

"Thursday night?" The woman seemed to know the routine.

Pearson looked at Conway, but he was focused on the neighbor now.

"Yes. It would have been Thursday night. Did you see anyone?"

"See? No. I didn't see them. But I heard them. I hear them *every* Thursday." She said this with amusement. "If you're looking for him, though, he's not here. He's never here on the weekends. Something about his job—I think he works here but lives somewhere else. Comes and goes during the week. I have a key—I bring up his mail from the box downstairs. It's mostly junk, but it fills up fast in those small boxes and then the manager gets pissed off."

Rosie shuddered—this was him! It had to be. Thursday nights. Women.

"Can you open it?" Rosie asked.

Conway jumped in before the woman could answer. "That won't be necessary. . . ."

But the woman was already walking toward 2L, looking through the keys on her chain.

"I don't mind," she said. "He's not home. It's Saturday."

Now Gabe, finally, coming to the rescue. "It's okay if we go in," he said to the officers. "He gave consent by giving his key. We're not the police. . . ."

Rosie broke free of his hold and rushed to stand behind the neighbor as she slid the key into the lock.

Pearson and Conway didn't move. There was nothing they could do to stop her, or Gabe, from entering that apartment.

The door opened. The neighbor walked in, bent down to pick up a few fliers that had been slid under the door.

But Rosie was already in front of her. Calling her sister's name. "Laura!"

Gabe was there now. "Can we look around a little?" he asked the neighbor.

Rosie could sense that the neighbor was starting to question her decision to let them in—starting to see that this was not about finding a friend of her neighbor.

"Just a little—and quickly, okay?" she said. She sounded nervous.

"Laura!" Rosie raced into the living room, spinning around in a circle. Then to the bedroom, the bathroom, the closets, opening doors, calling out the name.

"Laura!"

Gabe stood quietly in the foyer with the neighbor and her dog. Rosie stared at them as the information settled into her bones. This had been everything—finding the women who knew this man. Finding out where he lived. And now, here she was—in the place where her sister must have been, and maybe just hours before. But there was nothing. No signs of her sister. No signs of a struggle. Not even a glass in the sink.

"The cleaning service comes on Fridays," the woman said. "Do you want the name?"

Gabe said something. The woman said something back. She pulled out her phone. He pulled out his phone. But none of it mattered. If the cleaning people had seen something wrong, they would have called the police. And if they didn't think what they found was wrong, they would have cleaned it up and erased it forever. All evidence of her sister—gone.

"Gabe!" Rosie cried out. She could feel the tears sting her dry skin.

The woman stood against the open door. "I think I should lock it up," she said. "I have Eddie's number. I can call him for you. . . ."

Gabe walked the few steps to Rosie and pulled her in tight. "It's okay," he said. "This is good news. Nothing happened here—look. Nothing happened. . . ."

Rosie looked up and found his eyes. "There was a number," she said in a whisper. "On the list . . . calls and texts going back weeks. There are so many of them. . . ."

"What number?" Gabe asked.

But she choked on the answer.

"Rosie! What number is it?" he asked again.

"Joe's—it's Joe's number."

THIRTY-FOUR

Laura. Session Number Twelve. Two Months Ago. New York City.

Dr. Brody: Calm down, Laura. I've never seen you like this. . . .

Laura: No! You need to tell me! Right now! Right this second!

Dr. Brody: It's complicated. I wanted you to be ready to understand. . . .

Laura: We're past that, Kevin. I need to know. Just tell me! Stop treating me like a patient.

Dr. Brody: Laura . . . that's not fair.

Laura: You said I do this to myself—to prove a point. You said I would come to know what that meant, what fucking point I'm always trying to prove. . . .

Dr. Brody: Okay, just calm down. You're distraught. What's brought this on?

Laura: Just. Tell. Me!

Dr. Brody: Fine. You want to know what point you're always trying prove to yourself, with scores of men who will never love you, who probably can't love anyone, and why you throw yourself at them and let them into your mind and your heart and your body . . . ?

Laura: Yes, tell me why I do all of those disgusting, reprehensible things that you obviously think are unworthy of your pristine self-awareness!

Dr. Brody: You are unlovable!

Laura: What?

Dr. Brody: The point you try to prove to yourself over and over so you can feel as shitty as you have your whole life . . . so you can be sure to repeat the past until you're dead and buried, never changing, never moving forward. Laura Lochner, men don't love you in spite of everything you give them because you are unlovable. Are you happy now? Now that you know?

Laura: Jesus Christ, Kevin.

Dr. Brody: But it's not true. It's never been true. That's what I wanted you to understand! That this truth you keep trying to prove over and over is a lie. You are lovable. And I love you, Laura. I love you.

Laura: Kevin . . .

Dr. Brody: Tell me what happened. Tell me why you're so upset.

Laura: I can't. I promised.

Dr. Brody: Whom did you promise?

Laura: Joe. I promised Joe. My sister's husband.

THIRTY-FIVE

Laura. The Night Before. Friday, 1 a.m. Branston, CT.

Jonathan eats pizza. He eats it standing at the kitchen counter, without a plate or a napkin. He found a beer in the back of the fridge and he split it in two. A glass for me, and what was left in the bottle for him.

He eats the pizza and drinks the beer like he hasn't a care in the world beyond hunger. He groans with satisfaction.

"Oh my God," he says. "What is it about late-night pizza?"

I've joined him on the other side of the counter, but I can't manage to eat because I've already downed a plateful of anxiety.

I drink the beer.

"I'm sorry," I say.

He looks at me and shrugs. "Don't worry about it. I'm sure I'll finish the leftovers tomorrow."

"Not about the pizza. About everything else." I think about the "everything else" as I say the words, and a shudder rolls through my body.

Everything else: (a) freaking out in his car and running through the park; (b) revealing my dark, twisted past; (c) seducing him; (d) freaking out in his kitchen; and (e) accusing him of numerous crimes he didn't commit.

He looks at me with a wry smile this time, and I can't stand how cute he is. His shirt hangs loosely now, sleeves rolled up, two buttons undone at the top. His hair is disheveled from my hands, my fingers running through it. And I want to do it again. Touch his hair. Touch his chest, his back, his face. I have spun around in circles as conclusions have come and gone, pulling me in sharp turns. It's made me dizzy. It's made me spent. I want to fall into his arms and let it all pour out of me until I'm fast asleep. Finally, my mind at rest.

"I kind of liked the everything else," he says between bites. "Some of it more than the rest, but that's the way life is, right?"

It's hard for me to believe in his kindness. But I do. I force it down my throat and swallow it because I will not repeat the past. Not anymore. And because I can't make one more turn.

"I probably started dating again too soon," I say. This is now damage control. If he opened me up and saw what was inside my head, he would shove me out the door and turn the bolts.

"After the bad breakup?" he asks.

I nod yes, but then also no. "It's more than that. I learned some things over the summer. About myself and my childhood. Things that I'm still sorting out."

He drops a piece of crust into the box and picks up a fresh slice. "Well, since this is technically our second date, let's hear it. All of it," he says. "Tell me what you learned this summer that you can't sort out."

I lean against the counter, bare feet planted firmly on the linoleum floor.

"It's about my father. And my mother, really."

"You said your father cheated and then left all of you for another woman. You haven't seen him for sixteen years, right?"

"We were supposed to go for weekends. Up to Boston, twice a month. Rosie went until she was seventeen, but I refused. I could see it made my mother happy when I did, and Dick never pushed it. At least, that's what I was told. *Your father said you can go if you want, but you don't have to.* I think it would have been different if Rosie had refused."

"Why? Did he love her more?"

I look at him now with profound curiosity. It's such a horrible question, and yet also dead-on. I like how smart Jonathan is, and how honest. Yes, I think. He is honest.

He offered to show me, to find himself on the Internet, to pull up emails. But I've done enough damage tonight. I'll have time tomorrow—I'll have all day because Rosie will wake me up, sneaking in my room to make sure I'm all right, the door squeaking, the floor creaking. She can't help herself.

"Yes," I answer just as boldly. "He loved her more. I've just recently been able to admit it. I had to be shown. I had to have the evidence laid out before me."

I tell him then about the picture I found in a box my mother sent me when she moved to California. It has all of my old junk from my room—plastic trophies and medals, art projects, letters I wrote home from summer camp. And pictures.

"I made it my screen saver," I tell him.

He stops eating and leans against the counter next to me. "Wait—you took the one photo from that box where you can actually see the sadness on your face—your little childhood face, sad because you knew your father loved your sister more—and you put it in a place where you had to look at it every day?"

I laugh a little because he's right. It is absurd. Except that it also makes perfect sense.

"I didn't want to forget. I wanted to see that face, looking at my father behind the camera, and know beyond any doubt that it lives inside me."

"That's horrible," he says. "It's so sad. I'm sorry, Laura. Really—I can't imagine thinking that my parents didn't love me. Even when my sister and I complain about the terrible things they did as parents . . ."

"Was your mother late to pick you up from soccer practice?"

"All the time! How did you know?"

We both smile now.

"But even when we complain about those things, there's never a question about whether they loved us."

I think to myself how normal that must be. How most adults in our world—the world of the privileged—take this for granted. And I realize how hard it is for me to imagine it.

"I'm happy for you," I say. "And I'm happy for Rosie."

I go on then, with these things I learned from Dr. Brody. How I choose men who would never love me so I could repeat the past. Craving that feeling that was so familiar. Craving the chance to finally be enough, enough to fix him and make him love me. How I did that with Mitch Adler.

It struck me one day in the West Hotel, lying in bed with Dr. Brody, Kevin, after making love. Feeling safe and protected. We spoke of these things, and I suddenly realized that all of these pieces fell into place. That Mitch was dead because they did.

I don't tell Jonathan about Dr. Brody or how I came to understand all of these things about myself.

And I don't tell him about Joe and the secret we now share.

I only say that I figured it out and that I now feel responsible for Mitch. He wouldn't have been in that car with me if I had done what any normal girl would have done. If I had told him to go straight to hell when we were kissing behind a tree.

Jonathan is quiet suddenly, and it has me unnerved. Something about Mitch Adler gets under his skin. Maybe because he can't believe he's here with me—the woman who might have killed someone. Or because it reminds him of the man who drowned when he was in high school. Or, maybe, because of something else. Something I can't even imagine. And I have a very colorful imagination.

"Are you wondering if I'm one of them?" Jonathan says after a little while. "One of your wrong men?"

Now it's my turn to be honest. "I wouldn't know if you were. That's the problem now. It's like knowing you're color-blind and then someone asks you the color of the leaves on the trees."

"So you gather evidence—is it spring or fall? Are they maples or oaks? Why is he driving that shitty little car?"

I answer with a nod and a smile as I stare at my naked toes.

"If it makes you feel any better, I do that more now. Now that I've been dating for a while on that godforsaken website. Everyone lies. You have to read between the lines, look for clues hidden in photos. Sometimes you don't know until you meet face-to-face."

"Or you Google them—and hope they've used their real names."

"Haha," he says. "But you did it too, Laura *Heart*."

Yes, I did.

"So where does that leave us?" he asks.

"I don't know."

He slips an arm behind my back and pulls me into him. Our bodies press together as we lean against the counter. His body is warm and strangely familiar now.

I wrap my arms around his neck and rest my cheek against his chest. I hear his heart beating and it soothes me.

But then everything changes.

"I think . . ." he says, moving one hand down my thigh until it finds the hem of Rosie's dress. Then it moves beneath the fabric, up and up and inside.

He whispers in my ear.

"I think we should fuck again."

His voice is deep and lurid and it sends my body into lockdown. Every muscle stiffens against the pull of his hands on my dress and my hair. His mouth is wet, kissing my neck, devouring me suddenly like he devoured that pizza.

What is happening? The question has nowhere to go for an answer. It searches for the place where instinct should be, where reason should sound out, and finds an empty hole.

This is my defect. This is my Achilles' heel. All I can do is look at the evidence.

Where is the kindness? Where is the honesty? I've just stripped my soul bare. I've told him how vulnerable I am to this very thing—to uncertainty about men, to regret. And to the violence that resulted years ago.

He says it again. "I want to fuck you right now," and I feel my hand squeeze tight. A ball of stiff, folded fingers. Nails digging into my palm. A fist.

I open my eyes when he moves his head away and I see my purse on the counter. I have one thought now—one thought about what I have to do.

RUN!

Maybe this is nothing. I know that. Some people like this—the physical passion, the verbal vulgarity. But it stands beside the soft touch of his hands less than an hour before. It stands beside the intimate conversation that has barely ended. I don't have the tools to understand.

"I have to go," I say. Though the words are not easy to get out. That sad child, that *stupid* child, does not want to disappoint him.

I hate her. She never listens.

He doesn't stop, so I say it again, fueled by anger now.

"I have to go."

I push him off me and grab my purse. I reach inside and look for my keys. Jonathan stands still. He seems embarrassed, but I don't care. I don't care if he was trying to be seductive or sexy or whatever. I have to leave.

"Laura," he says. "I'm sorry—did I misread something? I thought we were really connecting."

Fuck! Where are my keys?

My hand brushes a piece of paper, and I remember the same feeling from earlier. From before I lost control. Got in his bed. Found his ring.

I grab it this time and pull it out. It's heavy and when it is freed from the purse, my keys fall out from between the folds. Jonathan reaches down to pick them up and I hate him for doing it. For being nice again. So much hatred runs wild.

Who are you, Jonathan Fielding?

I unfold the paper. It's just like the others. One sentence typed in black ink. Only this one scares me even more. This one is not a threat. It's a conclusion.

"What is that?" Jonathan says. "What does it say? You just turned as white as a ghost."

I look up from the note. I don't need to read it again—they're words I will never forget. So I just say them as I stare at this stranger.

You should have left while you had the chance.

THIRTY-SIX

Rosie. Present Day. Saturday, 1 p.m. Branston, CT.

Rosie followed Conway and Pearson to the police station. Gabe offered to go with her, but she needed him to go home, where he could research Edward Rittle and the two companies he was involved with.

The first was the LLC that leased the apartment—*362 Maple Street*. The name of the company was the address of the building. Gabe said he had no doubt it was formed simply to hold the lease so it wouldn't be in Rittle's name.

The second was a financial firm—*Klayburn Capital*. Laura had made calls to a number registered to the hedge fund. It was the number Laura had used to contact the man she believed to be Jonathan Fields.

Rosie sat now in a small conference room staring at a printout of the numbers from Laura's phone.

Pearson sat with her, flipping through notes from the morning.

The young officer looked up suddenly with a question. "I thought you said Edward Rittle worked in construction—window replacements, right? What does that have to do with a hedge fund?" But Rosie only heard the voice, not the words that were spoken. Her mind was on something else.

She'd been staring at her husband's phone number. Counting the calls and the texts. Trying to remember what happened on the days when there were many, and the days when there were none. Trying to find a pattern that might explain this connection between her husband and her sister that began over the summer.

Pearson repeated the question, and this time Rosie forced herself to listen.

"I don't know," she said. "Maybe the hedge fund owns the window company. Maybe he works for the window company. Or the hedge fund. This woman, Kimmie Taylor—I didn't ask her details about the things she knew. But Gabe will find out. This is what he does."

Pearson nodded, her lips closed tight and pulled up at the corners in a smile. It was meant to be sympathetic, but Rosie found it patronizing, just like before. She didn't want sympathy. She wanted to find her sister.

A text lit up her phone. It was Joe, asking if she was still at the police station. She'd lied earlier about being there, only now she actually was. Rosie stared at her husband's name on the screen. She wanted to throw the phone against the wall.

"May I use the restroom?" Rosie asked. She had to call him and check in. If she didn't, he would just keep at it, texting with questions. Eventually he would find her, and she wasn't ready to see him.

Pearson pushed back her chair and stood up. "I'll take you," she said.

They left the room and turned a corner. Rosie heard a voice—a man's voice—yelling something about *Thursday night*.

She walked faster, following the voice, Pearson on her heels.

"Is that him?" she asked, now in a large room where a man was yelling at a desk sergeant.

She glanced quickly at Pearson, who tried to pull her away, back into the hall.

"That's him! That's Edward Rittle!"

Pearson's hand grabbed her arm, but Rosie pushed her away quickly. A moment later, she was standing in front of the man whose picture she and Gabe had found on findlove.com. The man who'd last seen her sister.

"Jonathan Fields!" she yelled.

She took hold of his arms. Officer Pearson was right behind her. The man pulled away.

"What are you doing?" he demanded. He looked at Rosie with trepidation.

The desperation of the past two days came crashing down and Rosie lost herself. She started screaming.

"Are you Jonathan Fields? Tell me! Where is my sister!" She reached out to grab him again, and again he pushed her away.

"Someone do something!" he shouted.

"Mrs. Ferro!" Pearson tried to contain Rosie. She grabbed her arms and held them behind her back with both hands. But Rosie was strong. She pulled away again, this time pushing the man with two open palms against his chest. He stumbled backward.

"What the hell? Someone stop her! She assaulted me!"

"Mrs. Ferro!" Pearson yelled, then took a zip tie from her pocket. She found Rosie's arms again and held them tight. "Don't make me restrain you. . . ."

Officer Conway was there now, and he ushered the man away while Pearson held on to Rosie.

"It's him!" Rosie cried out, pulling against Pearson's grip. "It's him! He has my sister!" She fell into Pearson, who opened her arms and held her.

"Shhh . . . Calm down, Mrs. Ferro."

"It's him. . . . It's him. . . ." Rosie repeated the words, though her voice began to soften as the man disappeared down the hall.

Twenty minutes later Joe walked into the same conference room where Rosie had been counting his calls and texts to her sister. She sat still, staring at her folded hands. She couldn't look at him.

"Jesus, Rosie . . ." Joe moved cautiously around the small table and knelt beside her. "What the hell happened? They said you attacked some man in the waiting room."

"It was him, Joe. It was Jonathan Fields. Only that's not his real name. He was at an apartment two blocks from here on Thursday night. With a woman—the neighbor heard them. He was with Laura."

Joe sighed and hung his head. "Okay, but did you have to attack him? They're questioning him now, about Laura. But he wants to press charges."

Perfect, Rosie thought. "He's done something to Laura—I know it. I can feel it. She was in that apartment! And now he wants to press charges against me for demanding to know what he did? Has everyone lost their mind?"

Joe touched Rosie's back. "It's okay. Just calm down."

Rosie stood up abruptly, pushing him away. "I won't calm down! This is crazy—they should have a team of forensic people in that apartment. They should be interrogating him, not asking polite questions. Do you know what he's done to other women? He's a monster!"

Joe stared at her as she paced the room. He wouldn't speak now because he knew he wouldn't convince her that she was wrong, or that she shouldn't be this upset about what was happening two doors down where they'd taken that man. But that didn't mean he believed her. Or that he thought she was being rational.

"Where's Mason?" she asked. Her eyes opened wildly as she remembered Joe had been alone with their son. "What did you do with him?"

"Rosie!" Joe was angry now. "I called Zoe. I texted you that. What did you think I did with him? What's wrong with you?"

Shit. He had told her that. Zoe had come to the house. She knew she should apologize. But she couldn't bring herself to do it.

Joe saw the papers on the table. He looked once, quickly, then back again when he realized what they were.

"The phone records?" he asked cautiously. "What did they find?"

Rosie watched as he picked up the pages. She'd marked his number with a pencil—a small gray dot in front of every one of the calls and texts between his phone and Laura's.

His face didn't change when he saw the markings, but she knew he was seeing it. The evidence.

"Rosie . . ." Now his voice was contrite. He set the papers down, then looked back up at her.

"It went on for weeks," she said, folding her arms across her chest. "And you visited her in New York—at her apartment. And all those nights when you stayed up together, getting drunk and laughing. I could hear you all the way upstairs. Lying in bed with our son, thinking how happy it made me that you were being so generous with her. Making her laugh again when she'd been so sad. I never thought . . . It never crossed my mind. . . ."

"What didn't you think?" Joe looked confused. "What are thinking now? What do you think you've discovered?"

Rosie felt the clutch in her chest like she was about to cry, but no tears came. She was too exhausted.

She held her hands to the sky. "Is that what happened to her?" Rosie asked the question at the same time it entered her consciousness. Maybe it had been there since Laura's roommate had said his name. Or maybe it had come only after she'd seen his phone number in Laura's records. It didn't matter—it was here now. The pieces falling into place. "Did you have something to do with her disappearance?"

Joe was frozen, though Rosie could see his world coming apart.

But was it coming apart because she'd stumbled on the truth? Or because she had just wielded a fatal blow to everything that was between them? A lifetime of friendship and trust. And love.

"What am I supposed to make of this, Joe? You've been seeing my sister behind my back. Calling and texting her. Staying up late with her. And the one night she decides to start over, to meet another man, she disappears."

Oh God . . . Another thought. Another piece of evidence was suddenly before her.

"Where were you Thursday night—after you left our bed? I don't even know what time you left because I was passed out cold from the Benadryl and the wine, which you saw me take."

Still, nothing. Not a sound or a movement from her husband. There was no turning back now. She had crossed the line into this dark place where nothing was what it seemed. She stared at her husband, this man she'd known her entire life, and allowed herself to believe that she had never known him at all. It was terrifying, but in the same moment, a relief to know the truth.

"Were you jealous? Did you follow her? God, Joe . . . what? What happened?"

When he didn't answer, Rosie sat down at the table and collapsed into her hands.

She heard Joe pull out a chair and sit down across from her. He shifted in his seat nervously.

"Whatever you think is between me and Laura, I promise you—you're wrong. And I would never . . ." He stopped then, choking on his own words. "I would never hurt her. Never."

Rosie looked up and saw tears flood his eyes. But his jaw was stern and filled with anger and regret.

"How do I know? How can I believe you? People do all kinds of things when they love someone. When they want someone . . ."

"No . . ." Joe said again. "I would never hurt Laura!"

Rosie repeated her words as well. "How do I know?"

Then he paused as though he was considering his answer. And it was nothing she could have ever imagined.

"Because Laura is my sister. My *biological* sister."

THIRTY-SEVEN

Laura. Session Number Fifteen.
Six Weeks Ago. New York City.

Dr. Brody: I'm glad you've finally told me about Joe. How do you feel about it?

Laura: Confused at first. Disbelieving. I had so many questions—how long did my mother have an affair with his father? Who knew and for how long? How did they find out?

Dr. Brody: Your father knew before you were born, didn't he?

Laura: How did you know?

Dr. Brody: Because it explains everything. Don't you see it? It's the missing piece to the puzzle.

Laura: Dick couldn't love me because he knew I wasn't his daughter?

Dr. Brody: And more than that, Laura—you were the living embodiment of his wife's betrayal. An assault to his manhood—and with a neighbor. Then he had to pretend that you were his to protect the family, and he had to do it in front of everyone. You said the neighborhood was close, parties and impromptu gatherings. Joe's family didn't move away until he was in high school, right?

Laura: Yes. Joe said his father didn't tell his mother until then—which explains so much . . . why Mrs. Ferro was so friendly with our family, but Mr. Ferro kept his distance. We thought he was just antisocial.

Dr. Brody: I hope you realize that this doesn't excuse your father's behavior. You were a child. It wasn't your fault. He should have found a way to give you what you needed—what any child needs.

Laura: You think this should help me—this information?

Dr. Brody: Doesn't it? That child inside you asking why her father couldn't love her—now she knows. It had nothing to do with her. Now she can stop choosing the wrong men so she can repeat the past. It can all stop!

Laura: You try telling her that, Kevin. She doesn't listen to me.

THIRTY-EIGHT

Laura. The Night Before. Friday, 1:15 a.m. Branston, CT.

Jonathan reads the note. He looks at me with concern.

"What does this mean?" he asks.

I tell him it's the fourth note I've received since returning home. I tell him what each one said and where I found it, and while I do, I search for clues on his face and in the way his body moves. I do this even though I know I have no ability to decipher them. My brain is hobbled by this defect, this giant hole where instinct and reason should be.

"Laura . . ." he says. His surprise appears to be genuine, but I don't let myself trust it. "Why haven't you gone to the police? This is serious."

I take the note back into my hands. I fold it and put it in the purse.

"I don't know." This is the truth.

"Do you have any idea who would do this? Mitch Adler's family? Or a friend? And what about the homeless man who was sent to that institution?"

"No one from either family is local, but that doesn't mean they didn't come back when they heard I had returned. And friends—my God, it could be any of them. Mitch was really popular. But who would go to all this trouble after so many years?"

Jonathan's eyes light up. "What about that other girl? What was her name? Britney—the one from the party the night he was killed? His girlfriend for over a year. What if she was in love with him and blames you for taking that away from her?"

My head feels light suddenly as I see her face. *Britney*. Long blond hair. Big blue eyes. Puffy baby cheeks even at sixteen. I had never considered this. I never saw her again after that night.

"But why wait so long?"

Jonathan looks at the ground and shakes his head. His eyebrows scrunch together as he strains his brain for answers at one in the morning after scotch and sex and beer. And pizza. *Half a pizza*. Would he be able to eat if he wasn't just who he says he is—Jonathan Fielding, divorced hedge fund manager whose car is in the shop?

I stare at him. I study him. I wait for an answer, but it doesn't come.

I remember Dr. Brody explaining all of this to me. How this hole came to be, this defect. A child is told she is loved but then feels nothing. Tugging at a sleeve, waiting for a head to turn her way. Confusion is all she will ever know. And that's exactly what I feel as I watch this man in front of me.

Nothing but confusion.

I have to get out of here. My mind turns to my keys, the ones that fell to the ground and that he picked up. What did he do with them?

I remember—he put them on the counter—and I start to turn my head that way.

But he looks up suddenly with a new thought.

"What about the guy from New York? What if this has nothing to do with the past—but the present?"

I stop in my tracks and confront this new absurdity.

"It doesn't make sense. He dumped me. We haven't been in touch for weeks."

But Jonathan is not deterred.

"What if he expected you to do what you used to do—come back, do anything to make him love you again? Isn't that what you said? Your pattern with wrong men?"

He speaks of these things as though we are lab partners conducting a science experiment. He speaks of them and they are punches to my gut, forcing the air out of my body with the violent strikes.

Maybe I've spoken of them the way he now does, with detachment as though it's all in the past. As though I haven't spent every minute of the past six hours wondering if I'm doing it again, right here and right now with him. And my God, is that all it's been? Six hours? It feels like a lifetime that I've been with Jonathan Fielding.

He keeps on with his new theory about Dr. Kevin Brody, and I hate that I am even considering it. If Kevin was a wrong man, then I am truly lost. He said he loved me and he said it knowing every piece of me and how they all fit together in a broken heap. He had started to fix them. To fix me. The tables turned on my pattern of fixing broken men.

"I don't know," I say. "That would make him pretty crazy."

Jonathan likes his new theory.

"People are crazy," he says. "Haven't you figured that out? No one is what they seem."

I stare at him now. What is he trying to tell me? I think about his lurid voice telling me how he wanted to *fuck me* again. I think of the soft touch of his hands, and the sweet sighs when we did a drive-by in his bed. Yes, it was short, but it was sweet and passionate.

Wasn't it? Wasn't he?

Wasn't Dr. Brody, when he told me he loved me?

Jonathan looks at my purse. "When did you last look in there?" he asks.

I take a moment, because he is moving too fast now. From theory to theory to pontifications about mankind and now to his Sherlock Holmes Q&A.

"Uh . . ." I stammer. "At the house. It's Rosie's purse. I borrowed it."

He rubs his chin, thinking and thinking. Then he says, "Was it empty when she gave it to you?"

Where the hell are you going with this, Jonathan Fielding, the liar?

"I thought so," I say. But I really don't know.

"Did you get it yourself, or did she give it to you?"

Shit. Now he has me thinking absurd thoughts right along with him. I try to recall the exact series of events that led to my departure in Rosie's dress, with the cherry-red lipstick that I put in the purse. . . . I can see it on the counter in the kitchen. Rosie and Joe were cooking. Mason was running around half naked, glee on his face. Gabe had left sometime earlier when I went up to get ready. There was laughter. . . . *You could always hit up nursing homes next.* . . . Haha, yes, he's forty. Who had said it, Gabe or Joe? Joe, I think. It's more like Joe to tease me that way.

Rosie brought the purse. I remember that now. She set it down on the kitchen counter, but I didn't bring it with me because I had nothing upstairs that needed to go inside. Except the lipstick, which I carried in my hand when I came back down.

I opened the purse and shoved things in it—the lipstick in the kitchen, and then my wallet and other things from my purse I'd left in the car. I would have seen the note. I would have felt it.

Wouldn't I?

"It was empty when I got it," I tell him. But I'm not at all sure.

"Are you sure?" he asks, right on cue, like he's just read my mind. Again.

I won't think it. That note was not put in this purse by Rosie or Joe or Gabe.

How devious he is to make me question them. How ruthless. I feel my eyes narrow as I look at him.

"How about this for a theory: I left the purse in your car when I ran into the park. Remember?"

Silence descends. Jonathan stares. I stare back.

Then he breaks it. "What are you saying?"

"I'm saying that the note was not in the purse when I left the house. I'm saying that I left it alone—with you. First in your car . . . and in this apartment," I say, realizing this just now. "It's been on the counter the whole time."

"So you think I did this? That's insane! I didn't even know you before tonight. You said there were three notes, right? I saw you on the website a week ago—well after the first note was left on your windshield. Jesus Christ! I feel like we just drove off a cliff here."

He walks away, starts cleaning things up. The pizza box to the fridge. The glasses to the sink.

"I can't believe you just said that." He doesn't look at me.

And suddenly I'm the one who can't believe I just said that.

The voice is so loud as it rumbles through my mind. *This is why no one loves you. You are damaged and broken and no one ever will . . .*

I told Dr. Brody that she wouldn't listen—that little girl

tugging on a sleeve. The face in that photo. That starving child who lives inside me. I told him and he told me that I was wrong. He told me it would all get better now that I knew the truth about my childhood.

But he told me a lot of things.

And the last thing, the worst of all.

I saved the text on my phone so I would never forget it. The text that ended everything between us.

I don't love you. I love my wife. Please don't contact me ever again.

I'm about to do what that starving child asks of me, to fix things with this man—with Jonathan Fielding. That is the only voice I hear now, and it is loud and desperate. I start to plot ways to make him believe I'm worthy. To trick him into thinking I'm not what I seem even though I've just accused him of something horrible.

"I'm sorry . . ." I say.

But the doorbell rings before I can go on.

He looks up, past me to the door. He's frustrated and angry as he storms around the counter to the small entryway.

"It's probably my neighbor," he says. "We're being too loud."

He walks to the door as though he's walked to it before, explaining why he and some woman are making too much noise in the middle of the night. He turns the locks, his mouth already forming an apology.

But then the door slams hard against him, pushed with extreme force from the outside as soon as the locks give way and he's shown himself. He's stunned as he falls back against the wall and just as he leans forward, the door slams him a second time and he falls to the floor. It slams again, the hard metal of the bottom corner catching him right in the forehead.

I am perfectly still now, staring at Jonathan Fielding as his head bleeds. As the blood pools around his face.

I have been here before. I have seen this before.

I look to the door.

"Laura!"

It's a man standing there. I don't recognize him at first because he wears a baseball cap and a hoodie over it.

But then he looks up at me after he sees the damage he's inflicted on his victim.

"Gabe?" I say. I am hallucinating. "Gabe?"

I say it again, but he has already moved into the apartment. He grabs the purse on the counter. Sees my keys beside them and puts them in his pocket.

Then he looks at me, head to toe.

"Where are your shoes?" But he finds them in the corner behind the door before I can answer.

"Did you have a coat?" he asks, and I shake my head, still staring at him in a daze.

My eyes find Jonathan Fielding and the small but growing pool of blood. He doesn't move. He doesn't make a sound. He lies in a fetal position right where he fell. A large gash exposes bone at the top of his head where the sharp edge of the door struck it just right.

Gabe sees me and stops looking for my things. He stands in front of me and blocks my view.

"Laura," he says firmly. He waits until my eyes move, slowly, from the man on the floor, to find his eyes. "We have to get out of here. Right now!"

I have no words. I am back on that gravel road at the edge of the woods. A bat in my hand and a boy at my feet.

"Laura!" Gabe commands me now. He grabs my arm and starts to pull me toward the door.

My bare feet begin to move and I stumble behind him. Gabe blocks my line of sight until we are clear of the body. He pulls the door closed behind us.

And then we are gone.

THIRTY-NINE

Rosie. Present Day. Saturday, 1:30 p.m. Branston, CT.

Rosie listened to Joe's story, each and every sentence ushering forth memories that now had a new context.

I found out just before the summer, when my father died. . . .

Joe's parents had lived in Maine for over a decade. She and Joe had started to see them twice a year after Mason was born. He liked the beach. Rosie liked having free babysitters. She had never cared for his parents. His mother was flighty and his father distant. Then, and now, right up until his father died last summer.

My mother found out when we were in ninth grade. . . . That's why we moved.

Before they moved from the neighborhood, Mrs. Ferro was a frequent visitor to their kitchen, along with Mrs. Wallace. Rosie's mother would serve the ladies coffee and they would speak about their husbands and their children. Their voices were at times exuberant and filled with laughter. At other times, hushed and tearful. Rosie had never wondered why Joe's father rarely joined her father for beers on Sunday afternoons, or why the Ferros never came to their annual holiday party.

She didn't want us to know—not ever. But my father left a note. . . .

All those years, the Ferros kept the secret.

And all those years, so did Rosie's parents.

"Well," Rosie said when Joe paused, "it explains why your mother always hated me. Why she didn't want us to date and nearly had a stroke when we got married."

Joe didn't respond. He sat across from Rosie and stared at his hands, which were folded in a prayer at the table.

"Why did you tell Laura and not me?" That was the question of the hour.

Joe's chest puffed up with air as he leaned back in his seat. He was stalling for time.

Rosie didn't ask again. She stared at her husband and waited for the answer.

"I promised my mother not to tell anyone. Not you. Not Laura," he said, finally. "Do you remember when my mother wanted to see me alone, when we went for the funeral?"

She remembered. She'd felt guilty because it had annoyed her—they were about to go to bed after a long, emotional day.

"It was late at night. After we'd gone to sleep . . ." Rosie began. But Joe interrupted her.

"She came to our room and asked me to join her in my father's study. I had already received the note from his lawyer, and she knew it. She was hysterical. Begged me not to tell anyone—not my siblings, and not you or Laura. She said she'd suffered a lifetime of humiliation and she wanted to bury it along with my father. She begged me, Rosie," Joe said, pleading now for her to understand. "I felt I owed it to her after what my father had done."

Rosie wanted to scream. She wanted to whale her fists into

people who were not in the room—her mother, her father. Joe's father. And even Joe's mother. Yes, she had been a victim of her husband's infidelity and lies. But she had chosen to suffer the humiliation that she described. That was her choice. She had no right to poison her son's marriage.

"How long did he know?" Rosie asked. She could see them all—the "grown-ups" on their street. She used to think they were wise. She used to watch the women and imagine herself in their shoes one day, married with a house full of children. She had looked to them to show her how to be a woman, even when she pretended not to. This thought now disgusted her.

"He knew when your mother got pregnant. Their affair began six months before. Your mother told him she had stopped sleeping with your father."

"Jesus Christ!" Rosie exploded. "He put that in a note? A note he left with his lawyer?"

Joe shook his head. "My mother told me that part. That was also how your father knew—they had grown distant after you were born. Tired and busy. He probably thought nothing of it—until your mother was suddenly pregnant. I can see how that happens. Can't you? After Mason, things changed between us."

"Not like that! What are you saying, Joe?"

"Nothing, Rosie. I'm just trying to make sense of it. I'm trying to understand how these people we looked up to, people who raised us, who toasted us at our wedding and were there when Mason was born—those people. I'm trying to make sense of what they did."

Rosie let her thoughts settle before she said things she couldn't take back. This would have been a hard secret for Joe to carry. She knew that. Still, if Laura hadn't gone missing, she may never have known. She'd seen no signs of the distress Joe was now saying he'd felt. No signs that he was holding on to such a monumental secret.

And that was exactly how *those people* had held on to theirs.

People could hide. And hide well. Even the people you love the most.

"Why did you tell Laura?" Rosie asked again. He still hadn't answered.

It was not easy to look at him when he did.

"I decided to tell Laura *first*. I couldn't keep the secret any longer. I knew she'd struggled with your father, and with every other man in her life. This information—it felt important. It made sense why your father always favored you. And why he started cheating on your mother. And why he left."

"And you didn't think it was important information for me? I had to live through the affairs. I had to listen to my mother crying. Do you have any idea how much she told us? Knowing we would feel sorry for her? How could you not know this would help me—to find peace with my father leaving us?"

Now she saw it. For the first time since Laura had been home, she saw a trace of guilt.

"I had no idea those things still bothered you."

"Well then, I guess you don't really know me. How is that possible?"

Now he was silent. Rosie pushed on.

"So you told Laura because you thought you could help her with her problems?"

"Yes. And I told her *first*, Rosie. I thought we should make sure before deciding whether to tell you—get a DNA test done, which we did."

"Why last summer?"

"Because it was unbearable to keep this secret. And because

she told you she was talking to a therapist, right? And that she had a boyfriend who loved her. She had support to help her deal with it. I didn't know if that chance would come again. So I went to the city and I took her to lunch. And I told her."

"What about all the calls and texts . . . ?"

"She had questions, just like you. And we had to arrange for the DNA test, and then wait for the results, which was hard. She wanted me to tell you. She begged me to tell you, or to give her permission to tell you herself. She wanted to be able to talk to you about it, Rosie. You are the only person she's ever really trusted. But I was scared of how you might look at me. If it would change things between us. And then Laura fell apart and moved back home and the fear grew—we've been holding Laura together for weeks. It didn't seem like the best time to drop this bombshell too."

Rosie felt her throat close tight. *Goddamn it,* she thought. She did not want to cry. She did not want to feel anything but anger for all of them. Her mother for a lifetime of lies, even as she saw her girls suffering. And Joe for keeping this from her. And Laura . . . she wanted to hate Laura right now. Everything was always about Laura. Poor, sad Laura. Hurt Laura. Broken Laura. And now, missing Laura.

"Does Gabe know?" Rosie asked, suddenly wondering if he was another traitor.

Joe shook his head. "I don't think so. I didn't tell him and Laura promised not to."

"I can't believe this," Rosie said. "I can't believe any of this is happening."

The door opened. Conway was there now. And Rosie could tell from his demeanor that he did not have good news.

"What? What's happened?" she demanded.

Conway sat down at the head of the table. He slid a piece of paper, a black-and-white photograph, in between Rosie and Joe.

Joe turned it slightly so he could see what it was.

"Who is that?" he asked.

But Rosie knew. It was Jonathan Fields. Buck or Billy. Or Edward Rittle. Take your pick.

He was in the hallway of his apartment building, stopped in front of his door—the door she had been pounding on. The door she'd walked through, certain she'd find her sister behind it.

In the photo, this man was with a woman.

"That's not Laura," Rosie said, looking up from the photograph.

"Exactly," Conway said. "That's a still shot from video surveillance in the suspect's building. Look at the time stamp."

In the bottom right-hand corner was a date. And a time.

"This can't be right," Rosie said. "This was from Thursday night?"

Conway nodded. "This is the suspect and a woman entering the apartment just after ten p.m. There's footage of her leaving around midnight. He doesn't leave until the next morning, dressed for work. The cleaning service arrives later that morning. The neighbor drops the mail that afternoon. And then we arrive this morning. That's it—your sister was never at that apartment."

Rosie looked at Joe, confused and disoriented. Nothing was what it seemed. Nothing was what she thought.

"I don't understand," Joe said, staring at the photograph. "How did he wind up with this woman and not Laura?"

Conway shook his head. "No," he said. "Laura was never with the suspect. He showed us his account on the dating website. We've spoken to his date. They made a plan for Thursday night. They met at that bar by the harbor, like you said—he was there. But he was with this woman. Not with Laura. He never even contacted Laura—never."

Rosie dropped her head into her hands. "No!" she said. "That can't be right!"

Conway sighed, hard. "I'm afraid it is."

"But what about everything else—those women we found who knew things about him . . ."

"Well, all of that was accurate. He is married. He does lease the apartment under an LLC, a holding company, to hide it from his wife. He works for Eversource—the electric company. Does efficiency checks on houses. Sells new windows on the side. Probably breaching a whole ton of regulations, but that's for another day. And another cop. But if it makes you feel any better, his wife now knows, so there will be some payback for this asshole."

"Oh God!" Rosie was in a panic now. Her head spinning with theories and facts from the past two days that now had nowhere to go.

"What about the calls?" Joe asked. "On her phone log?"

"We did get something," Conway said. "The numbers around the time of the date belong to a company called Klayburn Capital. We got in touch with one of their administrative assistants—that number belongs to a man named Jonathan Fielding."

Rosie jumped from her chair. "That's it, then! Jonathan Fields . . . Jonathan Fielding. Do you know where he is? Can you find him?"

"All we have is an address in Boston. But he has an ex-wife here in Branston, and she gave us the name of a hotel where he was staying up until a few weeks ago. We'll find him."

Rosie leaned against the wall and stared at the photograph on the table. "So Jonathan Fields is Jonathan Fielding. Not Edward Rittle . . ."

"Yes. There's no doubt about it," Conway said.

Joe looked up then, surprised. "What did you just say? Edward Rittle? That was the man we've been chasing all this time?"

"Why?" Conway asked. "Do you know him?"

Joe stared straight ahead. "I'm trying to follow, that's all. We thought Edward Rittle was Laura's date because of the photo— because Edward Rittle was seen at the bar close to where her phone died? But he's not the guy. . . ."

"No—he's not the guy," Conway said again.

Rosie looked at Joe. He was speaking in a tone she hadn't heard before. Maybe this was how he sounded when he was with his clients or in front of a judge. Detached and analytical.

"I can't believe this," Rosie said. "What can I do?"

"Just stay put. We should have some emails and text messages soon. We may need you to go through them."

"I'll go," Joe offered. "I have something to take care of, and then I should get back to our son. We left him with a sitter."

He stood up, shook hands with the officer. He looked then to Rosie and started to move as though he wanted to walk around the table and hold her or kiss her—something. But she stood still, her body growing stiff. And Joe retreated, heading for the door.

"Joe . . ." Rosie said, making him turn. "I'm sorry." She had all but accused him of sleeping with her sister, and that could never be taken back.

He nodded, acknowledging her apology. But his face was cold.

"So am I."

FORTY

Laura. Session Number Five.
Three Months Ago. New York City.

Dr. Brody: Tell me more about Gabe Wallace.

Laura: We were friends. We still are.

Dr. Brody: Never more? Is he someone who loved you that you pushed away?

Laura: It was never like that. I kept his secret. I'm the only one who knew.

Dr. Brody: What kind of secret?

Laura: The kind I can't tell anyone. Not even you.

FORTY-ONE

Laura. The Night Before. Friday, 1:30 a.m. Branston, CT.

Gabe drives us away from downtown. Away from Jonathan Fielding, who lies on the floor of his apartment. Unconscious. Bleeding.

He drives slow and steady. Stopping at lights. Keeping within the speed limits. He is consumed with concentration. If I didn't know him so well, if he hadn't been my best friend all through childhood, it would have caused alarm. I am shocked and confused, but not that—not alarmed. I know there must be an explanation.

"Gabe," I say. "Please tell me what's going on." I've been asking him for the past five minutes. Since the moment we got in the car.

"No one saw us," he says, as though he doesn't understand my question. "I covered the security cameras with spray paint."

I stare at him now and he can feel it. He turns for a second to smile at me.

"What?" he asks. "You're safe now."

He says this like I should be relieved.

"Gabe . . . you have to tell me what's going on." I try to keep my voice calm, but I feel like reaching over and shaking him until the answers fall out. "What you did to him . . . we have to call the police. He could bleed to death."

His hands clench the wheel tighter. One hand at ten and one hand at two, just like they taught us in driving school. Eyes on the road. Back up straight. Gabe always followed the rules. Meticulously. Obsessively. If I hadn't been on the other side of that door, I would never suspect he'd done anything out of the ordinary before getting behind the wheel.

"Don't worry," he says now. "They'll notice the cameras aren't working and they'll check the apartments. They'll find him in time."

This does not settle me.

"No!" I insist now. "That could take hours. Did you see his head? All the blood . . ." He doesn't flinch. "Gabe!" I yell at him. "Tell me what the hell is going on!"

He sighs the way a parent sighs at an unruly teenager—frustrated that he has to deal with my insubordination.

"He was going to hurt you. Maybe even kill you," he says. "There. Are you satisfied now? Do you still want to save his life?"

I feel my mouth hang open. Wide-open as I stare at Gabe. His face has changed again; this time he looks smug.

"How do you know that? And why . . ."

He takes one hand off the wheel and holds it to face me.

"Stop," he says. "I'll explain everything when we get to the house."

I'm scared now. Scared like I've never been scared in my life. I'm so scared, I start to cry. "Gabe . . ."

I feel his frustration turn to anger.

"You've been getting notes. Threats. Haven't you?" he asks. "Joe told me."

"How does Joe know?"

"I didn't ask—does it matter? You've been getting them—threats, right?"

I nod. "I got one tonight. It was in my purse."

"And how do you think it got there?" he asks.

I think about the note and the conversation I had with Jonathan Fielding right before Gabe hit him with the door. How he suggested Rosie was the one leaving me the notes. And how I turned it right back on him. He was angry at the accusation, but now my mind is flooded with every moment I spent with him. I think about the list of wrong things. His fake name. The car. The story. The route he took to the bar and his bare apartment. The wedding ring in the medicine cabinet, hidden in a bottle of pills. He had excuses for everything, except for one thing—and it glares at me now. Why was he like a dog with a bone when it came to Mitch Adler's murder?

I hear his voice turn lurid. *I want to fuck you again.*

But I couldn't make sense of these things. I make mountains from molehills but then don't see danger when it's standing in front of me. When it's stroking my face and kissing my neck.

I am suddenly grateful.

"Who is he?" I ask. "Why did he want to hurt me?"

Gabe shakes his head now. "I don't know. I'm still trying to find out. I knew he wasn't real—Jonathan Fields. I looked into him for Joe. He was worried. And then I just wanted to get you out of there. Get you someplace safe."

"Rosie . . ." I start to say, suddenly picturing her and Joe standing in their kitchen, watching me leave last night. The fear in

Rosie's forced smile. The hope in Joe's eyes—or so I thought. Maybe I misread that too. Maybe he was fearful as well.

"I've been following you all night. You and this man."

A chill runs through me. He says the word "man" with disgust, like I've been spending time with a monster posing as a man.

"I told them I'd get you and keep you safe. The police won't look for you at my house. Not right away at least."

"Why would the police be looking for me?" Nothing is making sense. My mind spins and spins.

"Because," he says. And then he pauses as though it should be obvious. "Laura . . ." he continues. There is nothing but dismay on my face, so he lays it out. "He's bleeding on the floor. He's been struck in the head. And you were the last person seen with him. Given the past, I think it's only a matter of time before they put the pieces together."

"But he'll tell them, won't he? He'll tell them that I was with him when the doorbell rang."

"Will he? He lost his chance to hurt you one way. Now he has another."

Tears soak my skin. Gabe is right. If Jonathan Fielding was really out to punish me for what happened to Mitch Adler, he'll lie now. He'll tell them I assaulted him. Tried to kill him.

Maybe he's already dead. Maybe I'll have another murder to account for.

"It will never be over," I manage to say through the tears. "What happened that night . . . to Mitch. To his family. It will never end, will it?"

Gabe turns the wheel. We are at his house now, pulling into the driveway.

He puts the car in park. Turns off the engine.

"Melissa's traveling for work. It'll be safe here," he says.

I lean across the console and fall into his arms.

"It's going to be okay now," he says.

I don't answer. I don't know if I believe him.

A man found me. Lured me on a date. Wanted to hurt me. And I ignored every sign that appeared. I told him my darkest secrets. I slept with him. *Christ.* And now I will be a suspect in his assault. Or his murder. How can it possibly be okay?

Gabe rocks me back and forth.

"I always kept you safe and I always will," he says. And I pull away, startled by his words.

"What do you mean?" I ask. Gabe was never my protector. It was always the other way around. From the first time I saw his brother hit him, it's been me saving him. Me keeping him safe. Me keeping his secret from the world.

He looks at me, perplexed. "From my brother," he says. "Remember? He used to follow you into the woods. Stalking you. Hunting you. He would come out of nowhere, pin you to the ground. Try to smother you. Or hit you. Or strangle you. Or put a knife to your throat. Just enough . . ." he says, then he pauses to reflect, and remember carefully. "Just enough," he continues, "until you thought you were going to die. Only then would he let you go."

Am I losing my mind? He is dead serious as he describes these events, only I was the one watching as his brother did these things to him. I was the one who saw the bruises on his neck. I was the one who found them in the fort that day, Rick on top of him, a knife to Gabe's throat. I was the one who picked up a branch from a tree and struck Rick in the head. I told him I would kill him if he did it again. I told him, and he believed me because he knew it was true. I had more anger inside me than an army of men. He left for military school a few weeks later. Gabe said he'd asked to go and I had always thought it was because of me. Because I had put the fear of God into him.

But now I wonder if that's what happened. I wonder if Gabe invented this story about Rick hurting me, and used it to make his parents send him away.

I don't know how to ask him. Am I remembering it wrong? Have I lost my mind? I can see Rick holding that knife. I can feel the branch in my hands the same way I can feel the bat in my hands—the bat that killed Mitch Adler.

Gabe's eyes are wide with something soft and warm. Affection, I think. Affection like I'm his ward. His pet. His child.

"After this," he says, "you have to stop, okay?"

"Stop?" I ask, cautiously.

"No more of these men who want to hurt you. I know you can't help it, just like you couldn't help it when you kissed my brother. When you liked kissing him after everything he did to you."

I try to make sense of things, but I know I am incapable of making sense.

"And Mitch Adler. He just wanted to use you. And that doctor in New York—he had a wife and children. He was using you too. All of them just trying to hurt you. Don't you see that?"

The breath leaves quickly but rushes in again. The rest of me remains still. Frozen.

How does Gabe know that Kevin was married? Had children? I've told no one because I knew what they would have thought. I knew what they would have said. No one would have understood our situation.

I never told anyone his last name. I never told anyone that he was a shrink.

"Rick is in prison. Did you know that?" Gabe asks me. And I

shake my head. I had no idea. Neither did Rosie or Joe. Last we heard, he was stationed overseas somewhere.

"He killed a man in a bar fight. He had a military trial and he's in military prison. He got what he deserved. But it destroyed my poor mother. My father's dead. My brother's in jail. It's just me now. I'm all she has."

"Okay," I manage to say because I'm afraid to say nothing. Our mother told us Mrs. Wallace moved to a nursing home. Surely Mrs. Wallace would have told her if Rick was in prison. Or maybe not. Maybe she was too ashamed.

"We should get you inside," he says. "You should rest."

I look out the window at Deer Hill Lane. I can't see much in the darkness. I can barely make out the frame of Gabe's house. So many memories live in this neighborhood. Happy memories. Sad memories. Fear and trauma. They twist around one another in a tangled web. I haven't been back here since I left. Not to this street. I haven't come back because I want no part of them. I have that one picture on my screen so I won't forget what this place did to me.

Gabe opens his door and goes outside. He waits by the front of the car for me to join him.

Something is wrong. I don't know what it is. I don't know if it's Gabe. If it's Rosie or Joe. If it's Jonathan Fielding.

But I get out of the car anyway. I follow Gabe into the dark, quiet house. I let him close the door behind us because I don't know what it is that I think is wrong.

And because it's entirely possible that what is wrong is me.

FORTY-TWO

Rosie. Present Day. Saturday, 2:30 p.m.
Branston, CT.

Both officers sat with her now, with all of the evidence spread across the table. Rosie cradled a cup of stale coffee in her hands, trying to pull together thoughts amid the exhaustion and emotional turmoil.

"Let's go back to the very beginning," Pearson said. Her voice was calm and soothing, unlike earlier when she was screaming at Rosie in the open room. Rosie felt like an idiot for going after that man, Edward Rittle, who wasn't even with Laura Thursday night. But then she reminded herself of the other women he had lied to and used, and wished she'd gotten in at least one sucker punch. Laura would have done it. She would have leveled him and he would have deserved it.

At least now his wife knew. And his employer. The women he hurt got some payback for the pain he caused them.

"Okay," Rosie said. "The beginning."

"Start when she told you about the date."

Rosie remembered it clearly. Laura had come downstairs from

the attic, where she'd been working. She said she'd gone on a website, findlove.com, to look for older, divorced men. Men who had a proven track record for commitment. Men who were eager to settle down, and maybe one who already had his own children.

"She thought that would be perfect—a man with children who only came to visit every other weekend—"

Conway interrupted her. "Doesn't she like children?"

"She loves my child. Mason—her nephew. But we had a complicated childhood. Our father left when we were barely teenagers. So she's never been sure about wanting kids."

"Okay—so she said she found one. Did she tell you his screen name?" Pearson asked.

Rosie shook her head. "No. But she described him. And that description sounds a lot like Edward Rittle, but I guess now that doesn't mean much. All she really said was that he had a full head of brown hair, tall, in good shape. Handsome face. God, it could be a lot of men, now that I think about it. It sounded specific at the time, but it wasn't really."

"What about a picture? Didn't you ask to see it?" Pearson had obviously been down this road with other women.

"No, honestly. She only had the site on her laptop upstairs, and I didn't want to encourage it. I didn't think she should start dating so soon. She'd just been back five weeks after leaving her entire life in New York. And it was over a breakup with a man. It seemed pretty extreme to me."

Rosie's cheeks started to burn. She had not told them about Laura's breakup in New York. *Shit.* What if they asked? Would she have to tell them he was her therapist? That he was married and had children, and now—dead?

But Conway, mercifully, pushed ahead. "Did she say where he lived, what he did for work, anything more specific?"

"Only what I've told you—that he said his name was Jonathan Fields. That he worked for a hedge fund. Lived in Branston. Drove a black BMW. That all fits, right? With Jonathan Fielding? His company phone on Laura's records—Klayburn Capital—is a hedge fund. And the car—you said you got a license plate number?"

"In Massachusetts," Pearson said now. "A BMW. He doesn't have an address here in Branston. But the company said he was living here now to open a new office."

"So he lied to her—that's something, right? He was lying. And if she found out . . ." Rosie paused then and looked at their faces. Conway's was blank, but Pearson . . .

"You're afraid she might have turned violent. That's what this has been about all along," she said. "Because of what happened eleven years ago."

Rosie looked away then. Still, she defended her sister the way she always had, and the way she always would.

"Laura didn't kill that boy. It was a homeless man with mental health problems. He lived in those woods for years. He used to chase us, dress up like a vampire. They found him in the car. . . ."

Conway then: "We're not here to rehash that crime, Mrs. Ferro."

Rosie stopped talking, though she didn't believe him. Not entirely. That crime would never go away. She thought about the notes—more things she hadn't shared with them. Maybe it was time. Gabe had them, didn't he? She'd given them to him at the diner? So many questions, but her mind was shutting down.

"The night of the date, she took your car. The minivan, which you later found on Richmond Street with two parking tickets. One at seven forty-five p.m. and one at ten a.m. Correct?" Conway asked.

Rosie nodded.

"And then you went to the harbor with photos of possible men from findlove.com—men you found doing a search that you thought was similar to what Laura might have done?"

"Yes. Married men. Thirty-five to forty. Divorced and no kids. Then we ruled out men who were balding, under five-six, overweight, et cetera."

"And you took those photos to the harbor to see if anyone recognized him or your sister?"

"Yes."

Conway paused. He tilted his head and leaned forward like he just had a thought.

"Why the harbor? Why not Richmond Street where the car was parked?"

Rosie looked at him curiously. She'd already been over this with them.

"Because of her phone—her phone died and when we called the carrier, they said it last sent out a signal by the harbor. If her phone was there, then she was there."

Pearson picked up some papers and flipped through them until she found what she was looking for. She handed it to Conway, who looked it over, then passed it to Rosie.

"The records they gave us show the last signal on Richmond Street. Inside the Irish pub. Whom did you speak with at the carrier?" Conway asked.

Rosie stared at the paper and the information that could not be refuted.

"I don't know—it was Gabe. Gabe Wallace—he's an old friend of ours. He came over that morning to help us because he works in IT and because he's very close with my sister. Is it possible the phone went offline but then came back on briefly? Maybe that's what Gabe's contact saw—the first time it went offline but not the last?"

Conway shook his head. "I don't think so." Then he looked at Pearson. "Can you have them check again?"

Pearson got up and left the room.

"She might have found a charger at the harbor, right? But not for long—just enough to send out another signal before it died again. That's possible, right?"

"I don't know. Let's just see what they say."

"I'll call Gabe," Rosie said, picking up her phone. She dialed his number, but the call went straight to voicemail. She hung up and sent him a text to call her. She said it was urgent.

"This Gabe—was he ever romantically involved with your sister?" Conway asked then.

Rosie was indignant, though it was an obvious question. "No. Never. She was like a little sister to him."

Conway had another question on the heels of the first. "You said he works in IT?"

"Yes. He does home and office installations. Troubleshooting, that sort of thing. But also some forensic work for law firms. He works for my husband's firm sometimes, for the divorce lawyers, mostly. That's why he did the search for those men—he does that for clients trying to find cheating spouses. He knew how to create the fake account so we could find other women this man had been with."

"And it worked," Conway said. "You found women Rittle had lured into bed."

"Yes, we did. Our mistake was looking at the wrong bar—but wait!" Rosie suddenly had an idea. "If we show the photograph of Jonathan Fielding to people at the bar where her phone actually died—the Irish pub, right?—maybe someone saw them together! Where is his picture . . . ?"

Rosie started riffling through the stack of papers on the table. Conway seemed reluctant, but he began to help her.

They were interrupted by Pearson, who walked cautiously into the room.

"What is it?" Rosie asked. Her eyes were pinched together with apprehension.

"It's Jonathan Fielding. We put out a locate—he was admitted to Branston Hospital Friday afternoon. Severe trauma to the head. They've induced a coma until they can control the swelling."

"No!" Rosie gasped, and covered her mouth with her hand. "No . . ."

"A forensics team already worked his apartment. They haven't run the prints yet, but they have them."

"And Laura?" Rosie asked. "Was Laura . . ."

"No one was there. There was no sign of a struggle. They didn't know about Laura missing until just now—when we put out the locate on Fielding. Looks like someone pushed in when he unlocked the door. He was struck twice while he was standing, and a third time after he was on the ground. The corner caught his forehead dead-on. Doesn't look like anything was stolen."

Rosie was dizzy and began to sway. Conway took her by the arm and helped her sit down.

"There were two glasses in the sink. A half-eaten pizza from a local spot. The deliveryman said there was a woman with him, but he didn't get a good look at her. She had long hair. Light brown."

"What was she wearing?" Rosie asked, though she already knew the answer.

"A black dress."

Resignation came over her then. This was exactly what she thought it was. Right from the moment she opened her eyes and knew something was wrong. Before she found the car missing. Before she found the empty bed. She knew, in her heart, that this was what had happened. Just like before. With Mitch Adler. With Dr. Kevin Brody. And even before all of that—with Rick Wallace. With little fists punching through that wall.

Whatever happened now, she had to find Laura. And one way or another, they would help her through this. They would get her the help she needed to finally be well.

She looked at Pearson. "Is he going to make it?"

She nodded softly. "They think so."

Thank God.

Thank God!

Rosie stood up then. She had work to do. She had to gather their troops—Joe and Gabe, and maybe even their mother, now. Whatever sins they had all committed would be forgotten. They would find Laura. And they would save her.

"Can I go?" Rosie asked. "I need to speak with my family. I need to call my mother."

Pearson backed away from the door. "Just so you know, we'll have to send a unit to your house. They'll want to look through Laura's room, her computer. Can we get your consent to enter?"

"My son is there," Rosie said, thinking then about Mason and how he'd been without her all day. What must he be thinking? She knew he was safe, with Joe all morning and now with Zoe, but she was his mother. She felt torn in two.

"I'll call the sitter—maybe she can take him outside when the officers get there."

Conway got up and opened the door for her. "Make sure we can reach you, okay?"

Rosie didn't look back as she walked out of the room, down the hall, and out the front door to her car.

She pulled out her phone and started to call Gabe. Something made her stop. She didn't know why and she didn't have time to think about it—but she called her husband instead.

FORTY-THREE

Laura. Session Number Sixteen. Six Weeks Ago. New York City.

Dr. Brody: You must have wondered about who he was—that man who pulled Mitch Adler from the car and killed him in the road.

Laura: I told myself it was Lionel Casey. He was found living in the car. He drove it into the woods as far as it would go and then he used it for shelter.

Dr. Brody: But it's possible someone else drove it there—to hide it—and that Casey stumbled upon it after the fact. That's what his defense team said, right?

Laura: Who else, then? Who else wanted him dead? They obviously didn't want the car if they left it in the woods.

Dr. Brody: You had the bat in your hands. Blood on your clothing, even though you were standing several feet from the body. Do you remember, Laura? Do you remember if you swung that bat?

FORTY-FOUR

Laura. Present Day. Saturday, 2:30 p.m.
Branston, CT.

Thirty-six hours have passed and I am still in Gabe's house, hiding now behind the door of his basement.

I spent many afternoons here when I was a child, playing games in the dark with Gabe and other kids in our neighborhood, so I know it well. I know every window that looks to the outside. I know the door that leads to the boiler room, and how at the end of that room is a Bilco hatch that opens to his backyard. No one lived down here. The basement isn't finished, so it's clammy in the summer and ice-cold in the winter unless you huddle beside the water heater.

I wait now, hiding at the top of the stairs. Waiting for the door to open. Holding a bat in my hands.

Gabe had set up a makeshift bedroom here before we arrived. A mattress on the floor with a pillow and some old fleece blankets. A flashlight. And a bucket that he said I should use to go to the bathroom. He told me not to go upstairs, where a neighbor might see me through a window, or the police if they showed up.

He told me not to peek out the small basement windows for the same reason. And he told me to leave through the Bilco doors if I heard three thuds on the ceiling—he said he would stomp his feet three times on the floor above and that would be the signal to escape.

I have not slept. I have cycled through terror at being blamed for what happened to Jonathan Fielding, and relief that Gabe saved me and that I might not have been found. But then all of that disappeared and left me with the horror that another man might be dead, and dead because of me.

Gabe stayed with me until daybreak Friday morning. Sitting beside the bed watching me sleep, although I was only pretending. I didn't want him to know what was on my mind. The doubts about what he had done to Jonathan, whether it had been necessary and what that said about Gabe. And I didn't want him to come closer to me, to touch me or try to comfort me, because he had been looking at me and speaking to me in ways that were unfamiliar. And that made me worry that I never really understood him or our relationship. And why would I? This is my defect, and I should have known that it applied not just to men on dates, but to everyone. Even my closest friend. And, perhaps, even to my family.

In the morning, he got a call from Rosie. I saw him answer it and speak to her calmly, saying he would be right over.

"What happened?" I asked him when he ended the call.

"The police have come to her house. They're looking for you—just like I said they would."

"Does Rosie know where I am?" I asked.

"Of course she does. It was all part of our plan to keep you safe. But I have to go now and I might not be back for several hours. It would seem strange to the police if I didn't try to help them find you. There's food in the spare refrigerator—do you remember where it is?" he asked me.

"In the utility room," I answered him. We used to hide beer there when we were in high school.

"Right," he said. "And remember—if you hear three thuds from up above, that's your cue to go out the Bilco hatch. But not unless you hear them, okay? Do you understand? The neighbors could see you."

I nodded, and he leaned over onto the bed and kissed my forehead. His eyes were wide with excitement like this was some top secret military operation and he was our general. He had never been our leader when we were younger. It was always Joe, or me at times. He liked to follow. I used to think it made him feel safe to be with strong people, people who could stand up to his brother the way I had done. Maybe that's why I had never seen this look before. Maybe it wasn't strange but just new—a new Gabe who had grown from the shadows after Rick left for good to join the army.

This is what I told myself as he walked up the stairs. The bright light of day rushed into the dark space, but then disappeared along with Gabe when he closed the door behind him.

He returned sometime that afternoon. I don't know what time it was or how long he'd been gone. I only know that it had felt like forever.

I had found sandwiches in the refrigerator. Peanut butter and jelly on white bread. I used to eat those in hoards when I was little, and it was both sweet and eerie that he remembered and had gone to the trouble to fix them, wrapping them carefully in plastic baggies. There were bottles of water and grape soda.

I used the bucket to pee, like he said, and emptied it in a utility sink and ran the water hot for a long time. Then I ran it cold and splashed it on my face. I ran it through my hair, which still smelled of Jonathan Fielding, if that was even possible. But it had been wrapped in his hands, pressed against his chest. The smell of him, of his cologne and his sweat, made me feel sick inside.

Is he dead? I wondered this every minute Gabe was gone.

When he returned, the light was not as bright when it came through the door, or peeked through the tiny windows, so I imagined it was late afternoon.

"What happened?" I asked him. "Is he still alive?"

"I don't know," he said. "But Rosie and Joe are fine. The police won't leave them alone. We'll give it one more day and then I'll get you out of here. You'll ride in the trunk of my car and we'll drive until we find someplace safe."

"What about Melissa?" I asked. He'd said she was traveling for work, but surely she would be home for the weekend. And one more night would make it Saturday, unless I had lost track of time entirely.

"Don't worry about my wife. She's away for work. She won't come back until we're gone."

"And Rosie . . ." I started to cry then. "I don't want to leave, Gabe. I don't want to leave what's left of my life!"

He took me by the arms then and shook me hard. The excitement left his face and what came instead was anger. The general dressing down his soldier.

"I've gone to a lot of effort. Taken a lot of risks and thrown away my life to save you. You could be a little bit grateful and do what you're told!"

I was quiet then, choking back my tears. Choking back the terror that was now raw and full-on.

"Okay?" he asked me, his voice growing softer.

I nodded. "Okay, Gabe." I was afraid to say anything else.

"I have to leave as soon as Rosie calls again."

The call didn't come for a long time. Hours upon hours. I asked Gabe what time it was, but he said it was best if I didn't know. He said it would make me anxious.

He went upstairs to speak to her, then he returned. He said I should sleep. So I lay back down and pretended to sleep and felt his eyes never leave me as he sat by the mattress.

The next call came when it was light again. He shook me, though I wasn't asleep, and told me he had to go.

"Don't come upstairs," he reminded me. "Or go outside. Not unless you hear three thuds on the ceiling."

"I know," I said. He'd repeated the instructions over and over, so I didn't question him. I knew I could be wrong about what I was thinking. But in the end, I would have to decide. I had to trust reasoning that had proven to be untrustworthy without fail.

And what I was thinking was that Gabe had lost his mind.

He was gone for the second time, and when I heard the car pull away, I climbed up on an old trunk and peeked out the small window that faced the front of the house. I saw his car disappear down the driveway and toward the top of Deer Hill Lane.

I climbed down from the trunk and ran up the stairs to the door. I didn't know where I would go, but I would look for Rosie's purse, which had my phone, and try to charge it and call her. Or I would find a computer or a phone in the house. Or I would simply run—out of this house and through the woods that led to the preserve. I knew every inch of it, and I would hide until I could find out what was going on.

I reached the top step, crazy with fear, and I put my hand on the knob and turned. But it wouldn't open. I turned one way and it stopped. I turned the other way, and it stopped. The door was locked from the outside. I tried pulling on it, hard. Maybe it would break open. But it was strong and I remember when we entered that it had a dead bolt as well. I couldn't remember if I heard it slide closed when he left, but I didn't have time to find out.

I ran back down the stairs and through the door to the utility room, past the water heater and the refrigerator to the very back corner where there were cement steps and the two large folding doors of the Bilco hatch. I slid the latch to open them and pushed against the outer one. I'd opened these doors a hundred times and they hadn't been changed. But the door wouldn't budge more than an inch, and I could see through that inch the links of a metal chain, locking that door from the outside as well.

I screamed out in frustration. Once, twice. I folded over and screamed again, pounding my fists into my legs. There was no other way out. The windows didn't open and were too small for a body to squeeze through. Just two doors, that was it. And they were both locked.

I was not being rescued, saved from the police and the crimes I didn't commit. I was a prisoner. Gabe's prisoner.

Something inside me gave way then. Locked doors would not stop me from getting out of this house.

I began a search—every inch of this basement would be torn apart until I found something I could use to cut the chains or break down the door. I started in the corner by the mattress and worked my way around, opening boxes of old memorabilia, his mother's clothing, framed photos. One of them was of Rick—the one on top, and I wondered if Gabe came down here and stared at it and if that was what had made him crazy. Remembering the lifetime of abuse he suffered in this house at the hands of his brother.

So many secrets on this godforsaken road. How had his parents not seen it? How had they not stopped it until it was too late to undo the damage? It was becoming clear—this picture of Gabe, so different from the one I had growing up.

Dr. Brody had seen it. Kevin. He asked me frequently about the Wallace family as he got to know me. I thought he was just appalled by the negligence of his parents, but it was more than that.

I put the picture back in the box, and then remembered the last time he asked me about Gabe and Rick.

Where was Gabe the night Mitch Adler was killed?

I thought I had the answer. I believed what everyone believed— that he had gone back early to college. But then he was there the next day. He came to cheer me up after he found out what had happened. He came to be my protector, just like he'd done now.

He said he'd protected me my whole life. He said he'd protected me from his brother. And then he told me I had to stop being with men who wanted to hurt me and use me. He mentioned Mitch Adler when he said it. And Dr. Brody—he mentioned Kevin.

I didn't stop to put this together, although it was coming together all on its own. That night in the woods. The man who pulled Mitch Adler from the car was strong and quick. Not the body of an old man who lived in the woods.

It was Gabe.

The thought exploded in a violent scream. I closed my eyes and tried to see him, see his face as he opened that door and dragged Mitch from the car. But I didn't see it. I never saw the face. I hid in the bushes by the side of the road. I waited until the car was gone. And then I picked up the bat.

What did I do then? I can never remember.

I moved frantically then, tearing open every box and trunk, finding things—clothing and boots and luggage and, finally, a bag of sports equipment. I stopped with those. Golf club. Hockey skates. Baseball bat. Remnants from Gabe's childhood. If I could slip the blade through the crack in the Bilco doors, and then hit it hard with the club or bat, it might break the chain.

I took the skates and hockey stick back to the utility room and set them down next to the door. And when I did, I saw a small opening, a crawl space, with a duffel bag inside. It was strange, because that crawl space always flooded in the winter when the ground was too hard and cold to absorb the groundwater. They never kept anything in there.

I reached inside and pulled the strap. It was unbelievably heavy. I grabbed it with two hands and pulled with all my weight until, finally, it slid close enough for me to open the zipper.

A quick pull—it opened easily, but then I jerked my hands away and stared at the contents as the sides fell apart. It took a moment to understand what I saw, and every possible thought rushed in to make it not be what it was. *A doll. A mannequin. A Halloween prop.*

No. There were toes and feet and two grayish-white calves. The toes were painted red from a pedicure. Human toes. Human feet. Human legs.

I couldn't scream. My chest wouldn't move, wouldn't draw air. I pulled the zipper farther, knowing what I was about to find but still needing to see it with my eyes. As I unzipped the bag and the sides fell fully open, each part of her was revealed—feet, calves, thighs, folded up to her chest. Her side, an arm and then, at the top fold of the bag, Melissa's long black hair.

I did not see any blood. I did not know how long she had been there, but her limbs were stiff and cold. I zipped the bag up and pushed it back into the crawl space.

I was not able to escape. I was not able to break the chains with the hockey skate or the bat or the golf club. I was not able to break down the door.

So I did the only thing I could do.

Hours have passed again as I stand now behind the door at the top of the stairs. Waiting for my best friend. Waiting for my captor. This time, waiting to kill someone.

FORTY-FIVE

Rosie. Present Day. Saturday, 4 p.m. Branston, CT.

Joe didn't answer, so she left him a message. The same message she'd left for Gabe back at the police station. *Call me as soon as you get this. . . .*

She drove north, away from downtown, but now she didn't know where she was going. Home? The police would be there, going through Laura's things. Joe said he would go to the house to relieve the sitter, to be with Mason. God, what must he be thinking? Aunt Lala gone, his parents coming and going, on edge. Frantic. Maybe she should go there too. She also had to call her mother, tell her to get on the next plane. *Yes,* she thought. Home was where she should go, but something was tugging at her, a thought. A question.

How did they get so far afield? Chasing a man who had no connection to Laura? She'd been so certain. Gabe had been so certain. Laura's phone had died at the harbor—only it hadn't. And Edward Rittle had fit the profile of Jonathan Fields—only he was a different man. Yet Edward Rittle was at the bar by the harbor.

He went there every Thursday night with a different woman. And—the biggest coincidence, though not really given the abundance of apartments—both men lived in apartments near Richmond Street.

Rosie pulled the car off to the side of the road. She grabbed her phone and tried Joe again. Still, no answer. She tried Gabe. No answer. She left a message for Laura's roommate in New York, though she couldn't imagine Laura would have gone there after so much time had passed.

Then she decided. It was Gabe who would know how all of this happened. Gabe could call the woman at the phone company and ask why she'd told them the wrong information. And . . . Gabe said he was going home to look into Jonathan Fielding, so maybe he would have something the police didn't. Something lurid or criminal. Something on another dating website, maybe with another woman. Maybe they could expose him as well— the way they'd exposed Edward Rittle. And maybe he was even worse. Maybe it would help Laura if they found out. *God help me!* These thoughts were terrible. The man had been assaulted and was in a coma—but maybe he did something and Laura had to defend herself. Or maybe it had nothing to do with Laura at all! Yes—that could be it. Maybe someone else attacked him and Laura had run for her life.

Raw, nervous energy surged through her as she thought her way out of that horrible box where her sister had committed this violent act. *Yes!* she thought. There were other possibilities. And as horrible as they were, they left a strange kind of hope that only one person would understand.

Rosie pulled back onto the road and headed toward Gabe's house.

FORTY-SIX

Laura. Present Day. Saturday, 4:15 p.m.
Branston, CT.

I hear his car pull into the driveway. I hear the garage door open, a silent hum that vibrates through the walls. I hear it close.

Footsteps now, across the floor in his kitchen. They are light and deliberate so as not to alarm me and make me run for the Bilco hatch to make my escape. How clever he was to tell me that—to make me believe the doors would open by repeating it over and over. I didn't even think to check, to doubt him, until I saw the change in his face and his voice.

It occurs to me now that I was right this time. That the broken reasoning inside my head worked. I had sensed something amiss, and for once in my life, I'd been right about it.

I squeeze the bat in my hands, but the tightening of my fingers does not soothe me. My fists for hands—they bring no comfort.

I want to turn back time and be in Rosie's attic, under the covers. Safe. Loved. It would be enough now. That would be enough.

The footsteps grow louder, the click of his heels against the wood, the floorboards creaking.

He's outside the door, just on the other side. I hold my breath for fear he can hear me. The air going in and out, heavy, and the pounding in my chest. He is so quiet. I can feel him, mere inches away now. My head grows light, dizzy. I wait for the sound of the dead bolt. I stare at the doorknob, waiting for it to turn.

But then another sound. Another car, pulling up the driveway. His feet move away. Two steps back. Then he is quiet. Listening the way I am. A car door opens and closes. And then the doorbell rings.

"Gabe?" the voice calls from outside the house. Rosie's voice. With the bat still in my hands, I race down the stairs and slide a trunk beneath one of the windows again. I look outside and see her car. The blue minivan. They found it. They found the car. I think now that they must know where I am. But then why is Rosie here alone? Where are the police?

Then a horrible thought. Gabe said Rosie and Joe were helping him. Maybe he's fooled them. Maybe they all think I hurt Jonathan Fielding and now I have to be saved from myself. But why? To what end? What does Gabe want with me?

Floorboards shift above my head as he walks to the front door. I can't see Rosie, but I can hear her voice clearer now, just outside.

"Gabe!" she calls out.

The footsteps turn to shuffles just outside the front door. Then the turn of a lock. And the door opens.

FORTY-SEVEN

Rosie. Present Day. Saturday, 4:20 p.m.
Branston, CT.

"Gabe! Where have you been? I've been calling you. . . ."

Rosie walked inside the house the way she always did. It was strangely quiet today. And dark. She looked around and noticed the shades and curtains were all pulled shut and the lights were off.

Gabe stood still, his hands in his pockets. His expression was strange, like a little boy caught stealing candy.

Rosie started rattling off the things that had happened. The man Laura called from her phone was named Jonathan Fielding—he'd been assaulted and was unconscious. They wouldn't know anything from him for a few days. The police were at her house, looking through Laura's things, her computer. Joe had rushed off to be with Mason and he wasn't answering his phone either.

"What is it with the two of you?" she asked. "Anyway . . ."

She told him about the records from the phone company—how they said Laura's phone died on Richmond Street, not by the harbor. Fielding's apartment was near Richmond Street, just like Rittle's. Which explained the car being found there.

"Can you call your contact back? Find out why she said that about the phone? Maybe Laura charged it in between the two signals. . . ."

Gabe didn't move. Not one muscle, not even his eyes blinked. If he hadn't been standing up, she would have wondered if he was even alive.

"I know you were researching Edward Rittle, but we need to find out more about Jonathan Fielding—that's the man she was with last night. The man in the coma. I think maybe he's into something bad. Something criminal. And Laura just got mixed up in it. Don't you think? Isn't that possible?"

The theories that had seemed possible inside her head were suddenly absurd as she said them out loud. Most things were exactly what they seemed. The simplest answer was usually right. These were things Joe used to say. *Joe . . . where are you?*

"Gabe . . . what if there's really something wrong with her? What if she hurt this man and is running now? Scared and alone . . ."

Rosie fell into Gabe, wrapping her arms around his neck as she started to cry. She waited to feel his arms wrap around her back, for his voice to calmly tell her it would all be okay. They would find Laura and they would help her through this. But he didn't move. He stood straight and stiff like a piece of wood.

Rosie didn't move either then, except to open her eyes. She looked beyond his shoulder into the next room, the kitchen, and then stopped breathing.

On the counter was her black purse.

FORTY-EIGHT

Laura. Present Day. Saturday, 4:25 p.m.
Branston, CT.

Rosie!

I climb down from the trunk and back up the stairs to the door. I press my ear against it, but all is quiet now.

I move quickly back down the stairs and into the utility room to the Bilco hatch. I don't look into the crawl space where Gabe's wife is folded into a bag. I have to create a distraction. Gabe won't want to hurt Rosie. He will want her to leave so he can finish his plan. Put me into the trunk of his car and drive out of town. I know that's what he wants. He's gone to great lengths to make this plan. To execute it. He's made me sandwiches and a soft bed. He's stroked my hair while he thought I was sleeping. He wants to finish the plan. And his plan does not include getting rid of Rosie's body.

Gabe told me to leave through the Bilco hatch if I heard three thuds on the ceiling. He had been careful with his footsteps, but maybe Rosie had been louder than he realized. Maybe I heard thuds when Rosie walked into the house. And maybe I'm trying to follow the plan and escape from the house.

I put the bat down against the wall and grab both handles of the Bilco hatch. Then I push—hard against the chains, making the doors rattle. I push again. And again. And again.

FORTY-NINE

Rosie. Present Day. Saturday, 4:25 p.m. Branston, CT.

Slowly, gently, she released her arms from around Gabe's neck.

Laura was inside this house. Gabe had been lying the whole time. That explained why he'd sent them off in the wrong direction. Chasing the wrong man at the wrong bar. It explained why he'd been so assertive, so strong for her and Joe in the face of Laura's disappearance. And it explained why he was behaving so strangely now that she was here, inside this house. So close to Laura.

The question now was whether Laura was safe here. Whether she was hiding somewhere, as desperate as Gabe was for Rosie to leave. Or whether she was hiding somewhere, desperate for Rosie to find her.

"I'm sorry," she said, the way she would have hours before, when she had no reason to doubt him. "I'm just so scared."

She turned to face the living room, away from the kitchen, so he would have no reason to wonder if she'd seen the purse.

"Is Melissa home?" she asked, now covering for why she had looked away and into another room.

She turned back to Gabe and he opened his mouth as though he was going to answer, but then they both turned toward the bay window that looked out into the backyard.

"What is that?" Rosie asked.

There was a banging sound, metal against metal.

She started to walk toward the window to open the curtains and look outside, but Gabe grabbed her arm, his fingers digging deeply into her skin.

"It's nothing," he said. "The screen door out back doesn't latch anymore. The slightest wind will blow it against the frame."

He smiled then, his face returning to normal. "It's been driving me crazy all summer. Melissa will be home soon. That's why I'm in a bit of a state, honestly. With everything happening with Laura—well, you know how she feels about her."

Rosie nodded. "I'm sorry, Gabe," she said. "I should go. I'm sure the police can find out about the phone. And they're already digging into Jonathan Fielding's past, so they'll find whatever there is to find. I'm just impatient and worried."

Gabe released his grip and led her back to the front door. "It's fine, Rosie. You know I want to help if I can. Call me later. I promise I'll answer this time."

Rosie felt a final surge of fear as she stepped outside the house. She could see her car. She was so close to safety. But then Laura . . .

The sound came again—metal on metal from behind the house. It was louder now that they were outside.

"You should get that fixed," Rosie said. Her mouth was dry, the words barely making it out.

"I know. I will." Gabe closed the door quickly and Rosie heard the turn of the locks.

She didn't look back. She got in her car, then took out her phone and called Joe.

FIFTY

Laura. Present Day. Saturday, 4:30 p.m. Branston, CT.

Loud footsteps across the floor above me. I let go of the doors and race back to the foot of the stairs, the bat in my hands. I hear the bolt. I see the doorknob turn. There's no time to get back up the stairs, behind the door where I can hide.

I place the bat against the wall near my feet. I hold on to the stair rail and look up to the door. I watch it open. And wait.

FIFTY-ONE

Rosie. Present Day. Saturday, 4:30 p.m.
Branston, CT.

"Joe!" Rosie was frantic as she sat in her car, staring at Gabe's house.

"Where are you?" Joe asked.

"I'm at Gabe's. I think Laura is here. I saw my purse—the one she borrowed. . . ."

Joe started yelling into the phone. "Get out of there! Right now!"

Back and forth. Short bursts of information, each of them trying to catch up with the other.

Joe was frantic as he told her what he'd found in his office files.

"That man—Edward Rittle. I remembered the name from a case. Gabe worked it. Rittle was seeing our client's wife. Gabe found him the same way he did yesterday. . . . He knew this guy was on the website. . . . He knew he was a cheater and a liar and he knew where he took women. . . . Rosie—it was all a setup. . . ."

"I know!" Rosie cried the words. "Why, Joe? Why would he do that?"

Joe was running now. She could hear his feet pounding against the pavement. "It's Laura. He wants Laura."

"Why? Why now . . . ?" Rosie's eyes never left the house. There was no movement inside. No lights coming on. No sound.

"It doesn't matter. Just get out of there! I'm calling the police."

Rosie grew silent, thinking. "What about the notes, Joe? And her boyfriend in New York? God, I never even told you what I found. He's dead, Joe. The boyfriend in New York was killed in a robbery. Laura had no idea. Do you think . . . ?"

Joe stopped running. "Rosie," he said, his voice serious now. "Get out of there!"

"Okay . . . call the police. I'm leaving. I promise."

Joe hung up and Rosie put the phone down on the passenger seat. She put her hand on the key and started to turn the ignition.

But then she stopped.

The sound was gone—the metal against metal. It wasn't the screen door banging in the wind.

She knew what it was now.

It was Laura.

FIFTY-TWO

Laura. Present Day. Saturday, 4:30 p.m. Branston, CT.

"Gabe!" I say in a whisper when he comes through the door. "I heard thuds! I tried to get out! What's going on?"

Gabe shuffles down the stairs quickly and in a panic.

He takes my arms and ushers me away from the stairs, out of the line of sight from anyone who might open that door.

"It was nothing. Just an unexpected guest. But you did the right thing. Just like I told you. Good girl," he says. "Good girl."

I say nothing about the doors being chained from the outside, and Gabe doesn't wonder why.

"Are they gone now?" I ask.

Gabe looks to the window that faces the driveway and strains his neck to see through it. "I can't tell," he says.

I moved the trunk from beneath the window. But just beyond it is the bag with the sports equipment, which I've left open. *Shit!*

I pull Gabe's attention back to me, hoping he won't see.

"Gabe!"

He looks at me again.

"What do we do now? Is it time to leave?"

He shakes his head. "No. There's been a complication. But it'll be fine."

"What complication? Do they know I'm here? Are they coming?"

Gabe pulls me to his chest and wraps his arms around me tight. Every inch of my skin crawls at his touch, at his smell, but I grab hold of his arms and squeeze them as though I never want to let him go.

"I'm scared," I say. I have to make him believe me. He wants to be my protector, and I will make him just that.

But then his body jerks away from me. His head turns back toward the window. Back to the open bag with the sports equipment.

He walks to it with large strides, looking inside.

"What were you doing while I was gone?" he asks.

When he looks back, I'm standing by the foot of the stairs, one foot on the first step, and the bat gripped tightly in my hands.

He freezes for a second, stunned by my deception, but I am already moving. Up the second step, and then the third.

He runs to the stairs. I bound them two at a time.

I reach the top and grab the doorknob, this time turning it all the way. The door opens into me and I have to step down to make way. And when I do, I feel his hand on my ankle, pulling me hard to my knees and then down the stairs. Toward the bottom. Toward Gabe.

"Why?" he yells as he grabs hold of my other ankle. He drags me to the bottom of the stairs like a rag doll, the bat releasing from my hands and falling through the railing to the floor below.

He climbs on top of me, hands gripping my wrists, legs pinning my thighs to the ground.

"I did everything for you. Don't you understand that? I saved you from my brother. And then I saved you from Mitch Adler. You knew it was me. I know you saw me. I looked at you when I opened that car door and saw you with your shirt pulled up and his hands on you. You would never let him do that to you. I know that. But you always got yourself into trouble, didn't you?"

I feel his hot breath against my skin. His eyes are crazy now, like a dam has broken and whatever he's been holding inside is now free.

"I saved you again from that monster in New York. I made him disappear and it never touched you, did it? I always clean up your messes and then make sure it never touches you. *Precious Laura.* Nothing can ever touch *precious Laura.*"

I look in his eyes then and let my face soften. I stop fighting against his hold and let my body go limp.

"I know, Gabe," I tell him. "I've caused so much trouble, haven't I? I'm sorry. You've always been so good to me. But I'm scared. Don't you understand? I don't know if I can trust you. I don't know if I can trust anyone. That's always been my problem, remember? I can't tell the good guys from the bad guys."

Gabe lifts my wrists and then slams them down in anger. "You never could!" he yells. "You liked it when he kissed you! I know you did! You kissed him for a long time and in front of everyone!" But then the anger subsides. "I thought you would finally understand. When the notes started to come, I thought you would realize that I was the good guy. I was the one you could turn to. But you didn't, did you? You went on a dating website and put on makeup like a little whore. I couldn't let you do that again. I couldn't let you not see the truth—that I am the one who protects you! I am the only one!"

I nod and try to smile, though my mouth is trembling.

Gabe killed Mitch Adler. Gabe sent the notes. And Kevin—what did he mean about making him disappear?

My voice trembles when I speak. "I know, Gabe. Give me some time. Teach me. I can learn. I can be better."

We both hear footsteps coming from above. Gabe looks to the top of the stairs and the door that is now open. He climbs off me and pulls us both to the wall at the foot of the stairway, where we can't be seen.

In the corner I see the bat, and I break free long enough to get to it.

I stand tall now, Gabe right in front of me.

And I clutch the bat in both hands.

Sirens pierce the silence that has filled the room.

Sirens, and then the sound of my sister's voice calling my name.

---

FIFTY-THREE

*Rosie. Present Day. Saturday, 4:32 p.m.
Branston, CT.*

Rosie couldn't wait. Not one second longer.

She left the car and ran to the door at the side of garage. It opened the same way it always had, from the time they were kids. The frame was warped, the lock misaligned. She moved quickly to the toolbox on a small workbench in the corner and lifted it. The key was there—just like always. She ran to the side door that led to the house, turned the key, and opened the door, stepping just inside.

The side door led to the mudroom and then the kitchen. She slowed herself now because the house was quiet. Gabe would have heard her enter. He could be anywhere, around any corner. She walked past the small island and then the counter where he'd placed her black purse.

She saw a butcher block with a set of knives and grabbed one from the back, one with a large blade. She held it with both hands, propped in front of her, and walked slowly with her back against the wall until she reached the entrance to the living room.

She heard voices coming from the basement. The door was open. She approached it slowly, listening, the knife in her hands.

At the top of the stairs, she stopped.

"Laura!" she called out.

Sirens rang out in the distance. The police would be here in mere moments.

"Laura!" she called out again. Then she walked through the door.

FIFTY-FOUR

Laura. Present Day. Saturday, 4:35 p.m. Branston, CT.

Gabe turns to see Rosie standing at the top of the stairs. But I don't look away from my target. I raise the bat high behind my head.

"Gabe!" Rosie calls his name now. "Just back away. Everything is all right now. The police are just up the street—can't you hear them? Step away from Laura."

My knuckles go white. I can feel them the way I always do when the fists come. I want to swing it down against him. Strike him in the chest. Send him to the ground. My mind flashes back to the night in the woods. The bat in my hands. Mitch Adler at my feet, blood pooling around his head.

I tell my arms to move, but they don't listen.

And then I know. With every part of me, I know the answer to the last question Dr. Brody asked me.

I did not swing the bat. I did not level the fatal blow to Mitch Adler.

Rosie is moving down the stairs now, the knife in her hands.

Gabe is afraid of her. I can see it in his eyes. He's afraid of Rosie and what she might do to him.

Rosie, who's never lifted her finger against a living soul. But Rosie, who would give her life for mine. Who would take a life for mine.

Gabe lifts his hands in the air and steps back just as Rosie reaches the last step. We hear knocking on the front door and then feet pounding the floorboards. Officers appear at the top of the stairs, guns drawn.

I feel my fingers release. The bat drops to the ground. And my fists turn to open hands just as Rosie pulls me into her open arms.

FIFTY-FIVE

Laura. Before the Sessions.
Five Months Ago. New York City.

Dr. Brody: Is it strange dating a shrink?

Laura: As long as you don't try to shrink me.

Dr. Brody: I'll try.

Laura: It is strange dating a man with kids. And a wife.

Dr. Brody: It won't be strange when you meet them, finally. And she's a soon-to-be ex-wife. She left me, remember? For her high school boyfriend, no less. But then I met you.

Laura: But then you met me.... I hope you're not sorry about that day.

Dr. Brody: How could I ever be sorry I met you?

FIFTY-SIX

Laura. Present Day. Saturday, 10 p.m.
Branston, CT.

I feel cold.

Joe has brought a blanket and Rosie has wrapped it around me. But it can't touch the place where I feel it most.

Two men are dead. Another came close. *Jonathan Fielding.* Where this latest chapter began. They say he'll make it. His body will recover. But he won't recover in other ways. Every time his hand reaches for a lock to open a door, he will feel the fear. I think about his caution. His concerns about my past, all the questions—relentless questions. I convinced myself they were unusual, that they made him suspect. But in the end, he was right to be concerned, wasn't he?

Two men are dead.

Two men. The first, Mitch Adler. My high school obsession. Dragged from his car and beaten to death with a baseball bat. Gabe had been watching from deep in the woods, the preserve where we spent days upon days together, alone, and with Rosie and Joe. Hours, days, years—none of us ever saw it. None of us ever knew what was happening inside our friend. His brother's abuse was worse than even I knew, and I thought I knew everything. It had been going on for years. There was a file at social services. Visits from caseworkers to their home—right next door to us. Our mother now says that Mrs. Wallace confided in her about Rick, all those afternoons when they were in the kitchen together. Our mother crying about Dick and his infidelities. Mrs. Wallace crying about her twisted, violent son who enjoyed tormenting his little brother. Both women keeping secrets that would lead to people dying.

Our mother is on a plane now. She has no idea what she will face when she sees us. Me, Rosie. And Joe. My half brother.

The second man, Dr. Kevin Brody, was killed in an alley outside his gym in the early morning hours. I am in shock, they say, which is why I haven't cried yet. But the tears will come.

I met Kevin at a coffee shop one Saturday morning. His wife was leaving him, but they couldn't afford for either to move out of the apartment. Kevin left on Saturdays. She left on Sundays. They both needed some space, and to be alone with their children.

It was crowded that morning, and he asked if he could sit with me at my small table with the extra chair. I moved my bag and let him sit.

Four weeks later he told me he loved me, and it was the first time I ever believed it. Now I wonder if it will be the last.

I am the reason he's dead. I am the reason his children don't have a father. I may as well have beaten him myself and left him to die. It might as well have been me.

They found Kevin's phone in Gabe's house. He sent me the text I thought was from Kevin—the one ending things for good. It was so concise and so believable that I didn't question it. I didn't try to reach him or see him. I didn't seek out a more complicated explanation. Instead I invited the pain in—opened the door wide and put out a welcome mat. And I let it nearly destroy me, leaving my job. My home. My life. Returning to the scene of the crime. The place of my childhood, where it all began.

I know what he would say, because after a short while, I asked him to help me understand my mind. I could see that he was different. That he was not like the other men I had pulled close only to push them away or be hurt by them. Devastated. Immersed in pain that was so familiar.

I suppose this is a gift he left me. This understanding of my mind, which, ironically, I can now believe in.

Jonathan Fielding. The third man. He is everything he said he was. Just a man. A guy. Stumbling his way through life. Through his mother's death and his divorce and his job and his car needing a repair and trying to be sexy again as a single man with a younger woman. Loneliness. Hope. Desire. All of it had been real. Everything he said to me had been true.

And now he has paid the price for that.

More facts have come out in the past several hours. Gabe had seen a therapist throughout his teen years. He had a breakdown in college and spent three months as an inpatient. We were all told he was studying abroad.

As for Rick, he joined the army right after he graduated from military school. After a long string of violent outbursts, he was eventually dishonorably discharged, and later sent to prison for a gruesome bar fight that left a man dead.

Violence. Secrets. Mental illness. Right next door in the Wallaces' house.

Two men dead. And also one woman.

Melissa Wallace was strangled to death and stuffed in a bag. She'd never gone on a business trip. She just got too nosy. Too angry at her husband's obsessions. She got in the way.

I've gone over every detail of my life with the investigators. From the first memory of my childhood to knocking Rick Wallace off Gabe by the fort, to kissing Rick in a game of spin the bottle and all of the things I knew about his violence toward Gabe. I told them about the night in the woods and how I didn't see him, how I didn't know it was Gabe. And how I now know that I did not swing that bat. Not once.

After I left for college, there were other strange incidents that now raise questions. Men who left suddenly and without much explanation. These were my wolves, the "wrong" men I chose so they would hurt me. So I could try to make them love me, but then prove to myself I was unlovable so I could play the old record of my childhood over and over.

We are drawn to the familiar, even if it hurts us.

But now I wonder which ones were wolves, and which ones left because of Gabe. There was a guy freshman year who told me he *couldn't date someone with a crazy ex-boyfriend*. At the time I thought maybe he meant Mitch Adler. I thought he'd discovered my real last name, like Jonathan Fielding had, and read about my past and that night in the woods. I told the investigators about it and they are tracking him down. I suppose he will tell them that Gabe paid him a visit.

Gabe knew everything about my life because I told him. Every bad date. Every painful breakup. He was always there to comfort me. And, in his mind, to protect me. But what did he do with this knowledge? I fear what we will find.

Rosie and Joe sit with me in the room. Rosie says it is the same room where she saw my phone records, and where Joe confessed what he knew about the past just hours before.

A forensic psychologist is with us, along with a young man who is training to be one. He is going to learn a lot today.

"I just don't understand," Rosie says. She's said it a dozen times since we got here. I can feel her remorse, though she has been nothing but heroic.

Joe sits quietly now that he has the facts. He seems to understand Gabe in a way that we don't. He sits between us, one arm around Rosie and another around me. We huddle together in a giant heap of emotional chaos.

The forensic psychologist mostly asks questions, but she also tries to explain the possible scenarios.

"Sometimes during a childhood trauma, especially one that is ongoing, the child will create an unrealistic attachment to someone who makes him feel safe. That person becomes so crucial to his emotional survival that he has to have her all to himself. In this case, it is possible that Gabe developed that attachment to Laura. You said she was brave, even though she was just a little girl?"

Joe nods and even smiles a little like he's proud of me. Proud that he's my brother. "She was brave. And fierce."

But all I can think is that everything I was and everything I did back then contributed to this psychotic attachment that has now left three people dead.

The psychologist nods as well.

"And, Laura, you were the only one who knew about his brother, right?"

"Except for his mother. And my mother," I say, and I cannot hide my anger.

"But Gabe only told you. And you were the only one who tried to stop it. That's what matters. You became essential to his survival."

Rosie sniffles now even though the tears are gone. "I don't understand," she says again. "Why didn't he try to be with her? To date her or be physical with her in any way? Why didn't he try to marry her when they were older?"

Now a shrug and a tilt of the head. She doesn't know. But she offers a theory.

"It's likely he needed to keep those things separate. Sexualizing Laura risked making her vulnerable or weaker in his eyes. The act of sex involves a kind of submission by both parties. It exposes us in ways we don't share with everyone. I suspect he needed to keep her pure."

I lean forward now. Something bothers me about all this.

"Gabe said he was my protector. He said he had to protect me from the men I was with. But you're saying he saw me as *his* protector."

"Again, it's just a theory," she says. "But I think he needed to create a justification for making sure you were always available, because he needed you to belong only to him. That became difficult after you all grew up and started looking for partners. He found one, but I doubt she ever really knew him. He would have hidden himself from her. He would have compartmentalized her—his sexual partner. His roommate. His cover with the outside world to appear normal. But, Laura—he needed you to be alone so that in his mind, you belonged only to him. He told himself he was doing this all for you—to protect you—so he could justify it."

She leans her elbows on the table and shakes her head. Then she looks at her intern and speaks more to him than to us.

"These types of psychoses are extremely complex. There are

layers upon layers of ego that have to be managed. Gabe didn't want to see himself as a vulnerable, needy little boy who let his brother abuse him. Who needed a fierce but younger little girl to be his protector. So he created an alternate theory for why he had to keep her close and all to himself. *He* was the protector. *He* was the strong one. It made his ego happy while still allowing him to have his desperate attachment to Laura."

We all grew silent then because the picture was coming together clearly now. A clear, terrifying picture of our entire lives.

I think about Gabe the night I went on the date with Jonathan Fielding. I think about him in the kitchen, laughing with Joe about how old Jonathan Fielding was. And how he must have slipped that note in the purse that was on the kitchen counter. And then how he must have followed me downtown and then to the harbor and then back to Jonathan's apartment.

The police told us that he tried to get into the building several times before the pizza deliveryman held the door for him. Then he waited until the hallway was empty.

He knew about Edward Rittle from an old case he'd worked on. He had it all set up—how he would lead Rosie to the harbor and then to Rittle, where she would find an entire pool of disgruntled women. He was going to help in the search for a few days until Fielding was found and I became a suspect. And then he was going to disappear with me. Only, it would seem he'd gone on a last-minute vacation with his wife.

Gabe had a thick plastic bag in the trunk of his car—large enough for a body. There was also a shovel, and a passport with Melissa's information, but a photograph of me. And cash and plane tickets to Indonesia. There is no extradition treaty with Indonesia.

"He was going to bury her body along the way. By the time

her family started to wonder why she hadn't been in touch, it would have been too late," the psychologist says. "It was finally time. He couldn't keep you under control from afar anymore. You were starting to meet men who were serious about you. Who might want to marry you one day. He'd run out of road, so he started to pave a new one."

Nothing about this seems real to me. Not yet. But I know that day will come.

It will not be a good day.

"Where is he?" I ask. The police ushered us out of that basement before they'd even put handcuffs on Gabe. Joe had arrived and was waiting out on the street, held at bay by the police. We went to his car and stayed until they took Gabe.

"He's being evaluated. A lawyer has been assigned and will meet with him and begin the process," she says.

"The process of determining if he's fit to be charged?" I ask. I know how this goes. This was what happened to Lionel Casey.

Lionel Casey—another one of Gabe's victims. Another burden for me to carry.

She nods again. "Yes. The truth is that Gabe Wallace is a deeply disturbed man."

"What is he saying?" Rosie asks now.

The woman sighs. She doesn't want to answer.

But she does.

"He wants to see Laura."

Laura. I hear my name. I say it to myself, and I know others will be saying it now.

Laura, the reason my son is dead.

Laura, the reason my husband is dead.

Laura, the reason my father is dead.

Laura, the reason my husband left us years ago.

I feel the tears come again as I picture the faces of those who will be thinking my name. The Adler family. The Casey family. The Brody family. My family.

How do I live with this? How do I walk this earth knowing that I caused a man to do these unspeakable things? Knowing that he will, one day, likely be free and walking among us. I know how the system works. And Gabe is smart. He knows how to hide and pretend. He's done it his whole life. He may never pay for what he's done.

Kevin would tell me it's not my fault. Not any of it. He would tell me I was a victim as much as anyone else, even though I am still alive. And he would tell me not to punish myself but to move forward. To honor the lives taken by living a good life myself.

He would compare me to the sole survivor of a fatal car crash—maybe someone who insisted on sitting in the back. Or the target of a murder who stepped out of the way just as the gun went off, leaving another to take the bullet.

Survivor's guilt is nothing new. That's what Kevin would say.

Kevin was a good man. And Kevin loved me no matter how unworthy I may be.

"Are we done?" I ask.

"I think so. If we have more questions, you'll be at your sister's house?" she asks.

Joe and Rosie say yes together and emphatically. Joe's arm tightens around us both.

"I want to go to the hospital," I tell them. "I want to see Jonathan Fielding. I want to be there when he wakes up, even if his family won't let me near him. Even if he won't see me."

"Why, Laura?" Rosie asks. "You don't have to do that. You did nothing wrong."

And I think that maybe that's true. Or maybe it's not. But a thought has formed inside my heart more than my head. And I have no choice now but to trust it. And to follow it.

"I just need to do this," I say. But that's not entirely true.

The thought is this, and I hear it in the voice of Dr. Kevin Brody.

My only chance now is forgiveness. I have to forgive myself for the things Gabe Wallace has done in my name. And that forgiveness will not be easy. It will be a mountain I have to climb, step by step, inch by inch. It may take a lifetime. It may never come.

But the first step has to be with this man. Making peace with Jonathan Fielding.

And everything that happened the night before.

Acknowledgments

My grandmother, Estel Kempf, had the kind of life that could keep a writer very busy. And, yet, she had only one thing to say about it: *Who cares about the past!* She lived to be 101 years old looking only toward the future. I hope she's found a good one.

As always, I am indebted to many people for making this book happen. My sincerest gratitude goes out to: my amazing agent, Wendy Sherman, for flying all the way to Taiwan with me, talking me off ledges, and managing to be honest in the nicest possible way; my visionary editor and publisher, Jennifer Enderlin, who immediately got the concept for this book and then made it better; the magnificent team at St. Martin's Press, including Lisa Senz, Dori Weintraub, Katie Bassel, Brant Janeway, Erica Martirano and Jordan Hanley; the experts who shared their time and guidance—Detective Christy F. Girard; Attorney Mark Sherman; Dr. Felicia Rozek, Ph.D.; and author Lundy Bancroft; film and television agents Michelle Weiner and Olivia Blaustein at CAA; foreign rights agent Jenny Meyer; and Carol Fitzgerald at BookReporter.com for her enduring support of my work.

On a more personal note, I am profoundly thankful for the writers who let loose like nobody's business, sharing stories, hearing stories, loving stories the way writers do; my family for sticking together through thick and thin; my sons, Andrew, Ben, and Christopher, whom I adore beyond reason; and "the ladies" who prop me up, meet me for cocktails, and make me laugh—your friendship has saved me on more than one occasion.

And now, in memory of my grandmother, I look to the future. Onward!